'

Beautiful, fa levered back from her and lifted his hand to cradle the side of her face, the pad of his thumb feathering along the slope of her cheek. "A seemingly very strong woman and yet terrified of a kiss."

Rachel's lips went dry and she couldn't pry her tongue from the roof of her mouth. Her limbs trembled. Surely he had to hear how fiercely her heart was pounding, so loudly she heard it echoing in her ears.

His voice deepened, grew quieter until it was almost a whisper and she fought the urge to close her eyes and let the warmth in his voice wash fully over her. "A woman with a child but so frightened of intimacy." He leaned even closer to her, his mouth almost on hers, yet not touching her except where his warm palm held her face.

In the darkness, she could just make out his features. Her hands slid up his chest and she didn't know if it was to push him away or pull him closer. She was aware her breathing was shallow and she held her breath when he brushed the pad of his thumb against her lower lip.

"You have a mouth made for kissing, my beautiful wife, but I'm not going to kiss you. Not until you ask me. And, I promise, when that time comes, you'll be asking me to do a whole lot more than just kiss you."

*Carmen,*

*Readers like you have given me the gift of my career. Thank you!*

# West of Forgotten

by

Lynda J. Cox

*Lynda J. Cox*

*2018*

**West of Forgotten**

Cover Art by *Debbie Taylor*

The Wild Rose Press, Inc.
PO Box 708
Adams Basin, NY 14410-0708
Visit us at www.thewildrosepress.com

Publishing History
First Cactus Rose Edition, 2017
Print ISBN 978-1-5092-1562-1
Digital ISBN 978-1-5092-1563-8

Published in the United States of America

# Dedications

To all my readers who have asked for
Harrison and Rachel's story,
I dedicate *West of Forgotten*.
Your kind words and notes are so very much
appreciated. I hope you enjoy reading their story
as much as I have enjoyed crafting it for you.
~*~

To Jacque, Tenna, Nancy, Jerrica, Cheryl, Christine,
Lissy, Jan, Stacie, Erin, Lynn, Carol, Connie,
and all the other members of my street team—
you guys are the best in the world.
I love you and wouldn't be where I am now
without each and every one of you.
~*~

And to Salena
—the matriarch of my line of show collies—
you left me much too soon
and I still miss you.
My friend, my confidante, and some swore my familiar.
Until we meet again at the Rainbow Bridge...

Chapter One

*Between the towns of Forgotten and Federal, Wyoming Territory, late August 1875*

"Son of a—" Harrison Taylor bit off the curse as he struggled to bring his rearing horse under control. He pulled the black's head down to his right and shifted his weight forward to avoid being pitched from the saddle. When the horse dropped to all four hooves, he reined the snorting, startled animal in a tight circle. "I realize you haven't been shot at in ten years, Demon, but I'd think you'd remember not to throw me."

He ran a calming hand down the horse's sweat-soaked neck and used the moment to steal a glance in the direction that the shot had originated. It had been a shotgun, if the buzzing like so many angry hornets as the projectiles flew overhead was any indication. The question remained if the scatter-gun was a single shot. The figure in the shadows of the heavily shaded porch shifted and the late afternoon sunlight glinted on the muzzle.

"There's nothing here for you, mister."

Even though the voice in the shadows sounded young, there was no waver in the words. The levelness in the simple statement answered the question of whether the shotgun was a single shot. He nudged his hat back a little, unshrouding his face. "I just need water for my horse and me. I'm not looking for trouble."

The muzzle of the long gun emerged from the depths of the porch, gesturing toward the water trough he'd glimpsed in his attempt to calm the horse.

"Get a drink then move along. If you reach into those saddle bags when you dismount, I'll cut you in half." To emphasize the point, the sharp click of a hammer cocked back traveled across the hot land.

Smart kid. Even though he wasn't wearing his sidearm, the boy correctly guessed he had a weapon in the saddlebags. Harrison crossed his arm over his midsection and deliberately leaned his elbow onto the pommel. "I was told in town there might be work to be had here."

"You were told wrong." There was still a dead level cadence to the words. "You've got ten seconds to decide if you want a drink for you and your horse or if you're just going to keep riding."

He didn't need the ten seconds. Harrison tugged one rein, directing the large black to the water trough. He dismounted and worked the pump. Fresh, cold water filled the nearly empty tank. While his horse drank, he picked up the cup tied to the pump and worked the handle again. When he and his mount had quenched their thirst, he backed the animal from the trough. As he grabbed a hank of mane and put his foot into the stirrup, the kid on the porch asked, "Who told you in town there was work here?"

It wasn't so much curiosity he heard in the boy's voice, but anger. Aware of the shotgun still aimed at his midsection, Harrison stepped down and kept a firm grip on Demon's reins. "I stretched the truth just a bit." He nodded toward the remains of a garden near the house. "I figured from the looks of things when I rode up there was work to be had. Kinda hard to keep a garden growing when the fence is down and it looks like cows have been trampling it."

He took a step closer to the house and halted when the muzzle of the gun glinted again in the afternoon sunlight as it was pulled into a shooting position. He paused, weighing his options. "Look, kid—"

The kid stepped out of the shadows. Auburn hair was pulled up into a loose chignon, though several tendrils had escaped to frame a slender face. Harrison took in the faded chambray shirt, denim trousers patched repeatedly at the knees, and scuffed boots, all covering what was a decidedly feminine shape. Though the clothes were overly large and hung on her with as much form as a potato sack, there was no doubt it was a woman holding him at bay. He felt his jaw drop. "You're not a boy."

"I never said I was." She gestured with the shotgun. "Mount up, mister, and leave."

Harrison looked over his shoulder at the south-western horizon. Towering thunderheads rolled forward, churning over one another, growing darker with each passing minute. "Ma'am, if that sky is any indication, it's going to be a long, wet night. I'll admit I wasn't honest with you about being told in town there was work here. If you'll let me stay the night in your barn, at first light I'll get that garden fence repaired." He pulled his hat off, completely unshrouding his features. "I was honest when I said I'm not looking for trouble."

"And what guarantee do I have that you'll be here

at first light? Or that you won't try to rob us blind in the middle of the night?" She pointed the shotgun directly into his stomach, even as she descended the steps of the porch and closed the distance between them. "Or attempt to murder all of us in our sleep?"

Us? He would have bet she was the only one there. Her blunt questions raked over him even though he had given her cause to challenge his honesty. "Ma'am, if I give you my word, I aim to keep it." He didn't like being on the receiving end of any weapon but he pulled his gaze from the shotgun and scanned the ranch house, noting the faded whitewash, the boarded-up window on the second floor, the sagging step on the porch. He lowered his line of sight to her face and offered what he hoped was a friendly smile. "And, no offense meant, but it doesn't look like you have anything worth stealing. As to the other...I'm no killer. I'm not about to start now."

Her jaw clenched as she met his gaze. He'd never seen eyes quite like hers; almost a quicksilver gray with an undertone of deep blue. "Why should I believe you?"

"You've got every reason to keep that shotgun pointed at me and make me keep riding. All I can do is give you my word as a gentleman and hope you believe it."

Her unnerving stare never left him but her features softened while she appeared to weigh his words. He could rationalize her misgivings. She was a woman, alone on this wide open plain. Even dressed as a boy, there was no doubting she was a woman—and a rather becoming one at that. There wasn't a man on the place if the state of disrepair to the house was any indication.

A lack of male protection made her vulnerable. He was a total stranger and she'd be a fool to so lightly offer trust...He knew the moment she reached her decision as the quicksilver of her eyes darkened into a deeper blue-gray.

She lowered the shotgun in degrees and eased the hammer home. Harrison allowed himself a slow exhalation and relaxed his hold on the horse's reins.

"I've got three dairy cows. They go into the barn at night. You're more than welcome to bed your horse down in one of the other stalls and you can throw your bedroll out in an open stall or the tack room." Her gaze lifted to the horizon he had mentioned earlier. "I don't have a lot of grain, but I can spare a scoop of oats for your horse."

"Ma'am?" He wasn't sure what he was hearing, other than he wasn't going to be trying to find shelter in the middle of a thunderstorm.

"I was not raised to turn away those in need. You need a place out of the weather for the night." Resignation clung to the words before her voice firmed. "You may as well put your horse in the small corral next to the barn until that storm gets here. I would appreciate it if you clean his stall before you leave in the morning."

"Yes, ma'am." Harrison plopped his hat onto his head. He tugged on Demon's reins, then paused and asked, "What's the name of this place?"

Demon nudged the middle of his back, staggering him a step forward and closer to the woman.

"The town or the ranch?"

"Both, actually." He pushed the horse's head away from his shoulder, circumventing another hard nudge from the black. "I'm not sure where I am."

"It depends on which direction you rode in from. We're west of Forgotten and almost to Federal." The slightest hint of a smile tugged at a corner of her mouth and some of the tension faded from her features. He wondered if that was meant to be a joke. She paused, brushing a wayward tendril of hair from her face. "The name of the ranch is the Lazy L."

The last time he'd been this surprised Harrison was playing poker and saw a fifth ace dealt. "If this is the Lazy L, I need to see Sam Leonard. My name's Taylor. Harrison Taylor."

Her expression shuttered more quickly than he could have believed. Her pinched features tightened again and she drew back, sucking in a quick breath. "Why do you need to see him?"

Harrison didn't miss the small break in her voice, or the rapid manner the color leeched from her face. "I'm hoping that Sam can straighten something out for me. About six or seven years ago, I oversaw purchasing beef for the Army troops in the Western Theater and I met Sam at Fort Scott, Kansas."

Her posture stiffened and her chin jutted out at him. Those disconcerting eyes narrowed. "The Lazy L sold a lot of cattle to the Army then, Mr. Taylor."

He was startled by the vehemence with which she spat his name at him. "It's not about the beef. Sam and I were in the same poker game and he lost to me. He lost a lot."

She slowly shook her head. Harrison wondered what she was trying to negate.

"Sam couldn't cover his bet. He said he had the deed to a ranch. I've got what he wrote out for me in my saddle bag." Without waiting for her permission, he reached into the saddle bag. The muzzle of the shotgun lifting caught in the corner of his eye. He deliberately avoided the revolver resting in its holster in the depths of the leather pouch and pulled out a packet of often folded papers. He pulled one from the small group—the handwritten deed giving him one acre less than half of the total deeded ranch—and unfolded it. He glanced at the page. "I can read it for you if—"

"I can read." The sharp words were accompanied by her small hand thrusting out to take the paper from him.

Realizing his mistake, he let her take the creased page from him. He hadn't expected a woman on this frontier to be educated enough to read and certainly hadn't expected one dressed in denims to have that ability.

Her head dipped as she scanned the handwriting. The page crumpled with the tightening of her fingers.

"How could he do this?" Anger edged her thin whisper. She looked again at the paper. Her voice thickened and increased in volume with her distress. "He can't—This can't possibly be legal."

This young woman dressed in the most unladylike manner had to be Sam Leonard's daughter, the paragon Sam's bragging about had become almost tedious during their poker game. Harrison lifted his gaze to the house as he found he was unable to look at the woman in front of him, a woman who seemed to have the weight of the whole world on her slender shoulders. He couldn't shake the sensation he had just added to that heavy burden. "Ma'am, he was almost five thousand dollars into me when he wrote that to cover his last bet."

"I'm sure he was." Her hand closed around the paper, nearly wadding it into a ball before she thrust it in his direction. "He never did know when to walk away. Sam's in the house. I'll take you in to him, though I'm not sure what it will accomplish."

She rounded on her heel, leaving Harrison no choice but to follow. He couldn't stop the admiration coursing through him when he saw the butt of what appeared to be a heavy caliber revolver tucked into the waistband of her denims in the small of her back. The lady was well armed. Even though she had agreed to shelter him for the night in her barn and had lowered the shotgun, she still had a way to defend herself.

He released Demon's drop rein and jogged a few steps to catch up, shoving the paper into his trouser pocket. Just inside she paused only long enough to prop the shotgun near the door and settle the revolver on the counter. She then continued a determined march through the house.

Harrison raised a brow. He hadn't seen a Colt Dragoon in better than ten years. He noted the covered Dutch oven on the massive Hoosier stove in a corner of the kitchen and the scent of baking bread mingled with the mouth-watering aroma of what he guessed to be chicken stew. His rumbling stomach reminded him it had been several days since he'd had a decent meal. He looked at the floor, hoping she hadn't heard his growling stomach. The pine planking was scored in places. He guessed the gouging happened when any hands the ranch employed failed to remove their spurs before entering. His weren't going to add any more damage to the flooring as there was no rowel on the short shank, blunted ends.

Her footfalls faded when she left the kitchen and stepped onto a thick carpet runner in an Oriental pattern. He lengthened his stride to catch up to her again. This house wasn't the usual sod house he'd seen on the prairies. Unlike those soddies, this house hadn't grown up overnight. Despite the fact it needed maintenance and upkeep, this was a building that had been constructed to silently but firmly convey a message of wealth and authority.

He didn't know a lot about rugs or wall coverings or even construction. He'd never bothered to learn. Those aspects of a home had always been covered by his family's money, but even he could tell this wasn't the place of a dirt-poor homesteader. The ceiling in the kitchen was covered with patterned copper squares, though they needed burnishing as indicated by the green patina of the metal. The board running the length of the hallway above the dark wood wainscoting had been joined so it appeared seamless and had been carved with an intricate, twisting ivy pattern. Flocking embossed the wallpaper of the hallway. It was easy to see where someone—he guessed this young woman as her fingertips brushed along the wall while she led the way—had trailed a hand for years, leaving a shining path in the muted sunlight where the flocking had worn off the wallpaper.

The hallway ended in a large foyer. A set of double doors adorned with rippling leaded glass was to his right. To his left a flight of stairs made their way to a second floor. The young woman paused in front of a set of closed pocket doors. Next to those was an opened room—a less formal parlor, if the natural light and airiness of the room was any indication. A petticoat table with its mirror at floor level stood near the opened doors. Considering his guide's proclivity for denim trousers, boots, and chambray shirts, he didn't think that mirror was used often. He hadn't seen a home with a ladies' parlor since he left New Orleans more than two years earlier.

"You might not recognize my father. He was in an accident about six years ago and he's never recovered." She looked over her shoulder. An old pain defined the lines of her face, darkened her eyes, and layered her voice. "He hasn't been the same since then. Apoplexy shortly afterward exacerbated the damage caused by the accident."

His assumption that this was Sam's daughter had been correct. "You must be Rachel."

She nodded, once, and opened the doors to the closed parlor. Before he walked into the room, Rachel grabbed his shirt sleeve and stopped him. "Please don't upset him. He's very fragile."

Fragile was not a word he would have ever thought to use in conjunction with the man he so vividly remembered after only a few bare hours engaged in what became a high-stakes poker game. His recollections of Sam Leonard were of a barrel-chested giant of a man, capable of putting away copious amounts of alcohol, who became louder and brasher as the evening wore on, and of a man overbearingly proud of his only child. The paragon of feminine virtues created through Sam's bragging was far from the reality of the young woman impeding his entrance into the parlor.

"Why don't you stay for this conversation, then, so

I don't upset him?" Harrison made the offer after a single glance into the room. A wheeled chair bathed in the elongating rays of the late afternoon sun faced the southern exposed windows. What he could see of the individual slumped in the chair made him question if it was even the man he had known.

"It won't be a long conversation, Mr. Taylor." Rachel walked into the room and directly to the chair. "Daddy," she said and knelt at her father's side. "Someone is here to see you about the ranch."

The gurgling sounds from the hunched figure somehow still managed to sound angry and one hand flailed the air near Rachel's face. She stood and drew back.

Harrison crossed the room and stared down at the man imprisoned in the wicker wheelchair. The bull of a man he remembered was gone. Sam's complexion was ashen, half his face drooping. Drool had trickled from a side of his mouth and dried to a thick, white line. His left arm hung uselessly in his lap. The other was still flailing. From mid-thigh down, Sam's legs were missing. A heavy quilt covered his lap, while a wide swathe of what appeared to be linen wrapped around the man's once barrel chest, under his arms, and was tied around the back of the chair, to keep him from tumbling onto the floor.

It was the pure, stark terror crossing the old man's face though that tore through Harrison. The man thrashed his hand at Harrison, as if to push him away, and the incomprehensible sounds breaking from him were those of a frightened, wounded creature.

A long, low, distant rumble of thunder intruded into the room. Rachel stepped between Harrison and her father. "You might want to go put your horse up, Mr. Taylor. That storm is getting closer."

"What happened to him?" He couldn't take his gaze from the shell that stared up at him with undisguised fear.

"He was blasting a played-out silver mine shut and it collapsed on him. Please, go, now." She gestured at the opened doors. "You're upsetting him and Doc says anything that makes him upset could kill him."

Harrison wasn't sure if what was left of Sam was living and that death wouldn't be kinder, and even as he thought that, he bit the words back. He stepped away, hesitating just long enough to see Rachel lift a white rag from a wash basin near her father and gently dab at his face. "It's all right," he heard her murmur. "I'm right here, Daddy."

Chapter Two

Rachel wrung out the wash rag, her gaze drifting for a few seconds to the empty doorway. When that man first asked for water for his horse and himself, she heard the drawl and the cadence to his words and recognized that unique manner of speaking; something she had prayed to never hear anything the likes of again.

And then, dear, merciful Lord, he said his name was Taylor.

She should have told him to keep riding and emphasized her point with another load of buckshot. Instead, she had as much as invited the devil into her home.

Rachel wiped the dried spittle from Sam's chin, deftly dodging the badly aimed swing he took at her. Sam grabbed her shirt sleeve and shoved her hand away, sputtering his anger.

"I can't understand you." She dropped the rag into the wash basin. "Do as Dr. Hagar has said and speak slower. Try, Daddy. Please."

The old man's narrowed eyes blazed with impotent fury. He swung his right arm in an encompassing arc, then smacked his own chest, all the while vehemently shaking his head. He jabbed a finger at the floor, his head shaking not ceasing.

"Stop." Rachel forced herself to keep a soothing

tone, tamping down her own frustration at her inability to understand what he tried to communicate. "You're just making yourself more upset."

Sam shut his eyes and when he reopened them, Rachel drew back. Something she recognized as hatred glittered with bright flashes and twisted the half of his face not paralyzed by his stroke into something almost unrecognizable. With a deliberation born of fury, he tried to speak again. The words were still garbled and slurred but she made out one word: "mine."

It was the same pointless exercise in futility every time he tried to talk. "I know it was the mine that did this. Regardless of what you wanted, I was not about to just leave you there and let you die." She couldn't keep her defeat from her voice. Pulling him from what was left of the old silver mine had left her victim to Sam's vitriolic rage before the apoplexy deprived him of the ability to speak. For almost three months after his accident, Sam had berated her for saving him, cursing her for damning him to a life of utter dependency.

A sob of either frustration or anger ripped from her father. He beat his open palm on his chest, repeating that one less than garbled word.

Rachel tilted her head, considering another possibility other than the mine accident. An old pain twisted around her heart. She wasn't supposed to be dressed in denims and chambray. She was supposed to be the grand lady of the manor, as her mother had been—the perfect standard Sam had always held up as a pattern for her life. "Yes, the ranch is yours."

As she said those words, the hand-written deed she had seen less than fifteen minutes ago flashed in her memory. "That man who was just here—do you remember meeting him in a poker game at Fort Scott?"

Sam's involuntary, choked breath and the manner he flung his head back answered as clearly as any words he had once been able to speak.

"How could you be so foolish as to keep gambling? Your luck wasn't going to change if you continued to bet, no matter how much you had yourself convinced of that." She made herself take a step back because more than anything, she wanted to shake the infirm man. "How could you sign away half this ranch and not see fit to tell me about it?"

There wasn't an answer. Even if he had been able to speak, she knew he would have been able to justify what he did. In Sam's world, he was seldom if ever wrong and his ends were justification for the means he used. Without much effort, she could form his protests and his reasoning. She had heard those explanations so many times. It was his ranch, to do with as he wanted. The ranch was never meant to be hers, just held until she married. How dare she question him when she should be grateful he hadn't disowned her and thrown her out on her ear? She was a bitter disappointment in everything he had wanted for her and she dishonored her mother's memory. As if she could wipe away his harsh words, she rubbed her palms on her shirt sleeves. Needing an excuse to be gone from his anger and the betrayal she felt, she said, "Ben will be here shortly with Joshua. I have to finish up supper."

Sam growled and bared his teeth in a lop-sided, vicious snarl. He twisted his head away, pointedly staring out the windows.

She wanted to rail at him, scream until he understood, but she also knew he never would. He had never tried to understand her attachment to the ranch and her determination to never leave it. She had never been able to explain why it was that the mountains out her window had been and continued to be the only view she ever wanted. And as surely as if her soul were made of iron filings and those white granite peaks a lodestone they pulled her back to Wyoming every time she ever left.

With a small sigh and a shake of her head, she walked across the room. Anger made her pause in the open doorway. "You could have told me what you did when you got home from your last selling trip. With everything else you said to me then, I'm surprised you didn't deliver that news as your final blow."

Sam's indecipherable gibberish reached her.

"All my life, I've worked as hard as any man you ever hired. I knew I had to prove myself and prove I could run this spread. I rode for this brand. I rode drag for as long as you made me, choking on the dust from the herd and eating that dust for days afterward because if I had refused, you would have had your excuse to deny me ownership. I knew the only reason you kept me on drag was to try to force me to give up the 'foolish notion' of ever ramrodding the Lazy L. I roped our steers. I branded them. I dug screw worms out of them. I was covered more than once in blood and manure." As she spoke she retraced her steps to her father's side. She recalled the first time she had put a red-hot branding iron onto the flank of a bawling calf, the way the stench of seared flesh and burnt hair made her nauseous. None of the wranglers had dared to teach her to rope, so when she couldn't master the art she asked both Royce Majors and Drake Adams at the

Rocking Bar M to teach her. The uncomfortable silence when she roped her first bull calf, dragged him to the fire, threw him to the ground, and then branded and castrated him, still echoed in her. After that, she only dropped a rope on heifers.

"I had blisters on blisters and when they broke, I just wrapped my hands and kept on working." She glanced down at her palms and then closed her hands, hiding the callouses and the broken, ragged nails in clenched fists. Definitely not the soft, silky hands of a lady. "You never once heard me complain, never once heard me ask to do something less, even when I rode on the fall roundup with a broken collarbone. You taught me that I couldn't expect any more of the men hired at the Lazy L than what I was willing to do myself. Even with all of that, when you sent me to boarding school and then that finishing school, all I wanted was to be back here. Do you know how many nights I cried myself to sleep when I was there because I was so homesick?"

Did he know how many times she cut sage brush to hide in her trunk when he banished her to those schools? When the homesickness became so great and the need to see the mountains so intense it was a physical pain, the aroma of the crumbled sage leaves was the same scent of the land after a rain and offered her some comfort. A fist sized piece of white quartzite from the mountains had traveled to the East Coast and back every year, also hidden in the depths of her trunk. Her throat tightened with the memory of clutching that rock to her heart and she forced the next words out. "I may not be the lady you expected me to be and perhaps I've fallen far short of what you've told me my mother was, but I am your only child. This ranch is just as much mine as it is yours."

Her only answer was another unintelligible sound and a wave of his hand, as if she were an annoying fly he could swat away.

In the kitchen, Rachel leaned over the sink and struggled to push away a renewed sense of betrayal. Every hate-filled word Sam threw at her when she told him she was carrying a child echoed in her, pounded against her as painful as punches. Her fingers tightened on the galvanized metal, refusing to bend any further into the counter. Rachel shoved the litany of her short-comings according to her father away. Perhaps she was all those things but she was also the only reason the Lazy L was still solvent, though barely. With only the help of Ben and a few of the ranchers, she had managed for the last six years to keep their collective heads above water.

A steady, rhythmic "thunk" drew her attention. She forced herself to stand upright, tears held at bay. Following the sound, she made her way from the house to the woodshed and came to a halt.

Harrison Taylor was making short work of the woodpile. His hat and leather vest were on the ground near the chopping block. Her earlier suspicion that he had a revolver in his saddle bags was confirmed by a gun belt strategically laid across his vest. The sweat-darkened chambray strained across his back as he swung the axe into the smaller piece of wood. His sleeves were rolled up past his elbows. Clearly delineated muscling in his lower arms rippled with the upward swing of the axe. One strike and the aged, dry wood split cleanly in half. He bent, placed another piece of wood in position, and slid the axe through his palms for another chop.

When he bent to place yet another piece of the large pine on the block, she spoke. "Mr. Taylor, you don't need to do that."

He lowered the axe head to the ground and twisted his torso partially to her, all the while leaning on the handle. He needed a haircut. The dark stubble on his chin and cheeks said he hadn't shaved in several days. Sweat dripped down his face and soaked his hair, darkening the brown highlighted with gold. More droplets traced small rivulets down his neck, disappearing into the unbuttoned collar of his shirt. He was breathing heavily and he didn't answer her for a bit. After he caught his breath, he said, "When I went by the stove there were only a few pieces of wood left in the box. I probably don't have time to start working on that fence before the rain hits, but I can make sure you've got plenty of wood for the stove."

"Where are you from?" The words broke from her before she could stop them. So much for the vaunted upbringing Sam had insisted on. Instead of an expression of thankfulness for Taylor's assistance, she was interrogating him.

His mouth tightened and his posture stiffened. A forced smile eased the tightness but did little to erase the hard spark in the depths of his eyes. "I'm going to guess you don't want me to say I just rode up from around Denver."

Rachel fought the urge to step back, out of arm's reach. Drawing a breath became difficult with the manner her heart lodged in her throat. A cold sweat prickled on her back, dripping down her spine. "Where is your home, Mr. Taylor?"

"Here." He straightened but didn't release the axe handle. "Per that deed, I own half this ranch."

"It's rather convenient you've had that deed for at least six years, but you just get around to making a claim on it now when the only person who could dispute it will never be able to." Why did he dance around giving her a straight answer? "You're from Kentucky, aren't you?"

In the sudden silence between them, the gusting wind lifted to a mournful wail and another rumble of thunder rolled across the land. Uncomfortably aware both her shotgun and the Dragoon were in the kitchen and he was holding an axe tightened her throat even more.

"My drawl gives me away every time." The give-away thickened as he continued, "Always makes me sound like an uneducated, backwoods hick. How'd you know it's Kentucky?"

Rachel backed a step. "Some years ago, the Lazy L hired a hand named Jason Taylor. His drawl was just like yours."

The change in Harrison was instant. He straightened even more, his jaw clenched, and his fingers tightened on the axe handle. "Jason Taylor? A little taller than me, heavier? Black hair, black eyes? Bad temper on a hair trigger?"

She nodded. Just hearing Jason described brought up every memory she had tried over the years to suppress. Without a conscious thought, her arms crossed over her stomach and she fought the urge to hunch into herself.

"Where is he now?"

The question barked out like gunfire and drove her away another step. "I don't know. He disappeared from these parts some years ago. No one has seen him since."

The axe handle hit the ground with a dull thud. Rachel flinched and studied the tiny dust cloud raised by the impact. He walked to the small pile of his belongings. Her breath caught when he bent and reached for the gun belt, only to be released when he simply moved the weapon and shrugged into his vest. When he muttered, "I was hoping he was dead," her tongue felt glued to the roof of her mouth and she was unable to form a word.

He walked past her, set the axe inside the small wood shed that was not much more than a lean-to and scooped up a load of wood. Without another word, he carried the split logs away. She assumed he went to the house.

Rachel studied the dusty ground at her feet. Harrison's comment about hoping for Jason's death left little doubt in her mind he knew the man. They shared the same surname, the same marked drawl which meant Harrison was probably originally from the same area of Kentucky Jason had hailed from. There was no doubt in her mind he was related to Jason. Heaven help her, she hadn't invited the devil into her home—her father had deeded half her ranch to him.

She looked to the western horizon, her gaze settling on the flat top of Tableau Mesa, barely visible with the storm clouds rolling over it and shrouding the summit in rain. Lightning snaked from the clouds, speared into the ground, followed a few seconds later with a sharp crack. A shiver raced over her. She hated thunderstorms.

The slamming of the screened door at the back of the house jolted her from her thoughts. She still had to finish supper preparations. With little thought, she lifted the hat and gun belt he left behind and walked to the house.

Her climb up the short flight of steps onto the back porch involved avoiding the sagging middle step. Harrison met her on the porch. She handed him the gun belt and hat, then asked, "How did you know Jason?"

He paused in the process of buckling the gun belt on, his brow lifting in silent query.

"You know him. Just remarking you hoped he was dead is proof of that." Her earlier shiver returned. Deciding to toss all caution to the wind, she added, "I wish I had never made his acquaintance."

Harrison inclined his head to the side. A humorless smile crossed his face even as he leaned over to tie the holster down on his leg. "Unfortunately, I didn't have that option." He straightened and looked over her shoulder at some point well beyond the ranch yard. "I guess I was born into the wrong family in Trapman County. If you will excuse me, I'll leave you to finish your preparations for supper."

"Your saddle bags appear to be quite empty." For her whole life, she had been raised to extend hospitality. Finishing school had taught her to be a gracious hostess. That habit, coupled with those lessons, was hard to break and she fell back onto those behaviors, even if belatedly. If she made more dumplings for the stew, she could stretch it to include Harrison. She hadn't missed the rumbling of his stomach earlier. The hollowness in his cheeks said he hadn't been eating on a regular basis. "You're welcome to join us, Mr. Taylor. Supper will be ready as soon as Ben and my son arrive."

He brought his gaze to her face, leaning in a little closer to her. Curiosity lightened the hazel color in his eyes and his brow lifted again with another silent query. Rachel steeled herself to answer the question she was certain he was trying to frame. He surprised her with his next words. "I appreciate that. Thank you."

"It's simple fare." She let a smile cross her face in her relief at not having to answer questions. "It will stick to your ribs, though. All I ask is that you come to the table with clean hands and that you not use vulgarity in front of my son. Joshua is only five."

Harrison straightened, a crooked grin etching his mouth. "Yes, ma'am. Clean hands and no vulgarity. What I smelled when I dropped that wood for you in the kitchen really made my mouth water." He touched two fingers to the bill of his hat. "I'm going to go put my tack in the barn before it starts raining."

He stepped off the porch, right onto the sagging step. With a nimbleness she didn't expect from one so tall, he leaped to the ground. "When I fix the fence in the morning, I'll see what I can do to shore up that step, too."

Rachel spent several seconds watching him, unable to explain why his form drew her attention. She doubted the top of her head even came to his chin. His long legs made short work of the distance from the house to the small corral next to the barn where his saddle was balanced on the top rail. With a practiced ease, he swung the saddle onto his shoulder and entered the barn. He had broad shoulders, she admitted.

She was testing the dumplings with a fork when

she heard two horses canter into the yard. A glance out the window reassured her that the only hand left at the Lazy L had returned with her son. Lowering the lid onto the simmering stew, she reminded herself to check the nesting boxes for eggs when she brought the dairy cows in after supper.

"Momma!" Joshua's shout announced his arrival in the house. "Ben says you gotta come out to the barn right away."

Knowing the former foreman's deeply suspicious nature and his sometimes over-bearing protectiveness, Rachel ran from the house and to the barn. Harrison was slumped, unmoving, against a stall wall. A thin trickle of blood ran down the side of his face and Ben stood over his still form, revolver cocked and pointed at the back of his head.

"Ben Hauser! Lower that gun." Not bothering to wait for him to do as ordered, Rachel pushed past Ben and knelt next to Harrison. He was breathing, apparently just unconscious. "What did you do?"

"I walk into the barn and see a strange man here, wearing a gun strapped down pretty low so before he got the draw on me, I cold-cocked him." Ben shoved his gun into its holster. "I promised you a long time ago no one was ever going to hurt you, again."

"Attacking him is a bit premature, don't you think?" She shot a glare up at him. "There's some ice in the tray in the ice box. Make yourself useful and wrap it up in a kitchen towel and bring it out here." The rapidly forming goose egg over Harrison's temple drew her attention and she cautiously probed the swelling. Relief loosened the tension in her chest as it didn't appear his skull was broken, but she would bet he would have a massive headache when he came to.

Joshua hovered in the doorway, his eyes wide with astonishment. "Is he dead?"

Rachel spared him a smile. "No. Ben just knocked him out."

"Who is he, Momma?" Joshua crept a step closer.

She struggled with an answer and was spared by Ben's return with the ice. "Help me lay him out. It has to be hard to breathe huddled over like that."

The foreman's mouth compressed into a thin line, but he bent over and slipped his arms under Harrison's, then pulled him away from the stall. Hauser lowered him to the floor and straightened. "You going to tell me what's going on? Like who he is."

Rachel applied the ice to the side of Harrison's head, once more struggling to find an answer. She could tell Ben it was none of his business, but he was more than just the foreman. For most of her life, he had been a wrangler for the Lazy L. More than that, he was one of the few people who had stood by her and defended her from Sam's fury, even after Sam had fired the few men who had dared to brave his rage. "His name is Harrison Taylor—"

"*Harrison Taylor?*"

She didn't think it was possible for Ben's voice to reach such depths of disgust and disbelief at the same time. "Yes, Harrison Taylor. Apparently, on one of Daddy's selling trips back East, they met in a poker game."

Ben's mouth dropped open. She wondered if she had had the same incredulous expression when she read that hand-written deed Harrison handed to her. She hoped she had covered much of her unease when he had announced his name, but she wasn't willing to wager on that.

"Daddy made a bet he couldn't cover, so he put up half the Lazy L. He lost to Mr. Taylor, here." She glanced down at Harrison. "I saw the note Daddy wrote, giving him half the ranch. It's his handwriting. Lord knows, I saw it enough in the letters he wrote when I was at finishing school."

"Are you telling me your father gambled away the ranch? To *him*?" The foreman gestured at the man sprawled on the dusty floor and shook his head in what she could only define as disbelief. "To Jason's brother?"

"Yes, to him, and I don't know if he's Jason's brother. I doubt Daddy asked him if he was related." Of course Ben would remember Jason's contempt for his younger brother, the man Jason called a traitor to everything he had been raised to believe in and revere. Her stomach twisted with the recollection of Jason's pride in having fought for the Confederacy and that tattered shell jacket he wore.

"How many Harrison Taylors can there be?"

She didn't think he really wanted an answer. A low groan broke from Harrison as he stirred and allowed her an excuse to not respond to Ben. Rachel bent closer to Harrison. "Don't move. You took a pretty good blow to your head."

Rachel fought the urge to jerk free when he lifted a hand and covered hers but he did nothing more than move the linen-wrapped ice an inch or so closer to his temple. He opened his eyes, grimacing with pain. She extracted her hand and asked, "How many fingers am I holding up?"

To her relief, he seemed to be focusing when he squinted and then said, "Three, I think."

The sound of metal rasping against leather and then of a gun being cocked drew her attention from Harrison. Ben stood with gun drawn and pointed at Harrison's head. A multitude of emotions rippled through Rachel and she allowed the anger to edge her voice. "For heaven's sake, Ben, put it away. Take Joshua into the house, please, and get him some supper. Daddy also needs looked after."

Chapter Three

What the hell was it with these people drawing on him? He hadn't been on the receiving end of so many weapons since he rode with the Army of the Cumberland in the War of Southern Rebellion. Rachel he could understand but the other one? He was fairly certain he'd done absolutely nothing to merit a pistol butt to the side of the head. Which at the moment was pounding a nauseating tempo that not only doubled but reverberated in his whole body when his assailant stomped from the barn. A cautious tilt of his throbbing head brought Rachel into his view. "I'm going to guess the little one is your son and the other is your husband."

She rocked back onto her heels and shook her head once. "Yes and no. Joshua is my son." Surprisingly, a slash of bright color stained her cheeks. "Ben is not my husband."

Harrison grimaced. The water dripping through his hair and into his ear was annoying. He moved the ice away from his head, dropping the wet towel with its cold contents to the dirt floor. When had she slipped her hand away from his? Interesting the man wasn't her husband yet he seemed willing to assume responsibility for the boy. "Who is he?"

The color staining her cheeks deepened, while her features tightened with the same tension filling her voice. "I'm not sure that's any of your—" She let out a sigh as she broke that train of thought. "Daddy made it your business when he lost half the ranch to you. Ben is the foreman, or was, when I could afford to pay him."

Harrison pushed himself up into a sitting position. The interior of the barn spun, and forced him to close his eyes and draw in a deep breath to try to convince his stomach to stop roiling. Cold water dripped down his neck and spine from the melting ice she placed at the base of his skull. "You're a widow?"

A sharp hiss marked her intake of breath. Her voice broke on a single word. "No."

He twisted his head so quickly not only did the interior spin but black holes danced in his vision. Not succumbing to retching was a battle. Resisting the light pressure she applied to the back of his neck to lean forward wasn't an option.

"Slow, deep breaths, Mr. Taylor."

Her use of his surname reminded him he'd only known this woman for the better part of a few hours and despite her choice of attire, she did seem to be trying to hold onto propriety. The soothing, soft tone of her voice recalled a much gentler time in his life. When his vision stopped looping, Harrison risked another glance at her. He recognized the jut of her chin and the glitter in the depths of her gray eyes. She was waiting for his condemnation, perhaps because she'd received censure from too many people.

"It's none of my business." He attempted a smile. "If I overstep my boundaries, remind me of that."

"I will." Her smile was as tenuous as he felt his had been. She stood and he had enough of his wits about him to appreciate how fluidly she accomplished that act. "I have to go into the house. Don't try to stand on your own. Ben hit you harder than I hope he intended. I'll send him out to help you in to the house."

"No." Harrison rolled up onto his knees. "I'd rather not have help, even though this is a mite embarrassing." He forced himself to his feet. His head swam and he staggered a step forward, trying to catch his balance, but the floor rushed up to him.

Before he fell, Rachel caught him, palms pressed against his chest. Concerned only with not falling onto her, Harrison gripped her shoulders to steady himself. The moment his hands closed on her, he felt her frame tense. However if he released her, he knew he would fall to his knees.

The sudden silence held between them for what felt like an eternity. A tantalizing aroma of roses and vanilla drifted up from her hair and the strength in her shoulders and arms was a startling revelation. As slender as she was, this wasn't a frail or fragile woman. He loosened his hold but didn't release her. Lightning in the approaching storm flickered, illuminating the gloom. She raised her head and her gaze skipped over his face. Some of the tension in her shoulders eased, even though her breathing grew shallow. A renewed hint of color crept into her cheeks.

"Before the foreman discovers us in a compromising situation, perhaps, I should try to stand on my own."

"Yes." The grumbling thunder almost overwhelmed her whispered agreement.

Neither of them moved. The loose chignon she had gathered her hair into had loosened even more. Auburn strands framed her face, and one long length swept across her throat. The warmth of her palms against him radiated into his chest, while the swirling aroma of roses and vanilla teased him with a promise of what she might taste like if he pressed his lips to her throat. Harrison pulled his hands off her shoulders as if scalded and forced himself to take a step away.

She was off limits. She wasn't a widow, so that meant one of two things and he quickly eliminated her being light-skirted. She didn't strike him as the type. Somewhere, there was a husband—even if the bastard had left her and her child. The storm cooled air was a marked contrast where just moments before her hands had pressed against his shirt. Her wide-eyed pewter gaze never left his face.

"Rachel, Sam refuses to eat."

The foreman's announcement from the doorway drove Rachel a step back but she still didn't look away. Harrison pulled in a short breath. "I'm not going to fall on my face. I'll come to the house in a few minutes."

With only a half-nod, she walked from him. Harrison watched her retreat, cautious to avoid any rapid movement which would leave him dizzy again. The foreman stood in the open doorway, a scowl twisting his features. Mindful to keep his gun hand far from his holstered weapon, Harrison pulled his sight from Rachel's retreating back.

Hauser's gaze drifted from Harrison's boots to his face. "If you hurt her—"

"I have no intention of causing any harm to the lady." The nausea faded into tolerable and the throbbing in his head, while still painful, was no longer as intense as before. He debated asking what even gave the other man cause to believe he had plans to harm Rachel and decided against it. If the man objected,

Harrison was in no condition to counter.

Another bolt of lightning flickered, this time much brighter, and the accompanying thunder boomed sooner. The wind whistled and raised dust devils that whirled between the house and the barn in the fading light. The slamming of the screened back door alerted him Rachel was in the house. "If you'll excuse me, I'd like to move my horse in before it rains, and the lady in question mentioned there are three dairy cows that need to be milked."

If anything, the hostility from Ben increased. "You're Jason Taylor's brother, aren't you?"

"Half-brother." Harrison paused in the barn's doorway and met the foreman's heated glare. "The only thing Jason and I share is a surname."

\*\*\*\*

Thunderclaps shattered the usual late night quiet of the house. Unlike her son, who could sleep through just about anything, or her father who slept with the aid of laudanum, Rachel was awake and staring at the ceiling of her bedroom. Lightning flashed, creating dark and menacing shadows that skittered along the walls, despite the low-pitched lamp burning in her room. She settled her gaze on the flame dancing in the chimney, set into motion by the breezes gusting in the partially opened window.

She should extinguish the lamp, but she couldn't bring herself to do that. Even though it was an expense she could ill afford, it had been years since she had been able to sleep in a totally dark room. It was childish, according to Sam, and if he had his way, he would have allowed her to scream herself hoarse because he hadn't raised a coward.

She forced her thoughts away from the rest of that bitter memory and let her musings wander to the stranger in her barn. Ben told her and Harrison confirmed that he was Jason's sibling, though Harrison had been quick to point out they were only half-brothers. Perhaps that explained why they looked nothing alike. Yes, both men were tall. Harrison, though, was lean without being rangy, while Jason had been built like a bull bison, with the same unpredictable and dangerous temperament. And, black-hearted as the depths of any hell ever known.

Harrison had hazel eyes and she noticed that color shifted and changed in the light. At one time, he must have had a broken nose, if the slight ridge on his bridge was any indication. He had a thin scar just under his left eyebrow and she wondered if both the broken nose and that injury had occurred at the same time. He had a strong jaw, a firm chin, and the few times he had flashed a smile at her it had softened the hard lines of his face.

Her initial impression of him had been one of a grudging respect. Even though he'd been sweating profusely when he rode up in the brutal heat, his first care had been for his horse. That he later took it upon himself to cut firewood only increased her respect. He'd been comfortable with the use of an axe and when she'd pressed her palms to his chest to keep him from falling, the muscling under her hands was as solid as a wall.

A bright flash followed immediately by a sharp crack jolted Rachel upright with her heart racing. Realizing sleep would continue to elude her while the storm raged, she got out of the bed and padded over to the windows overlooking the ranch yard. She slipped into her robe while she crossed the floor.

Yellowed light spilled out the barn door, the reflection rippling with the heavy rain splattering into the puddles. Why was he still awake?

She squinted, trying to make out any movement in the barn through the rain streaked window. Another bolt of lightning illuminated the yard in harsh white light. The long flickering turned the falling rain into droplets of brilliant silver and revealed a massive buckskin horse standing next to the barn. His rider, dressed in a dark duster, sat straight in the saddle, though his head was dipped to shield his face from the rain. She leaned in closer to the window.

The rider lifted his head to her window, rain sluicing off his hat. Rachel gasped and jumped back. She raced to the lamp on the chest of drawers, and doused the flame.

It took her until the next flash of lightning to control her frightened breathing and slow her heart rate. "He's not there," she said, trying to convince herself what she saw hadn't been real. "No one has seen him for six years."

She forced herself to walk to the window and look out again. The horse and rider were still there, but moved further back along the barn wall, as if to melt into the pouring rain. Rachel ran from the room. Her bare feet carried her down the stairs and into the kitchen. She paused to pick up the shotgun as she bolted out the back door. A shell was levered into the chamber before she leaped down the porch steps.

Rachel reached the side of the barn and brought the long gun into a firing position.

There was nothing to aim at. With barely a thought, she retreated into the barn. Harrison was sitting on a saw horse, one of her saddles across another and he was rubbing saddle soap into the tooling.

He looked up at her and his mouth dropped open. "What is it with folks around here pointing guns at me?"

Rachel didn't lower the shotgun. "Is anyone in here with you?"

"No." Harrison rose. He set the rag in his hand into the seat of the saddle. "Did you see something?"

"I saw…" She trailed off, realizing how foolish it would sound if she stated what she'd seen. "I thought I saw…" Frustrated, frightened tears burned her eyes and tightened her throat. "But, it couldn't be."

Harrison's posture stiffened. He lowered the wick in the single lantern, and then his hand dropped onto the butt of his revolver, and slid the weapon from its holster. He leaned in closer to her, his voice little more than a whisper. "What did you see out there and where?"

She lowered the muzzle of the long gun and pointed to the side of the barn where she saw what she was beginning to believe was no more than an apparition. "I thought I saw a horse and rider. I saw him in two lightning flashes."

"Stay here. Keep that shotgun aimed at the doorway and if anyone other than me walks through it, don't hesitate. Shoot first and ask questions later." He slipped out of the barn, revolver leading the way into the thunder and lightning.

Rachel moved further back into the shadows, the shotgun drawn up to her shoulder, finger around the trigger, her thumb resting on the hammer. Harrison's horse thrust his head from the stall. His nostrils flared and he sniffed her, then nudged her. Unwilling to lower the long gun, she endured the large black's insistent nudging until he staggered her a step with his strength. She spared the animal a glare and muttered, "You're a nag."

The horse laced his ears, shuffled a step back into the depths of his stall and then presented his rump to her. It seemed being referenced as a "nag" insulted him. His loud snort emphasized his resentment.

"You're probably not even pedigreed." Rachel shook her head, bemused she was talking to the horse as if he could understand her.

"Actually, he is," Harrison said as he entered the barn. "His sire is an Arabian with a pedigree longer than my arm, and almost all of it is written in Arabic. His dam is a Thoroughbred mare with a fifteen-generation pedigree. And, do you always hold your shotgun like that?"

Rachel immediately noted his holstered revolver. She lowered the shotgun. "Yes, why?"

"I'm surprised you haven't broken your shoulder with the kick."

"It doesn't kick." When she broke her collarbone, that long gun mysteriously disappeared and this newer shotgun replaced it. Though Sam had denied switching the long guns, he was the only one who would or could have had access to replace the weapons. "What did you see out there?"

"There was nothing out there to see, Rachel." He pulled his fingers through his hair, shaking as much of the rain from his dripping scalp as possible. "No tracks, either."

"I know what I saw, Mr. Taylor. I saw—"

"Harrison," he easily corrected her. "I don't doubt you saw something. Maybe a shadow in the lightning, or just the way the lightning illuminated the side of the barn."

"There was someone out there." She gestured in the direction where she had seen the horse and rider. "I am not given to hysterics or hallucinations. I know what I saw."

He sank onto the saw horse. "Let's say for a moment you did see someone. It's rained enough for a horse to make fairly deep prints into the mud but not raining hard enough to wash those tracks away. My boot prints are still visible. If someone was out there, there would be hoof-prints and the only ones I saw were probably from either the boy's horse or Ben's." The smile he sent in her direction unnerved her with its charm. "I would also point out that I certainly don't believe you to be either the hysterical type or someone given to hallucinations."

He seemed convinced that no one was out in the storm. Perhaps, it had been simply the lightning and the shadows allowing her to see what wasn't there. However, the thought of going back to the house and leaving the relative safety his presence provided held no appeal. From her vantage point, she could see the back door. The front door was locked, a habit she had ingrained into her from a time before Joshua was born. She lowered the long gun and propped it against the second saw horse. Harrison's horse drew her attention.

Liquid black eyes regarded her calmly, while his nostrils flared to take in her scent when she moved closer. His muzzle was finely sculpted. She held her hand out to him and the horse slid his nose into her palm so she could scratch his chin. "You said he's pedigreed, but then said he's neither full Arabian nor Thoroughbred."

The black dropped his head as her fingers scratched the side of his face and then his poll.

"He's a cross of something my father was trying to perfect when the Southern Rebellion put the breeding farm under. Over about a mile and a half Demon's got the blazing speed of a Thoroughbred. That speed is combined with the stamina and docility of an Arabian. I'd like to see if I can't perfect the breeding my father saw." There was a distant quality to Harrison's voice, as if he was reminiscing about that those plans.

Rachel startled when he reached up to scratch the horse's ears. She hadn't heard him close the gap between them. As if aware he had alarmed her, Harrison moved a little to one side, and leaned against the stall wall. His elbows rested on the top of the half wall.

"You know there is going to be gossip in town. Not that I see you as anyone who really cares what the gossips say." His grin was at once charming and cynical. "If you cared, I seriously doubt you'd be out in the barn in your night clothes, barefoot, and muddied up to your ankles."

Her feet seemed rooted to the spot she stood. "Why would there be gossip?"

He dipped his head as if he was gathering his thoughts. "You asked me earlier where my home is. Other than what I will admit is a rather dubious claim to half of your ranch, I have no home." He drew a deep breath and lifted his head. A half grin dusted his features. "You need me here. You can't deny that."

"I do not need anyone, Mr. Taylor." Rachel ground out the words. She fought the urge to pull the collar of her night robe further closed even as she moved a step nearer to her shotgun.

"Harrison," he once more corrected. "Yes, you do. Ben can only do so much. Even I've seen that, in a few hours here. You have your hands full taking care of your father and your son. If nothing else, you need me to do the work that you and Ben don't have the time to do—like repairing the garden fence, fixing the steps, replacing the glass in the window on the second floor. Like it or not, your father deeded half this ranch to me when he lost that poker game. I'm not leaving because you need me."

The long gun was in her hands but she didn't point it in his direction. "I will repeat I do not need anyone. However, I expect you to comply with the original terms of our agreement: that in exchange for sleeping the night in my barn, you will repair my garden fence and then be on your way."

His smile grew icy. "We seem to be at an impasse, Rachel."

"Mr. Taylor, I find it highly inappropriate that you insist upon using my Christian name." Even as she said the words, she realized how ridiculous they sounded while she stood, as he put it earlier, wearing her night clothes, barefoot, and muddied to her ankles. Not to mention the highly inappropriate hour of the night.

"What name would you have me use?" He straightened off the stall wall, and to her relief, halted when she pulled the shotgun up.

"I don't want you to use any name for me. I just want you gone in the morning. You have no claim to this ranch. This is my home. I have literally put my blood and my sweat and my tears into this place. Wyoming is very unforgiving. It has destroyed many who tried to wrest a living from it. I'm still here and if you think I will allow you or anyone to take even an inch of my land without a fight, you are sorely mistaken. I will fight you in any manner I can."

He grabbed the saddle he had been cleaning and slid it back onto the stand mounted on the wall, then seized the bridle she knew usually was draped on the horn and placed it across the seat. The look he shot her over his shoulder chilled her to her bones. "If you're planning to fight me legally, good luck. And, I pray you're not planning on killing me to attempt to void that claim. In either scenario, I hope you have a damn good lawyer, *ma'am*."

Chapter Four

Harrison slammed his fist against a stall wall, startling not only the horses and the three milk cows in the barn, but several roosting swallows. The black and cream colored birds swooped around his head before they returned to their perches high in the rafters.

What the hell had he been thinking? He hadn't intended to stay long in any place and he needed to get the lay of the land if he was going to be effective in the position ordered on him. He certainly had no use for half a failing ranch and the thought of getting himself tangled up with another woman...If nothing else, he should have learned from Clarissa Howard women were nothing but devious, scheming creatures and heart-ache.

The darkened house, faintly illuminated in the far distant lightning, drew his glare. There was something different about Rachel, something that pulled him closer. He just couldn't find it possible to label her as devious or scheming. Fiercely independent. Yes. Gritty. Certainly. He'd gotten a good taste of her grit a few minutes ago. He hadn't missed her shock at the revelation her father had lost half the ranch in a poker game. When he told her his name she looked as frightened and desperate as a wild animal caught in a trap. And, the absolute terror gripping her when she had rushed out to the barn...whoever she had seen out there was gone by the time he went out to look. If anyone had been there.

Common sense dictated he should have heard anyone outside the barn ride away. But, her conviction that someone had been there wouldn't let him completely eliminate that possibility. The set of smeared prints he had found belonged to a horse with a unique shoe, on what appeared to be the animal's right front. Very few would be wearing a heart-bar because even fewer owners would keep a horse requiring such a shoe. Checking the shoes on the boy's horse would prove conclusively if it had been his horse next to the barn. And, all that brought him back to Rachel and her fear of whoever she had seen.

Still puzzling through the contradiction that seemed to be Rachel, he reached into his vest pocket and withdrew rolling paper and a small pouch of tobacco. Hefting the pouch, he realized he was going to have to have more money wired from the bank in New Orleans.

He rolled a tight cigarette, struck a match, and lit the tobacco. If her ease with milking the cows and moving the large creatures was any indication, she wasn't afraid of work, even though she seemed as fragile as his mother's fine porcelain and thin enough to blow away in a stiff breeze. He'd already determined that appearance of fragility was utterly inaccurate. Despite Rachel's choice of attire, it was her mannerisms, her actions, and her bearing that screamed what the denim trousers and chambray shirt tried to hide. She'd been raised to be a lady, he would bet a month of Sundays on that one. Her insistence on serving supper promptly at six, on having clean hands at the table, and not using vulgarity around her son all pointed to a woman raised to be more than she tried to portray herself as.

With one last drag on the cigarette, he flicked the glowing butt into a puddle and watched it go out in an instant. He went into the barn and returned to the bed he made in the empty stall next to Demon.

Harrison woke to Demon's terrified screams and the frightened, frantic lowing of the cows. The pungent tang of smoke assaulted his nostrils. He leaped to his feet. A quick look around momentarily froze him.

Angry red flames licked greedily at the loosely piled hay. The fire roared with hideous laughter. The back wall of the barn blazed out of control, the wood already beginning to crumble.

Harrison grabbed Demon's bridle and his saddle bags and flung open the horse's stall door. The stallion reared, terrified. Harrison slammed the stall door shut before the black trampled him in his instinctive fear of fire. He shouted to be heard over the roar of the flames. "Demon, easy, boy!"

Small brands dropped from the loft into the loose hay. More fires began blazing, adding to the hellish atmosphere. Shadows and smoke writhed in the fire's undulating dance. The choking smoke brought tears to Harrison's eyes.

The horse reared again, striking at the wall, and then whirled to the door. Harrison stripped off his shirt and flung it over Demon's head.

The improvised blindfold calmed the stallion so he stood still long enough for Harrison to throw the reins of the bridle around his neck into a makeshift lead rope. He grabbed his saddle off the stall wall, jumping out of the way of Demon's hooves. The black spun around him in mincing, frightened hops, snorting in terror.

Harrison flung the stall door of the mare open and led his horse out of the flaming, smoke-filled barn. He prayed the mare followed. Far enough from the fire to be safe, he directed the horse into a small paddock, heaving a deep breath when the mare bolted in behind the black.

He stripped the shirt off the horse's head. The shirt, bridle, saddle, and saddle bags dropped to the ground. Harrison slammed the gate shut and raced back into the barn. He opened two of the three stanchions holding the milk cows. The third stanchion was stuck but it was farthest from the flames, giving him hope he could return to save the cow. He then pulled the saddle he'd been cleaning earlier that night off the wall rack, and scooped up his vest.

The two freed cows stood blocking the exit. Harrison slapped the back end of the lead cow and she bolted out the door, the second following her. He ran behind the normally placid creatures until he was relatively sure they wouldn't go back into the inferno. He then dropped the saddle and his belongings to the ground.

One last time Harrison made his way into the oven-hot, blazing barn. Panic again paralyzed him. Rachel was trying to pull the last cow from her stanchion. The lunging cow made it impossible to break the stanchion open. Fire licked close to Rachel's feet. Larger and larger pieces of burning debris fell to the ground. The failing loft floor snapped his momentary paralysis. He jumped across a flare-up and heaved his weight against the jammed stanchion.

"Get out of here," he yelled over the roaring flames and pushed Rachel aside. "I've got it all under control."

Rachel returned to the battle to free the cow.

"Leave her," Harrison shouted, grabbing her arm. "We've got to get out of here. It's going to come down on our heads at any second. Leave her."

She flung his hand off and continued to pull on the stanchion. The cow screamed and lunged in terror.

Harrison grabbed Rachel around the waist, then lifted her over his shoulder like a sack of grain and carried her from the barn. She thumped on his back and he stumbled but refused to stop.

He hadn't taken more than two running steps out the door before the loft floor collapsed. When he set Rachel down in the yard at what he hoped was a safe distance from the inferno, he had to grab her arms to restrain her from going back into the blazing structure. "You can't go in there."

"She'll die if we don't get her out," Rachel screamed, thrashing in an attempt to break his grip.

"She's dead, already." He regretted those words with the look she shot over her shoulder.

The building collapsed in on itself with a loud, rumbling growl. The terrified, pained bellows of the trapped cow ceased.

Harrison pulled Rachel's suddenly passive frame back even further. He looked over at the fallen, flaming barn and started shaking. "Merciful God in Heaven, we could have been killed, for a damned cow, no less. Are you always this stubborn?"

"You set my barn on fire!"

"What?" How in the hell had she come to that conclusion? He'd been a lot of things in his life, he'd admit to that, but arsonist wasn't and never would be one of them. "Why would I do that? And then stick around to pull your horse and two of the cows from the barn if I did?"

"You deliberately burned my barn." The words were a growl. "It was you and your brother. I know I saw him!"

"Jason? Have you lost your mind?"

"The two of you burned my barn." She came at him with fists flying.

Harrison backed a step and caught her wrists, blunting her attack. With her fists stilled and no longer a danger, her response grew frantic in her attempts to free herself. He felt as if he was holding a wildcat by the ears—not sure what to do with her, but certain he didn't dare let go. He twisted his lower body away from her knees, but he couldn't avoid her relatively ineffective bare-footed kicks to his shins. "I didn't burn the barn."

He pulled her wrist up toward his shoulder when Rachel resorted to the only weapon she had left. "Don't you dare bite—"

Her teeth closed on his forearm and bit down.

"OW! Damn it! I should put you over my knee, you little hell cat."

His words garnered a response, but not the one he was expecting. Terror blanched her face and any hope for coherent thought from her at the moment vanished. Even more disturbing was she seemingly didn't recognize him and it was if she was fighting for her life. Other than her labored breathing as she battled to free herself, she was as silent as the grave, seeming terrified that any sound would go worse for her.

He released her wrists and leaped back. He dodged every punch and kick she tried to land, hoping she would soon either wear out or realize he wasn't a threat. He said as he avoided another punch, "I didn't set fire to the barn."

A momentary glance down at his forearm revealed blood welling where she had bitten him. In that second when his attention was off her, Rachel's fist connected with his jaw. Too late, Harrison realized his mistake. He'd let her in past his defensive posture. Even as his head snapped to a side with the force of her punch, he had to admire her tenacity and form. Someone had taught her to fight.

He let her fully into his defensive zone and before she realized where she was, he grabbed her shoulders and spun her around, and then pinned her arms to her sides in a bear hug. She tried to kick backward, but he had already spread his legs apart enough she couldn't do more than deliver a glancing blow. Her head slammed against him, connecting painfully with his collarbone. He grunted, grit his teeth, but didn't give her an inch of release.

She struggled with more and more frantic thrashings to break free. The back of her head repeatedly hit his collarbone and he wanted nothing more than to shake her until her teeth rattled but he sensed that would be the wrong thing to do.

A low moan broke from her. The sound grew until it was a high, thin sob and she went completely limp, all the fight escaping her. Harrison eased his hold. As soon as her arms were free enough, she drove her elbow into his ribs.

Harrison staggered a step, coughing and trying to

catch his breath. Her bare feet slapped in the mud as she ran to the house. With a shake of his head, he walked to the corral housing the two horses. He leaned his elbows onto the top rail and stared at the muddy ground, trying to make some sense of what had just happened. He cast a glance at the destroyed barn and the dying inferno.

She thought she saw his half-brother earlier that night? Was that why she accused him of deliberately burning the barn? And in a partnership with Jason? He hadn't seen his half-brother in better than a decade, not since the night Jason had called him a traitor for signing with the Union Army and the ensuing fisticuffs that had become deadly serious when Jason had pulled out a knife. Absent-mindedly he rubbed the bridge of his nose, the old break a constant reminder of the vicious fight.

What had Jason done to Rachel that she thought he could be the one responsible for the fire? By her own words, no one had seen him in this area for about six years. Why return now, if he was even alive? What purpose would returning now serve and unless Jason had drastically changed since he'd seen him last, Jason had never used subterfuge as a manner of intimidation. Jason had much preferred to use brute force, delivered personally through his own fists.

Something had happened between the two of them, but he just couldn't figure out what it was.

Demon and the mare jerked their heads up, alerting him to Rachel's return. The distinct sound of a gun being cocked carried to him. It didn't sound like her shotgun, though. "Are you really pointing a gun at me, again?"

"Saddle your horse and leave."

He craned his head over his shoulder. He hated being right. She held the heavy Colt Dragoon with both hands and it was pointed into the middle of his back.

"You sure that thing's loaded right?" Black powder, wad, ball, percussion cap—if it hadn't been loaded correctly, and she fired it, she could kill them both. Giving up the Dragoon for the newer Colt design of the Single Action Army with the metal cartridges hadn't been a hardship, not when more than once, the powder in his Dragoon had gotten damp and failed to fire.

"Go. Now."

He noted she didn't respond as to whether the Dragoon had been properly loaded. "You do know if that powder got damp even once, it won't fire. It's an annoyance."

"I will shoot you, if you do not saddle up and leave immediately."

He let a half smile cross his face with the tiniest of breaks in her voice on her threat to shoot. He faced her fully and leaned back against the corral fence. "You're bluffing. I'm not leaving, so you're going to have to shoot me."

She pulled the revolver up with a sharp, hissing intake of breath. Harrison stared down the wide bore barrel, and with a deliberation and calmness he wasn't feeling, crossed his arms over his chest. "Squeeze the trigger. You've already pulled the hammer back."

The strain of holding the nearly five pounds of the Dragoon steady was taking its toll on her arms and the muzzle wavered. The flames consuming the barn flared, washing her and the blued finish of the revolver in a deep contrast of shifting shadows and orange light.

"Would you prefer I turn around so you can shoot me in the back? Though I think if you're really going to shoot an unarmed man, you should look him in the eye when you squeeze that trigger."

He braced himself for the bullet with her harsh, sucked in breath. Demon's hoof-falls brought the stallion closer. "Just be sure my horse isn't behind me when you do fire, because at this distance, the ball will completely blow out the back of my skull and kill anything standing behind me."

The muzzle wavered a little more and her breath sounded like a choked off cry. Her jaw clenched with the strain of trying to hold the revolver steady. Indecision twisted her features and the gun shook in her hands. Taking the life of another human was never easy. He knew that from firsthand experience. The faces of so many young men dressed in butternut and gray still haunted him.

The very last flicker of lightning from the long past storm danced along the far horizon, brushing silver glints on the rain-covered landscape glowing orange-red. The final portion of the remaining wall of the barn collapsed with a groan. Her gaze darted to the building and Harrison lowered his arms and straightened. "The more you think about it, the harder it is to pull that trigger. So, either stop debating it with yourself and shoot, or put the gun down."

She moved the revolver away from him. Without lowering it, she took aim at a far distant point and squeezed the trigger. The resulting flash, smoke cloud, and loud report left Harrison's ears ringing. She lowered the weapon and said, "I have never aimed a gun at anything I didn't intend to shoot, Mr. Taylor.

Why won't you leave?"

He admitted he was wrong about whether she had been bluffing. The rain-cooled breeze brushed against his bared torso and without answering her, he looked around for his shirt. He pulled it out of the mud puddle where he had dropped it in his haste to return to the barn and attempt to save the dairy cows. Pulling on the wet, muddy garment held little appeal. He took the time it required to throw the shirt across the top rail of the corral to form an answer.

Why didn't he just saddle up and leave? There was nothing holding him here. Hell, he only agreed to accept Sam's hand-written deed to half of what appeared to be a failing ranch to soothe his own bruised ego for letting himself get that deep into a poker game without tangibles on the table. What was it about the woman standing in front of him that made him want to stay?

Sensing her discomfort with his silence, he tried to quiet her misgivings. "I didn't set fire to the barn. Why would I? I own half this ranch. A new barn is an expense that I doubt the Lazy L can spare."

Her shoulders rounded and she shook her head. "We're barely making ends meet."

Damn, he hated being right, again.

"So, you need me." He gestured at the house. "Let's try for some honesty here. Someone is making things deliberately hard on you. When I was chopping wood earlier, I took a good look at your garden. Unless you're putting horse shoes on your cows, it wasn't the cows that broke down the fence and trampled your vegetables. That broken window on the second floor has buck shot holes around it. I don't think you ventilated the house with your shotgun."

Her expression grew longer.

"When I rode in this afternoon, I noted several areas of burned acreage. What was left appeared to be prime grazing land. I don't know a lot about raising cows, but I do know about raising horses. You can't graze animals on burned out pasture land. On one of those pastures, there was a windmill that looked to be deliberately destroyed, so not only is there nothing to graze, there isn't any water."

"The windmill and the pump it's attached to were destroyed a month ago. I have no idea who shot the house or who trampled the garden. Both those events occurred when neither I nor Ben were here." She lowered her head as if something near her feet held her undivided attention. "The acreage burned two weeks ago, and I lost about fifteen head in that fire." She finally met his gaze. "We raise cattle, not cows, out here. And, you still haven't told me why I need you."

Harrison picked up his leather vest and dug into the inside pocket. He pulled out a silver badge and looked at it for several long seconds. He then handed it to Rachel.

Her mouth dropped open when she rotated the badge to read it in the flames still darting skyward from the barn. "You're a federal marshal?"

He nodded. "I've been appointed as the federal marshal for Laramie, Albany, and Carbon Counties for the next four years. I serve at the pleasure of President Grant and when he gave me this jurisdiction his exact words were 'I can't send you to the ends of the earth, but the Wyoming Territory is close enough.' He doesn't like losing in poker any more than your father does."

"If I still played poker, which I don't, I'd tell you to remind me to never play against you. Why didn't you tell me this when you first rode up?"

Harrison took the badge from her hand and secured it once more in the deep interior pocket of his vest. "It didn't seem important. Then when you told me where I was…" He trailed off. "It wasn't important then."

Rachel looked away and lifted her head skyward. Harrison followed her line of vision. The last of the storm was a darker ribbon on the far north-eastern horizon and the night sky was filled with stars.

"As long as we're trying honesty, to use your word, do you honestly think that little tin star will do anything to stop what's happening to my ranch?"

Even though there was doubt in her voice, he heard the hope, as well. Harrison closed the distance between them and stood behind her. "That little tin star carries a lot of weight."

Chapter Five

Rachel struggled with the urge to step away. She was much too aware of his large frame directly behind, close enough to touch her. Her mortification with so completely losing her wits and fighting him as if she were a caged wildcat still hissed in her and burned with more intensity than the flames consuming her barn. She hadn't made that mistake since before Joshua was born.

"As far as the ranch's creditors are concerned, the funds I have on deposit with a bank in New Orleans will carry a lot more weight than my badge," Harrison said.

She spun on her heel and found her nose mere inches from a very masculine, well-muscled bare torso. The mingling of smoke, saddle soap, and an earthy musk made her head spin. Her throat tightened. As if aware of her reaction, Harrison took a step back.

"What are you saying, Mr. Taylor?"

"It's Harrison. As your partner, I think we should be on a first name basis." A grin that was pure charm revealed his white, slightly uneven teeth. "I'm saying between that 'little tin star' and my money, you need me for this ranch."

Visions of buying more cattle and hiring enough hands to run those so far hypothetical herds on the massive acreage of the Lazy L, a newly built barn, a freshly whitewashed and repaired house, and even a refurbished buggy danced in her imagination. As tantalizing as the offer was, Rachel immediately squelched the idea. She shook her head. "I cannot and I will not become beholden to you and your money."

"Before we engage in another lively discussion about what I can and can't do for my interest in this ranch," he said and folded his arms across his chest, hands tucked under his upper arms, "do you think we could move the conversation into the house where it's a little warmer?"

Goose flesh pebbled his skin and he was shivering. With his arms flexed, the muscles defining his chest, shoulders, and upper arms were clearly delineated. The planes of his chest, lightly sprinkled with curling hair the same shade of golden-brown covering his head, drew her attention from his face. Heaven help her, he could have snapped her wrists as if they were twigs if he'd wanted, yet, he'd done nothing more than avoid her punches.

"Yes," she managed, at the same time noticing her bare feet felt encased in ice. "That would be a good idea."

She let him lead the way to the house, deciding as she walked behind him that was a mistake. The shifting flames writhing up from the destroyed barn washed his broad shoulders in a reddish haze, so he appeared cast of bronze. His shoulders tapered to narrow hips and the muscling across his back divided down his spine.

Just inside the back door, she pulled one of her father's brushed corduroy jackets off the coat tree and handed it to Harrison. "It should fit you."

"Thank you," he said, pulling the garment on and buttoning it shut. "I didn't expect it would turn so cold after a thunderstorm."

"I told you this is an unforgiving land. There are a thousand ways to die in the Wyoming Territory: snake bite, bears, getting lost and not being able to find water or finding only alkaline water. The weather around here is only one of those ways to die. With rain like tonight, I avoid the arroyos because of flash floods. And, when we don't have rain, we have dust storms that will choke you to death. There are tornados in the spring, drought by August, though not this year, fortunately." The kitchen table seemed as good as any place to set the Dragoon down. She tossed a few logs into the belly of the Hoosier and then set the coffee pot on to brew. "It's the blizzards in July that are the worst. Don't ever ride out without carrying a heavy coat and a fish with you at all times."

"I'll remember that." A chair creaked with his weight settling into the seat. "What kind of fish do I need?"

Rachel looked over at him, realizing her mistake in using the wranglers' name for their long, waxed overcoat. "The wranglers call their dusters a fish because it's waterproof and they swear it swims through the rain. Coffee will be done in a few minutes. I'm going to go wash the mud off my feet."

He was huddled in the jacket, still shivering. She hesitated and asked, "Are you all right?"

"I'm fully realizing how close we both came to dying when that barn came down." His grin was forced. "I survived the War of Southern Rebellion. I've been shot at, threatened with death a few times, but never came this close."

"I'm trying not to think about it." Rachel dipped

her head to the icebox. "There's cream for the coffee and some sugar in the bowl on the counter. I won't be long."

Halfway up the stairs to the second floor, she paused and glanced back. She was going to have to take the rugs out and beat them after this night as twice her foot prints left a trail of brown/yellow mud. There was no help for it now. Before entering her room, she eased open Joshua's door.

He was sound asleep, sprawled under the blankets, thumb in his mouth. She knew she should do something about Joshua's nightly thumb-sucking, but the one time she had tried to stop him by painting his thumbs with quinine, he'd refused to sleep for hours. Both of them had been miserable. And, he didn't suck his thumb during the daytime—only at night when he was falling asleep. She had learned a long time ago to pick her battles and this was one she chose not to fight.

When she finished cleaning the mud from her feet and ankles, the water in the wash basin had the consistency of thin gravy. She stared into the basin and tried to solve the enigma that was Harrison Taylor. She couldn't deny the hand-written deed he claimed gave him one acre less than half the Lazy L was in her father's handwriting. Why hadn't he staked his claim before? While Wyoming wasn't exactly on the beaten path for most people, it wasn't the other side of the world, either. Since the railroad had been completed, more and more people were flowing into the Territory.

Why, on this night, did she also think she had seen Jason Taylor—when no one had seen him for more than six years? The last person to have seen him in these parts had been her father, about a month before Joshua was born. When people started remarking about Jason's disappearance, Sam swore he saw both Jake Giles from the Crazy TG and Jason riding hard to the south, toward the railroad line. She had no reason not to believe her father.

There were no answers in the muddy waters of the wash basin. A single step from the wash stand made her realize she had to change out of her nightgown and robe, too. The hems of both garments were caked with sticky, drying mud. She pulled off the velvet robe and tossed it aside, then removed her cotton nightgown. Her skin pebbled in the chilly air invading the room and she quickly pulled on her only other nightgown. The flannel was worn so much it was nearly as soft as velvet. She hadn't been able to force herself to give it up or to make rags of it. Instead, she had patched the elbows and used scraps of other fabric to replace the cuffs and trim the fraying hem. Another glance at the velvet gown forced a sigh from her. Hopefully, the fabric wasn't ruined. Perhaps, when it dried, she could brush most of the mud from it.

A look around the room left her feeling uneasy. She would have sworn her silk slippers had been by her bedside. A search under the bed revealed nothing other than a few dust balls. The accumulation was a reminder to pay closer attention when she swept and mopped the house.

A sigh of frustration broke from her. Still barefoot it was then. As if she'd been the epitome of decorum and propriety lately...a snort broke from her. Finishing school had been a waste of good money. She had never had the slightest desire to ever be the lady of a grand manor and just who would her father have tried to marry her off to? Once it became common knowledge she was expecting a child, every negotiation Sam had engaged in for her hand fell to the wayside. That had been the only blessing to finding herself in a delicate condition, because God knew Sam had ignored every protest she had raised about being married off as if she were a prized heifer being sent to a prime bull.

She made her way to the kitchen. Harrison was still sitting at the table, but he held a steaming cup between his hands. Rachel poured a half cup of the dark brew and added six lumps of sugar and then cream to lighten the liquid to a caramel color.

"That's not coffee. That's a dessert," Harrison said.

A long, savoring sip of the sweetened drink slipped down her throat before she answered his observation. "Oh, I can drink it black. However, I was taught to brew coffee strong enough to do one of two things: either float a horse shoe or grow hair on one's chest. Haven't been able to float a horse shoe in it yet, and I am afraid that the latter just would not be becoming." As with every time she justified drinking sweetened and lightened coffee, her reply was delivered straight-faced.

Harrison quirked a brow, then a grin started which grew into a deep, dark chuckle. "I can understand how that would not be a becoming look for any woman."

It took biting the inside of her cheek to keep from smiling. His amusement threaded through her, causing her heart to skitter and settle in her with a curious warmth. "Then you understand my reason for diluting my coffee with copious amounts of sugar and cream." She sat across the table from him and began to trace a red square in the checked table cloth. "As generous as your offer of financial assistance is, I cannot accept it."

He released the cup and moved it away. "We're partners, like it or not, Rachel. Why don't you hear my terms for the use of those finances, before you reject the offer out of hand?"

The white square next to the red one beckoned her trailing finger. "And, just what guarantee do I have you will even abide by any terms either you or I set? You promised me that at first light you would be hard at work repairing my garden fence and then you would leave. However, you have also repeatedly stated you're not leaving."

He lifted his head to the windows over the sink. "It's not first light yet and I never said I would leave after I repaired the fence."

Rachel sucked in a deep breath to argue the point and slowly released it. He hadn't said he would leave. She bent her head to the table, blinking away sudden scalding tears. No matter what she did, holding onto the Lazy L intact was slipping out of her control. She cleared her throat and forced herself to ask, "What are your terms?"

"I haven't really thought about terms."

Out of the corner of her eye, she saw him reach for his cup. His silence weighed on her and her head dipped lower. A second later, she berated herself. It's just a business deal, and if she planned on keeping as much of the Lazy L as possible, sitting across the table from him as if she were awaiting a death sentence wasn't a position of strength. If nothing else, Sam had taught her how to fight for what she wanted in a business transaction: forcing her to negotiate with him for the licorice whips he brought home for her; to battle for what she saw as her right to ride for the brand; to war with him to not be sent away in shame to have her child and then return without "the bastard" as Sam had referred to Joshua. The only reason she had won that war was Sam had been caught in the collapsing mine before Joshua was born.

She slid clenched fists under the table and concentrated for a moment on the wind whispering across the roof. A long, slow, deep breath squared her shoulders and she met his gaze. Even the corners of his eyes crinkled with his broad smile.

"I was waiting for that," he admitted.

"Waiting for what?"

"You're not made of milk toast." The depths of the cup drew his gaze. "I would expect that Sam's only child would have learned something of negotiation from him. He did negotiate quite a bit the next morning after that poker game. If he hadn't, I would own the whole ranch: lock, stock, and barrel."

Her breath left her on a pained gasp. "What?" The realization that her father had gambled away the whole ranch, her home, left her reeling and nauseated.

"I told you he lost quite a bit to me in that game. I agreed to accept half because he didn't think I would want to displace a motherless child." His grin shifted and became less than amused. "He was right about that. Of course, I assumed you were much younger. That also explains why I never really had any intention to make good my claim on that deed he wrote."

"I don't know if I should be grateful you believed I was much younger, or livid that my father was so foolish." Rachel shoved way from the table and walked to the sink. From the moment Sam had stepped foot in the house after his last selling trip, he had been furious

61

and there had been no apparent reason. His rage, when she finally had screwed up the courage to tell him she was expecting a child, had terrified her. She gripped the edge of the metal sink so fiercely her knuckles whitened. "My earliest memories of this ranch involve me telling my father that it was mine, and that one day I would run it. When I was very young, he would laugh and humor me. When I grew older, I was told that it would never truly be mine, that my husband would be the one who would manage and operate the Lazy L."

There was no response from Harrison.

"For the last six years, I have been the one responsible for this ranch. I have fought to keep it financially sound. When it became apparent that my father was unable to manage the business, I was named the executor." She released the sink and turned with deliberation to face Harrison. "The Lazy L is the only home I have ever known and the only home I want. Knowing how foolish my father was only increases my resolve to hold onto this place. So, name your terms, Mr. Taylor."

As if deep in thought, he leaned his elbows onto the table. "First of all, I'd like for you to use my given name."

"So you've said." She just couldn't bring herself to use his first name. There was too much intimacy involved with that lack of formality. Hoping to hide how badly her hands were shaking, Rachel clasped them together. "What else?"

"I've assumed all this time that there is still the thirty-three thousand acres Sam split. Is all that still intact and is the acreage contiguous?"

"It's always been one large, contiguous parcel.

When the Homestead Act was passed, one of Daddy's conditions of employment for the wranglers was they would make claim on a tract in their name. Daddy paid them thirty cents an acre at the filing and at the end of the five-year homesteading period they would sign the tract over to him."

Even at thirty cents an acre, the price was still about a fourth less than the dollar and twenty-five cents an acre the government charged. The faint recollection of a small frame, one room, floorless cabin being dragged on skids from tract to tract to "prove up" the claim whispered in her memory. More than once she had seen money pass hands from her father to some bureaucrat sent by the land claim offices in Cheyenne. The manner Sam accumulated property was questionable at best and downright corrupt and riddled with bribery at its worst and she had promised herself at the time she was named executor that the Lazy L would never again engage in that kind of deception.

"It's all still there, except for fifteen acres I gave to Ben for wages I couldn't afford to pay him and fifteen acres I sold to the Rocking Bar M to pay the back taxes." Her chest tightened and breathing normally was a struggle. What if the acreage she gave to Ben or sold to Royce Majors was on the half Harrison claimed? What kind of a legal mess and headache would that cause?

Harrison stood and crossed the room to the stove. "So, that would technically make me the majority holder." The gurgling of coffee being poured into a cup underscored his words.

The implication hit her as hard as a mule kick. "Yes."

She waited with her heart in her throat for him to continue along that train of thought. Could he force her to leave, or force her to sell off the ranch? Would he even consider that?

"Take a breath, Rachel." He blew across the top of the cup, then sipped the steaming brew. "I have a hard time comprehending the kind of land ownership that encompasses God only knows how many sections of a county."

"A little more than fifty-one full sections," she automatically said. "The property straddles the Laramie/Albany county line."

"And, I thought one hundred acres in Kentucky was huge." He tilted his head to her. "I don't think the ranch should be divided into your half and my half, so I'm not going to tell you I want my acreage where this house is. Truth be told, what I know about raising cows"—he quickly corrected himself—"cattle— probably wouldn't fill a thimble."

She held her silence.

"When I'm done, you can make a counter-offer, but here's what I'm proposing: The ranch will not be divided up between you and me. We jointly own the ranch, as equal partners."

Her relief at hearing him say those words broke the tightness in her chest and she gulped in a deep breath. And then the relief died. If he wasn't planning to divide the ranch, what were his plans?

"I learned a long time ago, the only way to make more money was to spend money. The funds I have on deposit in New Orleans will be used to repair what has been vandalized, replenish the breeding stock, hire as many hands as you think we will need, and purchase whatever we require for the day to day operation of the ranch. I will defer all decisions on running this business to you, though I insist you keep me abreast of those. I will work on solving the problem of preventing any more destruction of Lazy L property and assets."

Rachel stared up at him. She couldn't possibly have heard him correctly. He was giving her free rein to do as she saw fit with the Lazy L. There had to be a fly in the ointment somewhere.

He leaned against the counter, crossing his legs at the ankles. "Are the terms I'm offering agreeable so far?"

"So far, yes. I can't promise you a return on the money you're offering." She backed a step. "There are too many things that can go wrong."

He took another sip of coffee. "We're dealing with living creatures and with the weather. I learned that lesson with the horse breeding farm my father had. There are some things that cannot be controlled and things can and will go wrong. As to splitting any profits—"

Profits…he was being deliberately cruel now. Despite her best efforts, cutting all possible corners, pinching every penny, the Lazy L hadn't seen a profit in three years. They had barely broken even. Her expression must have revealed her thoughts to him.

"How bad is it?"

Rachel dropped her head. "I had to let the last of the hands go at the end of the fall roundup. Most of the stock, including all the horses except for two older mares, was sold off to cover bank notes. The ranch has fewer than fifty head of breeding stock after that range fire. I have an outstanding balance at Burlington's

Mercantile, though Thom is willing to trade fresh eggs and butter for the necessities I need. I owe Mr. Greenburg for this month's grain that I have to have for the dairy cattle. The property taxes are due the first of the year."

His short, explosive exhalation was all the more telling coupled with his prolonged silence.

"I'm not frivolous," Rachel added, in her own defense when his silence bore down on her. "I have tried to prevent any debt and what I do purchase is no more than I absolutely need to keep food on the table and to feed the cows, chickens, and two horses. This last month, I've taken to butchering my older hens that aren't laying as many eggs as they did."

He grinned at her over the rim of his cup, and that strange warmth again invaded her chest.

"Rachel, unless your balances total more than eight thousand dollars, I don't think it's going to be a problem."

*Eight thousand?* She couldn't even envision having that much money in one place, at one time. Eight thousand...Was he saying he had that much to invest in the Lazy L?

## Chapter Six

"Eight thousand? You have…the Lazy L can use eight thou…eight thousand? How?"

Harrison almost laughed at her surprise and the manner she stumbled over her words. The way her brow knit and then smoothed out as she finally comprehended just what he could offer her for the ranch, and the way her eyes lit up with what he could only define as relief brought a renewed smile to his face. "Yes, I have that much available. It may take a few days to get it wired here, but I do have it. As to how, my father sold a lot of horses to the Army during the War and he continued to sell them to the government after the conflict for use out here. I brokered those sales and received a commission for every animal. Add to that I happen to be a fairly good poker player."

She staggered a step to the table and sank into a chair. "We could buy more cattle. There are always meat buyers from Chicago at the InterOcean in Cheyenne. They can't get enough Wyoming beef for back East." Her brow knit. "It costs about a dollar and a half to raise a steer on the range to market weight. Even after paying the hands to move them to the railhead in Cheyenne, and with shipping costs, we could still make over twenty dollars a head. Of course, we'll have to rebuild a bunk house so the hands have a place to stay."

He realized she was thinking out loud. "I'll leave all of that to you. And, I'll take it by your comments, we've reached terms."

Her hands clenched again and he wondered what pulled her up. She tilted her head to him in degrees and asked, "After operating costs are met, if we split the profits sixty/forty, would that be acceptable to you? We can renegotiate that split on an annual basis, once your eight-thousand-dollar loan to the ranch is repaid."

"Who gets the sixty percent?" Harrison set his cup on the counter. "This isn't a loan, Rachel. It's an investment in what I believe was and can again be a profitable livestock operation."

"It's your original capital going into the Lazy L to rebuild the ranch. You should receive the majority."

Her sense of fair play was frankly startling for its forthrightness. Harrison agreed with a nod of his head. Rachel rose from the table and met his gaze across the room.

"Mr. Tay—Harrison—it has been an incredibly long day, I believe, for the both of us. While this offer is very tempting, and one that I may be a fool to refuse, I would like a few hours of sleep before I commit to those terms."

A long day would be an understatement. From the looks of the eastern horizon, dawn was less than an hour away. He had no idea what time Rachel's day had started, but his had begun at first light. In the space of this one day he'd had a shotgun fired at him by what he had assumed to be a boy, then had learned he hadn't been shot at by a boy and that the property he'd ridden up to was the ranch he had been deeded half of. He then discovered the worthless bastard he was related to by virtue of having the same father had been here, and to top it all off, he'd almost died in a barn fire. Yeah, long day was a pretty good understatement.

"Take all the time you need to make that decision. But, we still have one problem." He drew a deep breath. "I can't throw my bedroll out in the barn."

The color drained from her face and her hand crept to her throat and clutched the collar more tightly closed. He'd wager every red cent he had in the bank in New Orleans she was debating turning and running from him as fast as she could. Even as he thought that, her posture stiffened and her jaw clenched.

"There is a leather chesterfield in the front parlor where you saw my father this afternoon. For a few nights, it's comfortable enough to sleep on." Her voice was tight with the tension marring her features. "You will find a pillow and a blanket folded in one corner of the chesterfield."

Before he could respond, she pivoted on a heel and fled the warmth of the kitchen. Harrison's gaze lingered on the darkened hallway that enveloped her. He dragged a hand down his face with a long sigh of exhaustion. He should go outside and move his saddle, the one other saddle he'd managed to save, and his saddle bags onto the porch, but that honestly sounded like too much effort at the moment. The rain was long gone and the sky was completely clear.

He looked around the kitchen, this time taking in the details without having to hurry behind her or maintain a polite air of disinterest. There was a lot here that spoke of Rachel and her care of this home.

In the dimmed light of the single lantern over the table, the counters gleamed with what he assumed to be lemon oil, if the scent in the air was any indication. The blacking on the stove had been recently reapplied because it shone with a dull luster in the low-pitched light. Fresh coats of grease glistened in the cast iron pans, a single pot, and the Dutch oven. Sometime after supper, she had mixed up fresh bread dough, which was rising on the back of the stove in two linen covered loaf pans.

He pushed off the counter next to the sink and made his way down the hallway to the front parlor. What he knew about running a household was less than minimal and he'd be the first to admit to that, yet from the tidiness of the kitchen and the preparations for the day already complete, it appeared Rachel was more than competent.

The large parlor where he had first seen Sam was shrouded in the gray half-light of the hour before sunrise. His shock over Sam's changed appearance hadn't allowed him to examine the room. Knowing sleep would be elusive, Harrison swept his gaze over the parlor. A massive desk of what he guessed to be black walnut dominated the front corner. A tattered green blotter, ink well, and pen covered the writing surface. Directly behind the desk, built into the bookshelves, was a small liquor cabinet.

In the opposite corner, close enough to the window that light would spill across the stand and keys, stood a piano. Its bench was pushed far under the key bed and both the cover and lid were closed. Harrison walked to the instrument. The amount of dust on its varnished surface was surprising. It was if Rachel had refused to touch it. If he had a mind to, he could write his name in the dust. And the dust was testament that no one had played this beauty in some time.

The leather chesterfield Rachel had spoken of was along the wall near the pocket doors. The walls on either side of the doors were covered with floor to ceiling book shelves. Every shelf should be groaning with the weight of the books, he mused. Whoever designed this room had considered the shade provided by the large, deep veranda wrapping around the front of the house. He doubted those book shelves had ever seen a direct ray of sunlight.

He raked both hands back through his hair, pausing at the base of his skull to press his fingertips into his neck. Rachel had been right when she said it'd been a long, exhausting day. He just needed a few minutes to close his eyes and rest. The couch beckoned and he collapsed into the middle and then eased into a reclining position. Harrison woke, he was sure, less than fifteen minutes later. To his surprise, full daylight illuminated the parlor. The aroma of strong coffee drifted in. He made his way to the kitchen, rubbing the last of the sleep from his eyes.

The coffee pot simmered on the stove. When he picked up the cup he'd used a few hours ago, he noticed a piece of paper under it. Unfolding the small sheet, he read "The garden needs tended to. If you need me, I am there."

Not a word about his promise to repair the fence. Harrison winced, realizing because he'd fallen asleep, she had probably already set to repairing the fence. As soon as he finished his coffee, he'd get on that.

With coffee in hand, Harrison walked onto the back porch. Sam was in his wheeled chair, shawl wrapped around his shoulders, a heavy blanket covering the lower half of his body.

"Good morning, Sam."

The old man didn't respond other than to lift his arm and point a shaking finger at the smoldering ruins of the barn.

"It went up fast. There was nothing Rachel and I could do to save it." Harrison leaned against a support for the overhang, looking at what was left of the barn. The sharp recollection of Rachel's struggle to free the third dairy cow flashed in his memory, complete with his momentary panic at seeing her in the flames. "You raised a very strong young woman. From what I've seen in the last day, she's more than capable of running this ranch."

He wasn't expecting an answer but Sam responded with a guttural growl.

"You probably didn't expect to ever see me again." The depths of his coffee cup drew his attention. "Honestly, if Grant hadn't decided to banish me to the ends of the earth, she never would have known you gambled away her home. It's funny I've ended up at the same place Jason did."

Sam's growl deepened with the mention of Jason's name. Before Harrison could puzzle why that was, movement at the edge of his vision caught his attention. Rachel rounded the corner of the house, deep in conversation with her son. Harrison's gaze skipped over the boy. Rachel had said she'd been frugal and the child's clothing attested to that. His trousers were at least two inches too short, and the sleeves of his shirt ended well above his wrists. He'd noticed how ill-fitting the boy's clothing was last night over supper. And, how painfully thin the child was.

His gaze shifted back to Sam. The old man was thin, also, and he suspected it wasn't just because of his accident or apoplexy. He looked to Rachel again, and felt his stomach falling. He should have noticed all this the night before. Hell, he'd seen it too often at the end of that damnable war when he'd made his way to New Orleans. He'd seen too many women and children and the few men returning from the conflict who were barely keeping body and soul together and slowly starving in the process.

The damn garden fence could wait. He had something else in mind that was far more pressing. "Does Ben come every day to help with your father?" he asked.

Rachel halted, her head tilting up to him. He noticed Joshua slipped behind her. There was hesitation in her voice when she said, "Yes." Her gaze focused on Sam for a few seconds and he was certain he saw respect and heartache vying on her face. "There are some things that I need Ben to do for my father, because if I did them, it would be too humiliating for Daddy."

The reality of how dependent Sam was hit Harrison in the gut. There was no polite manner to respond. He just nodded in acknowledgement. "As soon as Ben gets here, I'd like for you to go into town with me."

\*\*\*\*

Harrison walked out of the First Bank of Federal. Steve Hackett, the bank owner, had been more than accommodating in advancing him funds. Of course, the notarized letter from Dan Ball, on official letter head of the New Orleans bank probably made that accommodation easier.

He studied the town. Federal was similar to just about every other small town he'd ridden through in the past year or so—false fronts, a few saloons, livery, a boarding house, and more than a fair share of churches. Across the dusty street, a knot of women gathered, heads bent together. He'd be willing to put even money they were the local gossips and the self-proclaimed arbitrators of morality and decency. He snorted as that thought crossed his mind.

A steady, sharp metallic rapping filled the warm air, the sound originating at the blacksmith down the street. Demon and Rachel's mare dozed in the afternoon sun. He wasn't sure where he would find her and the boy, but he guessed the best place to start looking was in the mercantile, where they had left the horses hitched when they got into town.

A glance at the store front announced it to be both a general store and mercantile, with a sole proprietor named Thom Burlington. The name nudged his memory and he recalled this was one of the people Rachel said she had a balance with. He stepped out into the street and made his way there. As he passed the cluster of gossips, he tipped the bill of his hat. Three of the five women looked away as if he wasn't even there. One of them pulled her skirts in closer. The last one appeared offended by his show of courtesy.

Harrison pushed open the doors of Burlington's business, sparing a quick glance over his head at the jangling bells. A portly, slightly balding man behind the counter looked at him and said, "I'll be with you in just a few minutes."

"Has—" He almost used her given name and quickly corrected himself. No need to hand ammunition to the gossips. The trouble was he wasn't quite sure what her full name really was. "Has Mr. Leonard's daughter been here yet?"

The young woman with the store clerk glanced at him, curiosity openly defining her expression. Harrison dipped his head in greeting as he walked across the freshly oiled floor.

"I haven't seen her today." The other man rubbed his hands on the front of his apron before he took the bolt of pale yellow fabric from the young woman. "How much of this did you say you needed, Jessie?"

Harrison studied the mercantile's wares and interior. For a small town, the store was well-stocked, with products ranging from shovels and rakes to ribbons and lace. A small rack on the front counter held the latest offerings of dime novels. Food stuffs in tins lined a wall, while bulk items such as flour and sugar and beans were stacked in canvas sacks. Mingled spices scented the air, not completely hiding the odor of the kerosene he guessed had been used to oil the floors. A sizable selection of gleaming carbines stood at rigid attention along the whole of the back wall.

When the store clerk completed the young woman's order, she nodded a passing greeting to Harrison and left.

"Thom Burlington. How can I help you?"

Harrison pulled his attention from the table covered with bolts of fabric that ran the length of the store. "The Lazy L carries a balance here, doesn't it?"

Burlington shoved his hands into the pockets of his apron. "Yes," he said, drawing the word out.

Both men turned to the back of the store when the curtain separating what he assumed to be the private quarters from the store parted. Burlington gestured at the woman making her way toward them. "My wife, Mary. Rachel doesn't carry a big balance and I'm not worried about it."

"You might not be, but if it gets out that you've extended her credit, we'll have to do the same for everyone in this town," Mary said. "I don't know why you—"

Her husband cut her off. "You know why."

Harrison decided not to indulge his curiosity over the shopkeeper's sharp retort to his wife. He dug into his pocket and dropped a gold double eagle onto the glass counter, the coin spinning and chattering before it came to rest. "Will this cover her balance?"

The store owner looked down at the coin but didn't take it. "And then some. Who are you?"

"Harrison Taylor—"

Burlington's posture stiffened. He waved his hand at his wife. Mary scuttled away, toward the rear of the store.

"—I'm the half owner of the Leonards' ranch."

The owner backed a step away, closer to a small revolver on the counter behind him. "Any relation to Jason Taylor?"

What in the name of heaven had his half-brother done that brought about such a reaction? Harrison exhaled sharply. "What gave me away? The drawl or my last name?"

A door somewhere in the back of the building slammed. Harrison assumed the owner's wife had left the store.

"Mister, I know for a fact that Rachel would never agree to give up even an inch of that ranch of hers."

There was no point in telling the man Sam had been a fool and gambled it away and removed Rachel's ability to agree to anything. "Mr. Burlington, I'm just trying to help the lady. Since I arrived at the Lazy L yesterday, I've had a shotgun pointed at me, been hit over the head by her foreman—"

A faint smile jerked up a corner of the store owner's mouth.

"—almost died when her barn caught fire—"

"Is Rachel all right?" The change in Burlington was immediate.

"She's fine. She wasn't hurt. One of the dairy cows died and she lost all her hens, but the lady in question is fine." Harrison looked down at the twenty-dollar gold piece on the counter top. "We rode into town together. If you see Miss Rachel, will you tell her I'm looking for her?"

Without waiting for the man to answer, Harrison walked from the mercantile. The group of women on the boardwalk had been joined by another—Mary Burlington. He looked down the street, wondering where Rachel could have gone with Joshua. As he pondered where she might be, he heard the whispers from the women, most no more than unintelligible hissing, but what he did hear was more than enough.

He had to find Rachel. With a nod to the cluster of gossips and a touch of his fingers to the bill of his hat, he strode down the boardwalk. Several buildings away, the young woman he'd seen in the mercantile emerged from another business, and Rachel and Joshua were with her.

He recognized the gestures and the body posturing from the two women. Having three sisters sometimes did have a benefit. When women started talking fabrics—the younger woman had shoved the material recently purchased into Rachel's hands—he knew from experience with his sisters he would be risking life and limb if he cut that conversation short.

A supporting column for the overhang of the boardwalk took the weight of his shoulder as he settled in to wait. That Rachel had donned a riding habit to come into town both surprised and disconcerted him. The habit had a distinctly militaristic appearance, with the manner the jacket buttoned closed and the bright, canary yellow piping edging the pockets, the false cuffs, and the standup collar. It was the color of the fabric—in a gray so much like the Richmond gray he'd seen too much—that disconcerted him.

He hadn't seen a side saddle in the barn before it burned and when she saddled her mare, he had been left wondering just how she was going to ride astride. When she swung up, he realized the skirt was actually very wide legged trousers. The front pleat wasn't even a pleat, but a panel to hide the trouser legs and the extra-long tail of the severely tailored jacket served the same function for the back. It was ingenious, he admitted. The habit, coupled with what he guessed to be the yards and yards of lace and several dove-gray feathers adorning her hat, would have put her squarely into the most fashionable ladies he knew before or after the war. As much as he detested that color of gray, it was becoming on her.

Joshua was looking around and Harrison knew that expression. The child was seeking an avenue of escape. He waited until the boy glanced over at him. When he made eye contact across the street, Harrison gestured for Joshua to join him.

A large wagon rumbled down the street, blocking his view. The sight greeting him after the heavy wagon passed left him struggling to find a breath. Rachel was bent to Joshua but her face was tilted to him. If he hadn't briefly mistaken her for a boy the day before, he would swear there wasn't a chance in hell anyone could ever see the slender, curving figure as a boy. The thought of getting her alone and slowly opening each button on that jacket rippled through him. He reluctantly suppressed that thought. She was his business partner—nothing more—and everything he'd seen indicated she would not tolerate being trifled with.

Rachel released Joshua's hand, then straightened, and as soon as the boy stepped onto the boardwalk in front of Harrison, returned to her conversation with the other young woman. For what was probably the first time in his life, Harrison was thankful for a child's presence.

"What do you say we go down to that candy store I saw?" Harrison jerked his head up the street.

Joshua's eyes, shaded with more blue than his mother's, sparkled with the smile crossing his face. And, in an instant, the smile faded. "Momma says we don't have any money this time to buy candy."

"I think I have a penny or two I can spare." He started walking and the child fell in step with him. At the entrance to the candy store, Joshua grabbed Harrison's hand, stopping him.

"Can we go to Mr. Burlington's instead? Mr. Milton scares me."

Harrison looked down at the tow-headed boy. He was so terrified by the candy store owner his freckles stood in stark relief. "Why does he scare you?"

His chin jutted out, in exactly the same manner as Harrison had seen his mother's do. "He says I stole candy from him." Something shifted in the child's expression and the indignation faded. "He made Momma give him a whole nickel for what he says I took."

"That's a lot of penny candy. Did you steal from him?" The morose expression on the boy's face when he revealed what the confectioner demanded of Rachel twisted Harrison's heart.

"No, sir!" The boy shook his head as well. "It wasn't me. It was Donnie Morris. But, he said I was lying."

The other child had said Joshua lied, or the confectioner accused him of lying? Harrison wasn't sure he wanted to explore that. "If you didn't do anything wrong, let's see what Mr. Milton has in his store."

Joshua audibly gulped, then squared his shoulders, though his fingers tightened on Harrison's hand. Together they entered the small store and Harrison led him to a large glass display of various candies and sweet treats. The store owner wasn't in sight and Joshua's posture eased. Harrison noted that if Joshua had been involved with a theft of penny candy, he must have used a step stool to accomplish the deed. The glass jars with readily available candies were well above the boy's ability to reach. Everything else was secured within glass display cases.

The boy moved slowly down the case, never once glancing at the jars above his head, and Harrison noted which candies he hesitated at. Peppermint sticks, cherry drops, licorice whips, honey drops, and sugar plums…The floral print curtain at the back of the store was pulled sharply to a side. Joshua leaped away from the counter, thrusting his hands behind him. "I'm just looking, Mr. Milton."

"I told you the last time you were here not to come back." The store owner rounded the display case. "I don't want your kind in here."

"He's with me," Harrison said.

The confectioner marched into the center of the store, causing Joshua to duck behind Harrison. Milton didn't take his angry gaze from the boy. "I don't care who he's with, I don't want that little thief and liar in my store. To think that he'd blame such a good boy as Donnie Morris of stealing… Apple didn't fall far from the tree, considering his mother."

Harrison pulled himself to his full height and let his gaze drift down the candy maker, taking in the man's slight build, his balding pate, and the thin moustache. The slightly amusing thought occurred to him there was a dime novel villain somewhere based on a caricature of the candy-store owner.

Harrison slipped a hand onto Joshua's thin shoulder. "You're right," he said, speaking to the boy, but not looking at him. "There isn't anything in this store that's worth my money. Let's go to the mercantile."

## Chapter Seven

Rachel looked up and down the main street for Harrison and her son. The less than amused thought crossed her mind that Jessie could certainly chatter away about a lot of nothing for a long time. She located Joshua and Harrison, both seated on the bench outside Burlington's.

The closer she got to her son and Harrison, the more upset she grew. Joshua had a small brown bag clutched in one hand, and a peppermint stick in the other. What appeared to be several small toy soldiers and a tiny cannon were on the bench seat next to him. The peppermint stick she couldn't return, but hopefully Thom would let her return the other sweets in the bag and the toys. She had no manner to pay for those things.

Joshua spied her and he waved the bag. Rachel held her hand out to him. "Joshua, I have to take all that candy and the little soldiers and give them back to Mr. Burlington."

Joshua scooped up the toys and clutched them and the bag to his chest, staring up at her as if she had just promised to shoot his beloved old tom cat. Thankfully, she had seen the mangy creature that morning so she knew he had managed to survive the fire.

Harrison's head snapped toward her. "I've already paid for his toys and the candy."

She opened her mouth to argue, but no sound came

out.

"We got you a peppermint stick, too, Momma." Joshua pulled a red and white striped length of the confection from his bag and thrust it at her. His wide smile seemed at odds with what looked to be suspiciously like tear tracks down his cheeks. To ask him about her suspicions would only upset the boy and he seemed very happy at the moment. The times of genuine, childish happiness for Joshua had been few and far between, and she hesitated to shatter his light-heartedness.

She directed her full attention to the man seated next to her son. His long legs were stretched out, crossed at the ankles. He draped one arm across his stomach, the other casually slung across the back of the bench behind Joshua. Deep crinkles at the corners of his eyes and one side of his mouth quirked up with a smile. It was then she noticed the candy stick he held between his teeth. The half-smile grew, doing odd things to her. Her heart sped up, a strange warmth coiled through her chest, and butterflies fluttered in her stomach.

She didn't like peppermint but there was no way to graciously refuse and she was grateful for the distraction from the peculiar manner her body was reacting to Harrison's smile. She took the offered treat and sat on the other side of Joshua, then directed her gaze across the street at the sandstone façade of the Bank of Federal. By far, she was much too aware of the man sitting beside her son.

Like his half-brother, she had little doubt Harrison knew just how much attention he attracted from women. It would be hard not to notice him with his broad shoulders, long legs, and narrow hips. He stood at least a head taller than most men she knew.

The crunching from Joshua gave her a chance to study Harrison in a less than obvious manner. The sweet he'd held between his teeth had moved to the other side of his mouth. Without any prompting, she wondered if he would taste like peppermint if he kissed her and she immediately quashed any further thought moving along such a path. That kind of thinking led to dangerous and painful repercussions.

Harrison craned his head toward her, as if aware of her sidelong scrutiny. She never would have thought her father's shirt would fit him so well...and dear merciful God, when had he unbuttoned the collar? Not only was the hollow at the base of his throat visible, so were a few curling chest hairs.

The peppermint stick she clutched drew her attention. Her tightly fitted jacket was suddenly much too warm. Heat flooded her cheeks, making her long to unbutton the jacket. She didn't dare. If one of those gossiping hens saw that, any ground she might have gained in the last six years would be lost. By sheer force of will, she kept from snorting in self-deprecation. She hadn't gained any ground with them...and she realized Harrison had asked her a question she didn't hear.

"I'm sorry. I seem to have been wool-gathering." She handed the treat to Joshua, her fingers sticky with melting sugar. "Put that in your sack, please."

"I said, as soon as Thom brings the packages out, there's one other thing we need to do in town. Is there a justice of the peace?"

He was on a first name basis with the store owner all ready? "What packages?" she asked. Candy for

Joshua apparently wasn't the only thing he had purchased. "And, why do you need to see Mr. Pruitt?"

Before he answered, Harrison bent to Joshua. "I think now is the time to go see Mr. Burlington's beagle puppies."

Rachel nodded when Joshua looked up at her as if asking for her permission. "You may look, but we cannot take a puppy home, no matter how many runts Mr. Burlington says he has that no one will want."

Guilt flooded her with the sight of her son's crestfallen face. She tried to soften the blow. "Joshua, we can't afford to feed a dog."

"Yes, Momma," he said and made his way into the mercantile. Once the boy was out of earshot, Harrison said, "I don't want to intrude on how you're raising him, but we can afford to feed a puppy, if he really wants one."

"No," Rachel said. "*You* can afford to feed a puppy. I can't. Stop changing the subject on me. Why do we need to see Mr. Pruitt?"

Harrison lowered his gaze, seeming intent on the boardwalk under them. He twisted his head to her without raising it. "We need to be married."

Rachel shied back then shook her head. "That is not even amusing." Marriage also meant other things and surely he had to know that. The tightness in her chest constricted her breathing and painful knots coiled in her stomach. Bits and pieces of old memories hammered into her: huddling under her father's massive desk, a strange whimpering sound in her ears, only to realize she was the one keening; the loud boom of thunder accompanying her violent tumble to the floor... "No. I will not marry."

Harrison took the candy stick from between his teeth and twisted the treat between his fingers. "Marrying me will silence those gossips. Or, is there another reason you won't marry me? You said you're not a widow, so that leaves only a few possibilities: your husband isn't dead and he abandoned you and that boy or—"

"I was never married," Rachel said, surprised with the vehemence in her voice. "Was that the whole point of this exercise, getting me to acknowledge what those vile women said about me?" She jumped up and stalked a few paces away and then whirled to face him. She forced her fists to uncurl. "I've heard everything they've ever said, because at some point it was always said to my face."

"I'm not asking you to marry me as an exercise. I'm asking you so that you can silence them. Look at how you dressed to come into town." He leaned forward, elbows on his knees. The peppermint stick dropped to the boardwalk. "I fully expected you to be wearing your denims. Instead, you've clothed yourself exactly as a very proper lady would—and trust me, I know all about how proper ladies should dress. I have three sisters." He lifted his head, the intensity of his gaze forcing her to step back. "Marriage would be a united front to whoever is trying to make it harder for you to keep the Lazy L operational. As my wife, anything I own at my death becomes yours, so it keeps the ranch intact. It makes good business sense. Plus, there is Joshua to consider."

"What about him?" She teetered on the edge of the need to lift her skirts and run as fast as she could from this man, from this town, from everything. Sweat dripped down her back, dampened her palms. The maddened cadence of her heart thundered in her ears, roaring in her head.

He uncoiled his length from the bench but didn't approach her. "What are you going to tell him when he hears what those women are saying about you?" He tilted his head with the question, one brow slowly rising. "Or when he hears what they call him? I've already done a dance around a question he asked me after something Milton said to him."

Joshua was now the object of their verbal attacks. Somehow, that information didn't startle her but it did ignite her anger. It felt as if her heart was on fire. He was just a child. He was completely innocent. And, even as she contemplated the attacks on her son, she knew she had been foolish to ever hope he would remain out of the gossips' line of sight.

She could have told Harrison taking Joshua into the candy store would be a mistake. The incident the last time she had been in town with Joshua was proof of that. Donnie Morris was as pure as the driven snow in the confectioner's eyes and her son had to be guilty, only because of her.

Harrison drew her attention and she quelled her anger. He hadn't moved any closer. "If I even consider this strange proposal..." She trailed off, shaking her head. She couldn't consider it. Just the thought of everything else marriage entailed left her struggling to draw a breath.

A lopsided grin crossed his face. "I'm fairly certain as marriage proposals go this wasn't what any lady would have expected. Please understand that I will never try to replace Joshua's father in your affections."

A short, harsh laugh broke from her. "I hold no affection for him, I assure you of that, Mr. Taylor."

His grin faltered. "I'm certain it is difficult to hold fondness for a man who would take advantage of a lady and then leave her to raise his child." He paused a slight beat, and the grin returned, full force. "However, I would never do that. I was raised very differently. And, I thought we had agreed we are on a first name basis."

Rachel bit the inside of her cheek to keep a sharp retort corralled about his upbringing. She forced a deep breath and slowly let it go. "Yes, we did agree to that." She dropped her gaze to the wooden planks, drawn inexorably to the discarded peppermint stick. When she realized she could hold her silence no longer, she lifted her head. "If this marriage is to be no more than a business arrangement, it must remain in name only."

The bells over the mercantile door clanged before Harrison could respond and Thom Burlington walked out, three large packages wrapped in brown paper and secured with twine in his arms. Joshua followed with a fourth. Thom set the packages on the bench. Rachel looked from the brown-wrapped parcels to Harrison. A half smile pulled at his mouth. "Just some things that I asked Thom to put together that he figured you might need. As to the other, I accept your terms," he said, silencing any question she might have had about the contents.

Her head was spinning. Part of her screamed he couldn't be trusted, while another reasoned he had done nothing to merit her distrust. To give herself a few seconds to gather her thoughts, she studied the purchases shrouded in the paper wrapping. Did she dare trust Harrison to keep to those terms? What man in his right mind would agree to a demand of a marriage in name only?

"I notice the things that you would pause at, Rachel." The shop-keep broke into her tangled thoughts. "I know what Lily writes to me and tells me she uses in her home. I figured keeping house here isn't so different in Denver." He reached into the pocket of his apron and drew out a sealed envelope. "This was here this morning. Someone slid it under the door. It's addressed to you. Guess whoever left it knows you usually come into town once a week with eggs and butter."

Rachel took the envelope as if it would strike at her like an angry rattler. She stared at her name, not recognizing the handwriting and then tore the envelope open. Inside was a single sheet of paper. A sense of foreboding settled over her, tightening around her throat. One sentence marred the paper and after reading it, the page fluttered to the ground from her numb fingers.

She couldn't breathe. She couldn't bring anything into focus. Her knees buckled and only by sheer force of will did she keep from falling. A howling cry filled her ears and without caring about the consequences, she lifted her skirts and ran from the mercantile and to her horse.

As if from a long distance, she heard her name shouted.

Twinkle snorted when Rachel hammered her heels into her sides, but the mare willingly took off in a gallop. She bent lower over the mare's withers, panic making her demand more speed from the little bay, and she slashed the horse with the reins.

\*\*\*\*

Whatever was in that message terrified her. He had never seen the color drain from someone's face as it did from Rachel's when she scanned the missive. A low whimpering moan broke from her and the single page drifted to the ground, even as she spun on her heel and ran.

Harrison grabbed up the paper.

"*You won't be able to hide from me in the barn now.*"

There was no signature, no opening, just that single line. He shoved the threatening note into his pocket. "Joshua, stay here with Mr. Burlington."

He didn't bother to wait for the store-owner's consent. A small cloud of dust marked Rachel's headlong flight. He stepped into the saddle and pulled Demon's head around to give chase, putting his spurs into the black's sides before he had settled completely in the saddle.

A familiar bay mare stood outside the small Catholic church and Harrison reined Demon around and to a halt. Rachel huddled near a white headstone, the gleaming marble carved into a weeping angel. With her arms wrapped around her head, she matched the pose of the grieving sculpture.

Sage brush and sparse clumps of scrub grass dotted the area within the fencing, while faded bouquets adorned several of the graves. Gravel crunched underfoot with each step he took closer. The ever-present wind whispered through the row of pine trees marking the furthest reach of the cemetery's fence. Harrison read the legend adorning the base of the angel. *Rachel Anne Leonard. My heart and life.* According to the dates inscribed in the marble, the woman had been less than thirty when her life ended. Surrounding the woman's final resting place were little marble stones, each denoting a child who had passed: a son who bore Sam's name; a second son born stillborn, a daughter gone at only three years, a final son who didn't make a first birthday.

Rachel must have heard him approaching because when he was less than a foot from her side, she said, "My mother died from birthing fever when I was a month old. I never knew her." Her voice was muffled in her arms.

"Rachel, who's coming for you?"

She shuddered, as if severely chilled. Her only response to his question was to curl even further into herself. Harrison dropped to a knee next to her. After the manner she had fought him the night before, he hesitated to touch her. A thin, agonized keening sound emerged from her.

Harrison placed his hand on her back between her shoulder blades and waited for her reaction. There was none. Emboldened, he stroked her back. There was still no response. He murmured, "I wish you would trust me."

"Promise me," she said. The words sounded as if they were torn from her very depths.

"Anything you want." Even though he had no idea where her demand either came from or would lead, at that moment, he was willing to swear away his immortal soul. How had this happened that in less than one short day, he was willing to give up everything he had for this woman? He didn't have an answer and as he waited for her to tell him what she wanted him to promise, he realized it didn't matter that there was no answer.

"Promise me you won't let anything happen to my son." She reared back, arms dropping, and lifted her face to him. He had been expecting tears, but there were none. The gray there was as hard and unyielding as the granite slopes rising in the distance. "He said he would kill me when he came back. Promise me you'll protect my son and won't let him hurt Joshua."

A chill rippled up Harrison's spine. "Who said he'd kill you?"

She said, "It doesn't matter," and coupled the words with a minute shake of her head. "Promise me that I can trust you with Joshua's life."

"And, what about your life?" He lifted a hand to her face, pausing when she flinched. A tendril of hair fluttered across her cheek and he gently brushed it away. "What about yours?"

The tears he had expected earlier filled her eyes but didn't spill. "He's already here because he knows about the barn and he left that note. He said he would kill me when he came back."

"Whoever he is, he has to come through me first." The anger burning in his chest seeped into his whole body. She was convinced she would die and somehow was already so defeated she was more concerned with her child's life than her own. "No one is going to harm you or that little boy as long as I'm around."

"You won't stop him," she whispered and dropped her head.

The resignation echoing in her voice burned into him. Not that he couldn't stop this person terrorizing her, but just that he wouldn't do it. "I'm made of sterner material than you're giving me credit for, Rachel." He waited for her to meet his gaze again. When she finally did, he added, "I took an oath when I pinned that badge on. It's an oath I don't intend to ever betray."

"Regardless of the cost or who might be involved?" Her features tightened. "No one is that honorable."

He sensed there was more to her words than just what she asked of him, but her question also brought to mind the fleeting image of a man who had been a brother to him—a man he'd sent to a Union run prisoner of war camp and who'd perished in that veritable hell. He could tell her just what his own honor had cost him, the price it continued to extract from him. He drew a deep breath, unsuccessfully quelling the guilt. "I know very well the full cost of honor."

Her features softened as she searched his face for what felt like an eternity to Harrison. Finally, she said in little more than a whisper, "I believe you do."

"I promise that no one will harm you or your son." He pushed himself to stand and held his hand down to her. Without any hesitation, she slipped her hand into his palm and allowed him to pull her to her feet. "I think it's time I hang a shingle out on the town jail. There is a jail, isn't there?"

She nodded. "It was built but the town never saw fit to hire a sheriff. Other than the year Sam Greenburg stored grain there when his mill burned, it's never been used."

Harrison paused, allowing Rachel to exit the cemetery before him. Her posture stiffened when he caught her elbow, but she halted and looked back at him. He tilted his head toward the main section of town.

"Before I open the jail, we should see the justice of the peace."

Rachel minutely pulled away but didn't protest. He noted she also didn't agree with him. "After we see him, we need to let the biggest gossip in town know you've married the lawman."

She twisted her head to the church building, but it wasn't longing he saw in her features. If anything, there was anger. Her jaw clenched and her chin jutted ever so slightly. "They'll all probably say," she said, her gaze returning to him, "that someone has finally made an honest woman out of me."

"I have serious doubts that you've ever been anything but an honest woman, Rachel. Who do I have to see to get the keys to the jail?" He released his gentle hold on her elbow, trailing his hand down her lower arm.

"Harold Milton. He's the mayor." She caught Twinkle's reins and hoisted herself into the saddle.

"The candy store owner?" Harrison grinned. "This should be an interesting conversation."

## Chapter Eight

*Don't panic. Don't panic. Dear God, please don't let me panic.*

Adam Pruitt intoned the words with as much inflection as if he were repeating them in his sleep. Jessie Majors stood on Rachel's left, one of the required witnesses. On Harrison's right was Thom Burlington. Mary Burlington stood in the doorway of Pruitt's office, keeping the rest of the curiosity seekers outside. Joshua perched on a chair in the corner of the room, feet swinging.

Her hands tightened on the cluster of prairie sunflower and horsemint Jessie had collected to make an impromptu bouquet. One of the delicate horsemint stems broke and the purple-pink flower fell between her feet. So far, not an auspicious beginning to married life. Her chest ached and her stomach twisted into tight knots with the intense trembling racking her body.

"I will," Harrison said. Startled, Rachel tore her gaze from the flower head on the floor and looked up at him. For the first time in her life, she was certain she was suffering from the vapors. To catch herself from falling, she locked her knees, shifted the flowers to one hand, and caught Harrison's arm.

He bent closer to her, his eye brows lifting in a silent inquiry.

"I may faint," she managed.

If Pruitt noticed her extreme discomfort, he never wavered from his monotone recitation of the wedding vows. As casually as if he was taking a Sunday stroll, Harrison slipped his arm around her waist, giving her support. He bent his head even closer and his breath was warm against her ear as he whispered, "I won't let you fall."

The droning buzz ceased. Rachel realized everyone in the room was waiting for her response. Her mouth was drier than an arroyo in August and her tongue seemed numb. She wasn't even sure what response they were waiting for and hoped that repeating Harrison's deeply intoned "I will," would be the correct answer.

Apparently it was, because Pruitt said something about the power vested in him, something else about husband and wife. And, then, he said, "You may kiss your bride."

She sucked in a sharp breath but couldn't force the air past what she was certain was her heart lodged in her throat. Harrison's arm tightened around her waist to pull her closer. Her eyes closed with her effort to not push him away. His palm skimmed her cheek and she froze.

His lips brushed against her forehead and he dropped his arm from her waist. She opened her eyes in shock when he took her hand into his.

"I made a promise. Let's go home," he said.

****

"You did *what?*" Ben stared at her, mouth gaping.

"It's the only way to save the ranch." Rachel scrubbed a cast iron skillet with more force than necessary, ceasing her abuse of the metal when she realized she was going to have to season the pan, again.

"It is strictly business."

"That was your reason for marrying?" Ben stepped closer to her, halting when she moved away. "That sounds like some fool idea of your father's—when he was trying to marry you off to Jake Giles and every other single, rich rancher around trying to build a cattle dynasty."

"I have spent my whole life working and riding for this brand. I will not give up the Lazy L." She slammed the dried skillet into the belly of the stove and pulled off the apron protecting her gray habit. "I never would have married Jake and the rest of the men Daddy had in mind, well…Joshua put an end to all of that." Marriage to Jake had never been a serious consideration. Tom Giles had his sights on a much bigger prize than the Lazy L. He wanted his son to be the first governor when the Territory became a state and Rachel could do nothing to help with those political ambitions.

"So you marry a total stranger?" He shook his head. "Worse than that. He's Jason's brother."

"He's not like Jason." She looked out the window over the sink, praying she wasn't wrong in her assertion. Harrison was bent over, running a brush down Twinkle's front right leg, Joshua just a few feet away, intently watching the man.

"How do you know that? Damn it, Rachel, he could be as low as—or lower—than his brother." An angry breath escaped the foreman. "You couldn't wait a day or two?"

The recollection of the single sentence message left for her at Burlington's slithered through her thoughts. If she told Ben about that, somehow, he would find a way to connect Harrison to it. And, she just couldn't explain to the foreman what her heart was telling her, that Harrison was as different from his brother as day from night. As far as she was concerned, Jason would have to reach up to find a snake's belly. "No, Ben, it couldn't wait. You've seen what's happening here. It's getting worse. It started out as just a few head slaughtered and left for the scavengers. Whoever is doing this is getting more violent." She gestured out the window. "It could have just as easily been the house that was burned."

"He'll ride out of here one day, just like he rode in."

The proclamation caused her to look out the window again. Her husband—dear Lord, she was married—and her son had finished brushing Twinkle and were working on Demon. Harrison was bent over, one of the black's hooves held between his knees. Joshua was handing something—she guessed a hoof pick—to Harrison. From her vantage point, Harrison's shadow in the late afternoon sun was that of an old, stooped man walking through an archway, with a tall, slender image of her son assisting him. "He won't ride out."

"What happens when he decides your marriage is more than a business arrangement?"

"That is none of your concern." She finally turned away from the window, struggling to keep her anger in check. "You've been more than just the foreman, Ben, but I will not tolerate this from you. I won't tolerate it from anyone. For better or for worse, I am married. I have my reasons and the first is I have to do what I must to protect my son."

Ben threw his hands up in what she recognized as a gesture of both frustration and defeat.

"I have to go tell my father." Without a backward glance, she left the kitchen. When she less than a few steps down the hallway, she heard the back screened door slam shut. Rachel paused, dropping her head. As hard as the conversation had been with the foreman, she had the sinking feeling it was going to be more difficult with her father.

She lifted her head, looking down the passageway. She was a grown woman, with a child. Marrying Harrison might not have been the most prudent action in Ben's opinion, but her first concern was guaranteeing Joshua never came to any harm. In a distant second was her desire to restore the Lazy L to financial stability. Marriage to Harrison could assist with both. She supposed marriages had been arranged for lesser goals. A deep breath coupled with the squaring of her shoulders and she resumed walking.

Sam was in front of the southern exposed windows. His lap rug was pooled on the floor in front of the wheeled chair, while his left arm dangled.

Rachel hesitated in the center of the room at his lack of response to her entrance.

"Daddy?" He often fell into a deep sleep in the late afternoon. When he still failed to respond, she ran to him. Her hand darted out to shake his shoulder but she stopped herself. His eyes were glazed over, staring at a distant point but no longer seeing anything. At last, the anger was gone from his expression.

"I hope you're at peace, now," she whispered and backed away. Her throat tightened. Scalding tears filled her eyes but didn't fall. Too many times she had refused to give in to tears and now when she absolutely could surrender to that weakness Sam abhorred, she couldn't. Blinded with those unshed tears, she stumbled through the house and out the back door.

Ben and Harrison were engaged in a conversation, both men leaning elbows onto the corral fence. Joshua stood between them, mimicking their posture, though his body seemed much more relaxed than that of the two men.

"Daddy's gone," she said. All three rounded to her, their expressions varying from Joshua's confusion as to where Sam could have gone, to astonishment from Ben, and immediate concern from Harrison. In two long strides, Harrison closed the distance between them and gathered her into his arms.

Her response to the innocent gesture of comfort was immediate. A mountain settled on her chest, her heart pounded faster than a pronghorn bounding through the sage. A roaring filled her ears. Instinctively she pushed free, and said, "Don't."

Harrison lifted his hands chest high, brows furrowed with obvious confusion, and backed away from her. Ben put himself between Harrison and her and said, "He was fine when I got him his laudanum about three hours ago."

"No one is blaming you," Harrison said. He twisted his head to Rachel. "If there is an undertaker in town, one of us needs to ride into Federal and send him out here. And, I'm assuming, by where your mother and siblings are buried, the priest at the church needs to perform the Last Rites for your father."

She looked to Ben. "Will you do that, Ben?" Rachel thrust her hand out and caught Harrison's in hers. "Ben knows where Bob Young's place is and he knows where Father O'Cleary lives. I need you here."

The foreman nodded. "Yeah, I'll ride into town and send Bob and that priest out here."

Harrison's brow knit again with confusion, Rachel was sure, because of the manner she had shoved him away and moments later, took his hand. After a slight hesitation, Harrison's fingers tightened around hers.

\*\*\*\*

Watching Bob Young's hearse drive away from the house hurt more than she would have ever thought it could. Her father had looked so small, so frail, and so very, very worn when Bob and his son transferred Sam into the back of the predominantly glass hearse and then covered him with a black shroud. She walked from Sam's room on the first floor, pausing long enough to glance over her shoulder into the room before she eased the door closed. Tomorrow, she promised herself, she would decide what to do with this room.

Rachel stopped in the kitchen and poured a cup of coffee and doctored it to her taste. Absent-mindedly, she itched her stomach where the boning in her corset had dug into her skin and sipped the sweetened, lightened brew. Just to be out of the wool riding habit and once more wearing her comfortable denims and oversized chambray shirt felt good. She made her way out the back door and to the waist-high railing encircling the porch. Harrison sat in the rocking chair, the aroma of strong, black coffee mingling with the acrid tang of a burning cigarette. Closing her eyes and tilting her head back, she let the night wash over her.

A light breeze rustled over the sage and the summer-yellowed grasses. The scent of rain carried on the air. Somewhere in the darkness, in a high-pitched voice, a distant coyote's shrill yap and trill was joined with another voice. One of the two horses snorted. From the far south-west came a muted, low, long growl of rumbling thunder.

She looked to the horizon. Towering thunderheads were illuminated from within in shades of white and purple and blue as the lightning danced in their heights.

"Is it going to rain again tonight?"

Rachel continued to watch the play of light in the depths of the clouds. She tried to puzzle out why Harrison was engaging in trivial small talk. Perhaps he was on the same uncertain footing she was about their marriage, about Sam's sudden death, even what it was married couples talked about. "I don't think so. I think that one is going to miss us. We might get a few drops, but it will rain out before it gets here."

"Joshua asleep?"

She nodded. "I suppose we should discuss sleeping arrangements." Just saying those words twisted her stomach with painful knots. "My father's old room on the second floor hasn't been used since his accident." She had to stop thinking of that room as her father's. It hadn't been Sam's room since the day she had found him nearly crushed under the rubble of the mine collapse. There had been no manner to navigate him up and down the stairs.

"We don't have to discuss anything permanent tonight." The chair creaked with his shifting weight. He rose from the chair and set his coffee cup on the porch railing, then crossed the distance to her. Without a word, he took her hand and pulled her closer to him. He looked down into her face. "I can continue to sleep on the chesterfield for a few more nights. Not that it would be my first choice..." His voice trailed off.

"I will need to air the room out, change the bed linens, and dust in there, but it would be senseless for you to continue to sleep in the parlor." She freed her hand and walked a few paces away. She was talking nonsense, hoping to quell her unease. Even the most hastily arranged marriage had a wedding night. Yet he had agreed that for now, they would have a marriage in name only.

Harrison's boot heels echoed on the porch floor. She startled when his hands came to rest on her shoulders.

"You're terrified," he said.

"What makes you think that?" She couldn't make herself look at him. The knots in her stomach drew tighter, making breathing naturally more difficult, and forcing her heart to race.

He drew his hands down her arms and back to her shoulders. "Let's start with how stiff your spine is. Or that your voice is shaking. Every time I've touched you, you've either frozen or you panic." His breath whispered across the nape of her neck and ruffled the tendrils escaping her severe chignon. He turned her to him and caught her chin on the back of his hand, tilting her head up. "I made a promise, Rachel, and I will not break my word. *You* have to change the terms of our marriage."

She forced herself to draw a deep breath when his arms wrapped around her waist and he exerted gentle pressure to bring her against his chest. He enveloped her within his embrace and this time there wasn't panic or the desperate need to break free hammering in her. Rachel allowed herself to relax.

His cheek pressed into her crown. A self-deprecating laugh broke from him, and she admitted she liked how that sound rumbled in the depths of his chest.

"I really should have my head examined for agreeing to all of that."

His arms tightened around her. She forced herself to remain within the circle of his arms, the side of her face against him. He must have sensed her sudden unease as he loosened his hold.

"You are an interesting woman. Beautiful, fascinating, and so full of contradictions." He levered back from her and lifted his hand to cradle the side of her face, the pad of his thumb feathering along the slope of her cheek. "A seemingly very strong woman and yet terrified of a kiss."

Rachel's lips went dry and she couldn't pry her tongue from the roof of her mouth. Her limbs trembled. Surely he had to hear how fiercely her heart was pounding, so loudly she heard it echoing in her ears.

His voice deepened, grew quieter until it was almost a whisper and she fought the urge to close her eyes and let the warmth in his voice wash fully over her. "A woman with a child but so frightened of intimacy." He leaned even closer to her, his mouth almost on hers, yet not touching her except where his warm palm held her face.

In the darkness, she could just make out his features. Her hands slid up his chest and she didn't know if it was to push him away or pull him closer. She was aware her breathing was shallow and she held her breath when he brushed the pad of his thumb against her lower lip.

"You have a mouth made for kissing, my beautiful

wife, but I'm not going to kiss you. Not until you ask me. And, I promise, when that time comes, you'll be asking me to do a whole lot more than just kiss you."

He straightened and released her, moving away in the same fluid motion. His long strides carried him to the house, up the steps, and then through the door. Rachel sagged, pulling in a ragged, deep breath. A strange ache filled her lower belly, not painful but entirely confusing for its origin. She ran her tongue over her dry lips, staring into the night.

She twisted her head to the house. Part of her wanted to know if this time would be different. Fear of discovering that it wouldn't be kept her feet frozen, unable to move forward.

\*\*\*\*

Harrison lit one lamp in the parlor and then crossed the room to the desk. He sank into the chair and stared across the room without really seeing anything. He wasn't sure how long he spent wool-gathering before he craned his head to the small liquor cabinet behind him. He opened the doors, surprised to see a system that allowed a third length of highly polished wood to be lifted as a sideboard. A bit of maneuvering the board into place allowed him to peruse the cabinet's contents.

Though the bottles and decanters were dusty, the labels on the bottles all bespoke of a refined taste in alcohol: whiskey from the Casper Company of Winston-Salem, Old Overholt rye—President Lincoln's poison of choice and in Harrison's opinion poison was the right terminology for any rye—Old GrandDad Kentucky bourbon...He pulled the bourbon from the cabinet and worked the cork topper free. The heavy cut glass tumblers were as dusty as the bottles, but a swipe of the rag in the cabinet resolved that problem.

He poured about three fingers into the glass and took a swallow. The alcohol was beyond smooth. Aged ten years in Kentucky and heaven only knew how long in the cabinet gave the bourbon a mellow, warm taste. Leaning back in the chair, the tumbler settled on his knee, Harrison let his thoughts drift back to his wife.

If he hadn't walked away from her, any promise he'd made about keeping their marriage in name only would have vanished like a puff of smoke in the ever-present Wyoming wind. He couldn't miss the slight trembling of her lip when he'd dragged his thumb along it, or the manner her hands had curled against him instead of pushing on him. Not only did she have a mouth made for kissing, but after holding her more than once in his arms, he knew she had a body made for sinning.

There was no doubting she was terrified of intimacy…curious, also, but she just couldn't seem to move past that terror. He didn't think he was simple-minded by any means, but there was something that he just couldn't make fit. Ben's unfinished warning to not hurt Rachel, the mercantile owner's reaction when he told the man his name, Rachel's own response to any physical advance. She had been intimate at least once. Joshua was living proof of that.

He lifted the tumbler and took another sip. Somehow, Jason was involved in all of it, he just wasn't sure how.

*"I wish I'd never made his acquaintance."*

As surely as if she was standing in the room with him, Harrison heard Rachel say those words again. Was it possible Jason was the one who'd taken advantage of

Rachel and then left her high and dry when it became apparent she was carrying his child?

The boy didn't look anything like his older half-brother, if Jason was his father. Not with that head of tight bright blond curls and those freckles smattering over his nose and cheeks. Harrison stilled, recalling the many letters his sister Caroline had sent him over the years, always full of the most current gossip for Trapman County and her commentary of such, especially regarding the many tow-headed, freckle-faced children rumored to be Jason's doings.

"Harrison?"

He jerked away from his musings and looked to the opened doorway. Even though she was dressed in denims and an overly large chambray shirt, he still wondered how blind he had to have been to have thought for even a moment she was a boy. The single lamp illuminated her shifting from one foot to the other, revealing her discomfort.

He rose and walked out from behind the desk. "I'm sorry if it's too soon for anyone to be in that chair."

Her gaze darted from him to the desk chair and back. She shook her head, escaping tendrils of hair brushing along her cheeks. "That's not why I paused. I need to ask you something."

He set the nearly empty tumbler on the desk and leaned a hip into the edge of the dark wood.

She finally stepped into the room. Her fingers trailed along the back of the chesterfield as she rounded the couch but she didn't sit. "Would you consider being a pall bearer for my father? I have asked Ben and he's going to ask a few other people, but—"

"I'd be honored." The cut glass drew his attention

and he twisted the tumbler on the smooth surface of the desk. Aware she hadn't left the room but also hadn't relaxed enough to sit, he said, "It's a little early to turn in. I'd like to take a look at the financial records for the ranch. That is, if you don't mind and it's not too soon to be delving into them."

She dipped her head toward her father's desk. "I kept the books. They're in the top drawer on the left side."

He gestured to the chair. "They might make more sense if we go over them together."

Her brows snapped together in a fierce scowl and Harrison realized she regarded that comment as an insult to her book-keeping. Then, she exhaled sharply and the cloud lifted from her face. "They're fairly straight forward. One ledger was for expenditures and income. The other was kept for breeding results." She sat in the chair, pulled the drawer in question open, and placed two bound records on the desk.

Harrison twisted the wick in the lamp up and moved it closer to her. She flipped the first book open and leafed to the last page with entries recorded. "My father was particular about keeping track of every penny we made and spent. He didn't want me doing this, but he was never very good with figures."

Harrison made his way behind her and looked over her shoulder. Her fingertip trailed down the page, noting the funds going out, what monies came in. Even the few times she had purchased a piece of penny candy for Joshua was marked in the expenditures column. He set his hand down next to the ledger, leaning over her. The faint aroma of vanilla and rose water drifted up to him. "You can mark out the funds owed to the mercantile. That's been settled."

"I…I need to know what the other items you purchased at the mercantile amounted to."

"I have to go into town again tomorrow. I need a black frock coat." The long curls along the back of her neck that had escaped her chignon fluttered with his breath. He fought the urge to remove the combs and pins holding her hair captive and draw the tresses through his fingers. "I'll have Thom draw up a receipt then."

"That'll be—" She sucked in her breath when he brushed his fingertips the length of her neck. "That'll be fine."

"What about the other ledger?" He lifted his hand from the back of her neck but not before he slid one tendril of her scented hair through his fingers. It felt as cool and smooth as silk.

Even as she moved the first book aside and flipped open the second, he noted the tips of her ears coloring. He was certain discussing breeding practices wasn't anything she had ever planned on doing. A slight tilting of his upper body brought him closer to her ear. "It's just business, Rachel, even if that business involves breeding."

The red tint to her ear deepened and splashed along the slope of her cheek. Her hand shook when she flipped a page in the record book.

"At one time, the Lazy L had three bulls. I insisted on keeping them separate so we could track how many calves each of them sired." Her voice cracked. "The polled bull produced the least. He left a lot of heifers and cows open."

He hadn't even spared the ledger a glance. "If they

didn't have a calf one year, did you put those cows in with another bull?"

The color staining her face deepened. She nodded, the tantalizing aroma wafting up to him again. "We had a bull with a broken horn. By keeping track of how many calves he sired, I could argue to keep him and sell the polled bull. My father wasn't happy I was doing this when he found out. He was even less happy I insisted on selling his pedigreed, prize polled Hereford."

"Sometimes, a pedigree makes people believe an animal is worth more than it really is." Harrison could feel the heat radiating from her flushed cheeks. "Unfortunately, a pedigree doesn't guarantee results and you were making sure that the ranch made the most profit possible."

Her head bent more to the ledger in front of her. "According to most of the people of this town, I never should have involved myself with anything as vulgar as money. After his accident when I was the one dealing with the bank, I was told by several of those people just how vulgar it was." She slapped the book shut and forced him to step back as she flung herself from the chair. Sparks glittered in the depths of her eyes. "Do you know what people said about me when they learned I was the one managing the herds?"

"I can imagine." He gestured to the closed books. "I don't give a damn what anyone has said about you. You've done what you've had to do to keep this ranch. None of that makes you any less the lady you are."

The sparks faded and a tremulous smile lifted the corners of her mouth. "As my business partner, I suppose you're going to continue to flatter me."

Harrison offered her a grin. "As your business

partner, I'm supposed to make sure we stay in the black. As your husband, it's not flattery if I'm complimenting you. Mrs. Taylor, not only are you a lady, you're a very fine looking lady."

Her cheeks flooded with renewed color. "Now, you are flattering me."

"Simply stating the obvious."

Chapter Nine

The day of Sam's funeral started hot, a sunrise of burnished brass in a blood red sky. More than anything, Rachel wanted the agony of the funeral to be over. She hadn't been inside the church since the morning the former priest had made it plain he would not baptize Joshua unless and until she married the child's father. She had little dealings with the new priest, a middle-aged Irishman, though he often asked when he could expect to see her at Mass every time he came out to the ranch for her father. She had no manner to express her agony with the condemnation she felt in the one place where there should have been none.

The heat in the small church was stifling. Hopefully, it would be cooler outside for the short graveside service when the Mass concluded. The back and sides of her black mourning dress were soaked with perspiration and she briefly toyed with the idea of tugging the heavy fabric from her ribs. She stole a glance at Harrison. Sweat dampened his hair and trickled down the side of his face, but if he was otherwise affected by the heat, she didn't see any evidence of it. His attention was wholly on Drake Adams, Royce Majors's adopted son. Harrison startled with the sharp nudge of her elbow in his ribs and diverted his focus back to the Mass.

He had first seen Drake when her father's pall

bearers were instructed by O'Cleary on their duties during the Vigil and later funeral Mass. Harrison truly had the appearance of a man who had seen a ghost. "He reminds me of someone I once knew," was the only explanation he gave.

Mercifully, O'Cleary kept the graveside ceremony short. After the last words were spoken, Rachel walked in a measured tread to the opened earth, scooped up a small handful of dirt, and allowed the soil to fall from her fingers onto her father's coffin. The hollow, dull thud of a clump bouncing across the wood cover drove through her. She shut her eyes, willing herself to forget that sound, forget the sight of her father's frail form under the black shroud in the back of Bob Young's hearse, forget the anger and the pain Sam had caused.

When she turned from the grave, the landscape spun and she felt herself collapsing backward to the opening. Shocked gasps sounded as a loud hissing in her ears. Before she completely lost her balance, Harrison's strong arms encircled her shoulders and waist. She latched onto the front of his black frock coat, knowing only his strength kept her on her feet.

"I've got you," he said, barely above a murmur. "Let's go home. There's nothing more to do here."

She let herself crumble against him, her cheek against his chest. With his arms still around her, he guided her from the cemetery. Voices she couldn't place murmured platitudes of sympathy. A few feet from the carriage, a familiar voice called her name.

Though he stopped, Harrison didn't remove his stabilizing arm from around her waist. A smaller black buggy drew to a halt near them, and Dr. Hagar disembarked. "I'm sorry about your father," he said. "I delayed this until the funeral was over but I understand your husband is the new law in town."

"Can't this wait?" Harrison's voice rumbled through his chest and into her ear. Her head grew fuzzy and Rachel felt herself swaying. Nausea flipped her stomach over and over. Harrison's arm tightened on her and he added, "She really needs to be out of the sun."

"And out of that damn black wool and corset," Hagar added. "I'll make this very short. We can talk in detail later. Bob asked me to examine Sam because he found this tucked inside his shirt." The doctor handed a folded note to Harrison.

"I'll look at it when we're back at the ranch. Anything else?" Brusqueness added a sharp edge to Harrison's words.

"I think Sam was murdered."

If Harrison responded, Rachel never heard it. She heard only a fierce buzzing in her ears as if she was enveloped by a hive of angry bees before everything faded into darkness.

When she came to her senses, she didn't know where she was. Though the surface against her back was cool, it was also rigid and unyielding. Something pillowed her head. The low ceiling was composed of dark wood planks and heavy cross timbers. A slight twist of her head to one side revealed a wall made of yellowish bricks. Another tilt of her head and she saw floor to ceiling bars.

More sensations crept into her awareness: a cool, damp rag against her forehead, the chill of the stone floor on her bare arms. Her outer shirt was gone, as was the heavy wool skirt and her petticoats. And, blessedly, the corset. She was clad in no more than her chemise and knickers.

Harrison was sitting on the floor, propped in the corner, his head tilted back to the wall. He'd removed his frock coat, loosened the silk tie so that the ends dangled to either side of the opened collar of his shirt, and rolled his sleeves to mid-forearm. The vague recollection of being lifted into and then out of the carriage filtered through her thoughts. She tried to sit and gave up the effort. As soon as she made the attempt, Harrison raised his head and sent a roguish and slightly sheepish smile in her direction.

Heat filled her cheeks and she was uncomfortably aware of how little she wore.

"I apologize for the lack of accommodations." He crossed his long legs at the ankle. "However, I had to take you someplace to get you cooled down and I was fairly certain dropping you wholly clothed into a horse trough was not the best option."

"I appreciate that consideration." She cautiously sat up. Though she was a little light-headed, her earlier nausea didn't return. A slow dip of her head and what she hoped to be a delicate sniff of herself revealed she probably hadn't vomited on herself.

"You did throw up," Harrison said, the amusement in his voice telling her she hadn't been so subtle. Renewed heat filled her cheeks with her embarrassment. His voice deepened. "Doc and I made sure it was over the side of the buggy and not on yourself."

"I've never done that before." Now that she was divested of the heavy woolen garments and was no longer over-heated, a shiver skipped across her skin, raising gooseflesh. She drew her knees up to her chest and wrapped her arms around her bent legs. "Succumbed to the vapors, I mean. I've never done that."

"You've also never buried your father and then heard it was possible he was murdered." He levered himself off the floor.

Rachel watched him walk to the coat tree near the door. He lifted his frock coat from a branch, then returned to her. He draped the garment around her shoulders and dropped to one knee at her side. "For the record, I don't think Sam was murdered. I do think the note Young found tucked into your father's shirt may have caused another apoplexy which contributed to his death, but that's probably not murder."

The note. She'd forgotten about that. "What did it say?"

He stood, holding his hand down to her. "I don't want to talk about it here. I want to get you home. It'll be dark in another hour and it's probably going to storm again. There's been thunder rumbling for a little while now."

Rachel took his hand and let him assist her effort to stand. Again, she felt light-headed and she gripped his arm until the dizziness passed. "Where's Joshua?"

"Ben took him home. Said he'll keep him overnight and bring him to the ranch tomorrow when you're feeling better. He said it would probably be after a meeting here in town with the other ranchers." Harrison handed her clothing to her. He gestured to a door at the back corner of the jail. "There's a small room back there."

A laugh welled in her chest and she couldn't contain it. Perhaps it was everything in the last several days, but his suggestion she use a private room to put on her outer clothing struck her as amusing. "You've seen me in my night clothes and apparently removed enough of my clothing so that all I am attired in are my knickers and chemise, but you wish me to dress in a back room?" She shook the bustled petticoat so the multi layers of the fabric draped again over the bustle.

"Just how many petticoats does a lady need to wear at one time?" Harrison mused, his brow lifting with the query. "I fully understand why women faint in the heat."

Rachel gathered the petticoat and lifted it over her head. She tugged it down into place and around her waist so the bustle was properly situated, then pulled the drawstring tight and tied it. She repeated the process with the skirt. To make sure the skirt fell properly, she tugged it over the bustle and hopped a few times in place. Harrison turned his back to her, but not before she saw a flush of color creeping up his face. He was embarrassed. Amusement trickled through her again. She pulled her outer jacket on and began the tedious task of fastening the many, tiny black pearl buttons.

"I'm dressed, now," she said, even though she hadn't closed the top four buttons at the neck. Just putting the wool ensemble back on was making her warm, again. She picked up her small bonnet and gloves, noting the black lace was ruined from the handful of dirt she had dropped into her father's grave. While the gloves weren't the most current fashion, they were the only pair of lace ones she owned. With a small sigh, she dropped them onto the desk and tied the small hat onto her head.

Harrison's gaze rested briefly on her corset in full

view on the desk. "Why do you even wear a corset? You certainly don't need it."

"A proper lady never sets foot outside her home without the appropriate undergarments, Mr. Taylor." She hoped she put as much haughtiness and disdain into her voice as she had heard from her instructors at Miss Julianna's School for Young Ladies.

"Mrs. Taylor, I challenge any one to imply you are less than a proper lady." He shrugged into his frock coat. "My honor would require me to call out any one foolish enough to make that implication. Your person and your reputation will remain safe and unimpugned with me, ma'am."

She took his offered arm and cast a backward glance at the desk. "What about my corset? The whole town will be scandalized with it right there in full view."

"But, it's not in full view unless they peek through the window." His grin was a flash of rogue and devilment. "Whatever will they say? That I was so concerned with my wife's well-being after she was overcome by the heat that I took her someplace private to get her out of those horrid heavy wool garments before she became even more indisposed?"

The mental image of several of the town's gossips pressing their noses to the dusty glass just to see her undergarment gave her another set of the giggles. His deep chuckle mingled with hers. He walked her to the buggy. Before she could gather her skirts to climb into the seat, Harrison settled his hands on her waist and lifted her.

Her first instinct was to push him away and she grabbed his shoulders. As quickly as the urge to push him away invaded, Rachel quelled it and allowed him to settle her into the buggy. His hold lingered on her and he pulled her upper body closer to him.

Without making a scene, she couldn't resist. He didn't kiss her, though. When her face was inches from his, he grinned and said, "We can't scandalize the whole town, Mrs. Taylor, with a public display of affection. Plus, you haven't asked me to kiss you and I promised I wouldn't do that until you asked." He released her, adding, "Just for the record, I can state that you do not need a corset."

****

The thunder grumbled closer. Harrison guided the buggy onto the road leading to the Lazy L. He shot a sidelong glance at Rachel, noting her compressed lips, her hands clasped so tightly together her knuckles whitened, and her rigid posture. "You really don't like thunderstorms, do you?"

She shook her head.

He slapped the reins over Twinkle's haunches, urging her to a faster gait. "I'll try to get us home before that hits."

"Harrison, what did that note say?"

"I'll give it to you when we're at the house." He looked over at her. Her posture had grown more rigid and she stared straight ahead. The contents of the message left with Sam's body roiled his stomach. Even though it was short, the vitriol in the wording left little doubt in his mind that whoever wrote it posed an extreme danger to Rachel and Joshua.

The ranch house came into view as the wind began to gust with the approaching storm. When he reined Twinkle to a stop, the skies were nearly black. The wind whipped the scrub grasses into bent shapes and shook the sage. Dust devils formed and whistled and hissed across the landscape. He leaped down and helped Rachel from the conveyance. "Go on in the house. I'll get Twink put out with Demon and pull a tarp over the buggy."

The rain began in earnest just as he jogged up the porch steps. He walked into the kitchen, the aroma of coffee greeting him. Faltering notes from the piano drew his attention. The music softly challenged the angry howl of the wind, the cracking thunder, and the staccato rap of the rain against the windows.

He didn't bother with a cup of coffee. The folded paper in the breast pocket of his frock coat demanded something a lot stronger. The decanter of bourbon in the cabinet should work.

Rachel stopped playing when he walked into the parlor. He crossed the room to the sideboard. "Don't stop, please," he said.

"I'm surprised it's still in tune. I haven't played this piano since the night I told Daddy I was going to have a child." The music resonating in the body of the piano grew surer, the lament within the notes of "Oh, Shenandoah" more poignant. The embellishments she added heightened the longing inherent in the music.

Harrison walked to the windows and let the storm hold his attention. How often had he heard that tune from a jaw harp, or a fiddle, or even the voices of homesick men around a campfire during that damnable war? He tilted the small tumbler of bourbon back and downed the contents in one swallow. A small tap marked the contact of glass and desk top. The paper in his breast pocket crackled when he shrugged out of the frock coat. As if he could find either answers or divine assistance in its depths, he stared into the empty glass, at the same time pulling off the black silk tie dangling from either side of his open collar. Several buttons parted next. The shirt gaped further.

"Who is Joshua's father?"

The music stopped. He craned his head over his shoulder. Rachel stared down at the keys, her shoulders tense.

"Does it matter?" Her voice broke on the last word.

"I think it does." He picked up the glass and poured another drink. The tie dropped onto his coat. "I think it has everything to do with the note left for you at Burlington's and everything to do with the note that was with your father."

She hadn't lifted her head from her study of the keys. "What did that note say?"

Harrison pulled the wrinkled paper from his pocket and placed it on the keyboard. Her breathing grew rapid and shallow and she recoiled from it. He waited for her to unfold the thing. He'd already read it so many times in that afternoon he had the few, ugly lines memorized.

Rachel finally shook her head and looked up at him. "I can't."

He placed the tumbler on the sidearm and sat next to her on the bench. "It says that Sam tried to kill the author of that note when he blasted the mine shut. It also says that when he comes back he intends to finish what he started with you and that he intended to make Sam watch—but Sam had the bad graces to die while he was telling him what he planned to do to you." Just summarizing what he read in the note made Harrison's stomach knot. He made the deliberate decision to not tell her what the writer promised to do to Joshua.

Rachel wrapped her arms around her waist and she shrank into herself. She jumped at a brilliant flash of light and the subsequent immediate crack of thunder. As if she couldn't stay still, she bolted to her feet and paced the floor. "He never believed me."

"Sam?"

She stopped and nodded. "The night I told Daddy I was expecting a child, he slapped me so hard he knocked me to the floor. He had never raised his hand to me before. He then proceeded to call me every name in the book, including some things in Spanish. Just by the tone I could guess what they meant." She wrapped her arms around herself again. "Boarding school and finishing school were a waste of his good money, according to him. I was a disgrace. I wasn't fit to be his daughter any longer. I had dishonored my mother's memory. I wasn't a lady. I'm just a—" Another close lightning strike and a thin cry broke from her, halting her words.

"And, we both know just how wrong your father was. Being a lady involves a lot more than serving tea in fine china." Everything he knew told him to get up, go to her, and pull her into his arms and hold her—but where she was concerned, what he knew had proven to be the wrong thing. "The person who wrote these notes—the one left for you at Burlington's and this one—is that person Joshua's father?"

She dipped her head in one terse nod. "Daddy was away selling cattle when Joshua was…when it happened. By the time Daddy got back from Fort Scott, all the bruises had faded and I told him I had been thrown from a horse to explain my broken arm and ribs." The pain etched into the lines of her face knifed into him when she met his gaze across the floor. "I hoped I could just forget about it. But I can't." She shook her head, as if she was trying to shake off the memories. Deep tremors left her shuddering. "Every time there's a thunderstorm or if anyone tries to hold me...do you know how difficult it is to even let you hold my hand?" The last was asked on a breath that sounded almost like a cry. Before he could respond, she continued, "I made Dr. Hagar and Drake promise not to tell anyone what happened, what that man did, but everyone in town knew. Drake found me when I didn't come to the Rocking Bar M for Jessie's birthday party. He and Royce rode out here to check on me, because they'd already heard about the poker game and they were worried."

Harrison stood. He closed the distance between them, halting when she shied. "What poker game, Rachel? The one with your father at Fort Scott?"

"No." Once more, as if she couldn't hold still, she paced the floor. "The wranglers here, the Rocking Bar M, and the Crazy TG used to get together once a month after payday for a poker game. For months, all I heard was what a great poker player Jason was, so while my father was on that selling trip, I decided I'd get dealt into the game. I spent the first few hands learning his play, when he was likely to bluff, when he had a strong hand. And I played recklessly. I had nothing to lose."

*Jason?* He struggled to put the pieces together.

"By the end of the night, it was down to just him and me." Rachel paused by the windows, her back to him, and she moved a lace panel to one side. "Everyone else was out because it had gotten too pricy. Jason bet almost everything he had in front of him. I raised him to force him all in. He laid 'em down."

A chill chased the length of Harrison's spine. Too well he knew his half-brother's volatile anger because it was the same loss of control he often struggled with and more than once as a child, he'd been on the brunt end of Jason's temper. Combine that ugly temper with the alcohol he was willing to wager was flowing in the game and Jason's inability to calculate Rachel's manner of playing her cards because of her own admitted reckless play...Again a chill skittered up Harrison's back.

"He had a straight to the jack and he laid 'em down," she repeated, more forcefully. The lace panel fell into place. "I took the money on the table and he said he wanted to see what he lost to. I told him he paid to play, not see my cards." She looked over her shoulder at Harrison and the anguish darkening her eyes almost brought him to his knees. "I cut out the money I brought to the game and told the wranglers to get what they'd lost out of the pot. No one lost any money that night, including Jason."

"What cards did you have in your hand?"

"A pair of red deuces." A hint of a smile brushed her mouth then faded immediately. "I had a little more grit then, so I tossed my hand face up onto the table before I left the bunk house. He was furious. Said I'd humiliated him."

The bourbon he'd downed just a few moments ago felt as if was curdling in his gut.

She resumed pacing, pausing at the piano only to go back to the window. "The next day we had some of the worst thunderstorms anyone could ever remember. I was here alone." Her shoulders rounded and again she shrank into herself. "It was my fault. I never should have gotten dealt into the game."

"No." He crossed the floor in two strides, and caught her upper arms, pulling her around to him. "Whatever he did to you was not your fault, Rachel. If he did what I think you're saying—that he forced himself on you—there is no excuse for that and it will never be your fault."

A choked sob ripped from her. "I hadn't even been kissed before that."

Catching her face between his hands, giving her every opportunity to pull away, he bent closer to her. Even though her breathing was rapid and sharp, she didn't recoil. Kissing her at that exact moment would be the worst thing he could do, and he knew it. He lowered his hands and wrapped her in his embrace, pulling her against him. Her whole frame shook. He did no more than hold her and gradually, he felt her relax until her cheek was against the plane of his chest.

Thunder growled in the gathering gloom, louder this time and the wind gusted through the open window. The flame in the single lamp flickered, almost guttered. She stiffened and Harrison released her, taking a step from her at the same time. In what was a totally unconscious gesture, her arms wrapped around her mid-section and she whispered, "I hate this room."

Without saying as much, he understood she was trying to tell him where she had been when Jason attacked her.

She shifted her line of sight to the massive, dark desk in the corner. He followed her gaze. "When he left, I crawled under there. I felt so filthy." A visible shudder rippled over her. "He told people that I begged him."

And, like an idiot, he had told her he wouldn't kiss her until she asked him and when she did ask, it would be for a lot more than a kiss. "Rachel, I—"

She shook her head, cutting him off. "I did beg him, but not for the reason he told people." Her pacing steps carried her to the desk. She leaned her weight onto her palms, pressing her hands against the green blotter. The wind gusted through the open windows, billowing the lace curtains as if they were sails and again guttering the lantern. "He made me do things...I burned the dress I wore that day. I did the things he told me to do so he would stop hurting me." Her voice broke. "He didn't stop."

Close the distance between them and take her into his arms or make the offer and wait to see what she chose? Harrison knew what his instincts told him to do, but where Rachel was concerned, those instincts had proven wrong before. The pain his own brother had caused her was worse than a knife into his gut. No small wonder she panicked every time he had so much as tried to kiss her.

He crossed the room, halting directly behind her. To keep from pulling her into his arms, he clenched his fists. "I know I'm asking you to do something that's probably next to impossible." The wind howled around the house, and this time as it entered the room, it extinguished the lamp. Lightning filled the darkness while thunder rumbled low, like an angry growl. "I'm asking you to trust me and you can't because all you can see is someone who's bigger than you, stronger than you, and someone who could hurt you."

Chapter Ten

"...hurt you."

His frame behind her imprisoned her against the desk as surely as if he held her there. Rachel twisted her head over her shoulder, unable to even move away from him. Violent shuddering gripped her and she managed to move and put the desk at her back. Her throat closed. It was impossible to breathe. Impossible to think. Only react.

She couldn't contain her instinctive flinch when he lifted a hand to her face. Heedless of the consequences, she pushed him, trying to gain some space between them.

Another long, flickering stroke of lightning illuminated the room. His brow furrowed. The angle of his head tilt shadowed his features into sharp contrasts, leaving his expression dark and unreadable. The harsh, brilliant light glittered in his eyes.

She darted around him and ran through the pocket doors. Her room. Heavy bolt on the door. Her derringer. Safety. Up the stairs. Run faster. Turn at the landing.

Her feet slipped on the carpet runner and she fell against the wall.

Heavy footsteps on the stairs.

*Get up.*

The slick soles of her shoes slid on the carpet. She couldn't get purchase in her panicked state. Her knee caught in her skirt.

He had her arm. Blinded by terror, she struck out. He had her wrist. She was on her knees. Her back was pinned to the wall. He had both her wrists. She couldn't get away.

*Scream.*

No point. No one would hear her. She screwed her eyes shut. Waited for the pain.

He pressed her clenched fists to his chest, still holding her imprisoned with an iron grip on her wrists.

*Fight back.*

Nails were claws. His hissing breath filled her ears. He didn't strike and he didn't release her. She raked him again. Hurt him. Make him let her go. She tried to kick her legs free. The skirt still pinned her, trapped and vulnerable on her knees.

"…it's all right…Rachel, you're safe…"

Gradually, the soothing words filtered past the crazed panic. Confusion with the murmuring tempered the alarm. She opened her eyes. Raw, bloody scratches delved into the opened front of his shirt, marked his chest where her hands had been. Stunned, she lifted her gaze to his face—Harrison's face. A lop-sided grin curled up a corner of his lips and he released her wrists.

Her hands crept to her mouth. Her face was drenched with tears she didn't even realize she'd shed. "I'm so sorry," she whispered.

"You have nothing to apologize for. I shouldn't have made you feel trapped. I'm sorry I frightened you." He gently stroked the hair from her sweating brow and then cupped the back of her head. She couldn't resist when he pulled her head to his shoulder. Without warning, he pulled her away from the wall, onto his lap, and cradled her.

A deep sob tore its way free from her depths. The need to feel safe, to be held like this overwhelmed her. She wrapped her arms around his neck and surrendered to the tears, to the need to be held. The tears she had kept locked away for so long broke loose and she burrowed her face into him.

Harrison closed his arms more firmly. He pressed a lingering kiss to the top of her head and stroked her back. The muscles of his chest bunched and smoothed under her cheek as he shifted until he was leaning against the wall. Lulled by the gentle motion of his hand tracing a repeated path down her back, her tears dried and her sobs gradually faded to only shaking breaths.

"I never should have gotten dealt into that poker game."

She couldn't stop her squeak when his hands clamped down on her upper arms. Harrison pushed her back with a growl. "Let's get this straight now. What that bastard did to you will never be your fault." The words were clipped, full of an anger that seethed in the staccato cadence.

"If I hadn't been in the bunk house and playing poker…a lot of people said I led him on. I never should have been there. Father O'Reilly, the priest who used to be here, said I made Jason sin with my actions."

His hands tightened on her upper arms in a painful hold. Rachel managed a whispered, "Stop. You're hurting me."

"Jason isn't the victim in all this." The firmness in his grip eased but he didn't release her. He drew a long breath and the lines of his face softened. "There is nothing you could have done to make his actions your fault. It doesn't matter what anyone else has said—and I don't care what was said in trying to place the blame on you—what he did is not your fault. It doesn't matter that you got dealt into a poker game. It doesn't matter what you wore. It doesn't matter you cleaned him out. Hell, it doesn't even matter if you were flirting with him and every man in the room. He had no right to abuse you and force himself on you. No one will ever have that right, nor is there anything you could ever do that will ever give anyone that right."

She lowered her gaze, the angry, red scratches she left on his chest drawing her attention. The memory of similar claw marks on Jason's face and his subsequent heightened rage tore into her.

"Rachel, I meant it when I said there is nothing you could do to give anyone the right to hurt you. That includes me. Being married to you doesn't change that. No one has that right."

She forced herself to meet his eyes. "You're really not anything like him, are you?"

Harrison's brow shot up and he tilted his head to a side. "I've spent most of my life trying to *never* be anything like him." The slightest hint of a smile tugged a corner of his mouth. "And, if it takes the rest of my life to gain your trust and belief that I will never be anything like him, I'll willingly make that my life's avocation."

A long, tapering sigh eased from her and she didn't resist when he pulled her down against his chest again. She had almost fallen asleep when he shifted her weight in his arms and stood, holding her cradled to him. "What are you doing?"

"Taking you to your bed." His voice had a drowsy quality, as if he was fighting sleep. "And, then I'm going to my room and put myself to bed, too."

Before she lost every bit of her nerve, Rachel blurted out, "I don't want to be alone tonight. I can't sleep when it's storming."

Harrison lowered her to stand. She met his questioning gaze and added, "I can sleep in the chair in my room. I've done it before. I just don't want to be alone."

The grin that split his face held a hint of sadness. "Now, just what kind of gentleman would I be if I allowed you to try to sleep in a chair while I slept in a bed? That chesterfield is large enough for you to sleep against me."

In the parlor…sleeping in that room would never be an option for her. Her gaze lifted to the closed bedroom doors on the second floor. "Don't…don't married couples usually sleep in the same room?"

"Usually in the same bed, too. And, while I will not deny that I want you in my bed, even if you told me you want to change the terms of our agreement right now, I wouldn't consent to any changes. Not tonight, darlin'."

Confusion dulled her thoughts. "But…"

"I only want there to be the two of us in our bed and right now, there's someone else who'd be there." He gestured down the stairs. "I can wait until you feel safe enough. So, our options are the chesterfield or I sleep in the chair you said is in your room."

That he didn't know the furnishings of her room, that he hadn't looked into her room, and that he apparently saw that space as private for her, was comforting. "Well, you're not sleeping in a chair."

"The chesterfield it is, then." He took her hand and led her down the stairs. The mantel clock softly chimed the top of the hour.

"I don't know why I was so tired," she said, extracting her hand from his. Her steps carried her to the piano. The note which had been found with her father was on the bench and without even opening it, she crumbled it into a wad and threw the paper ball onto the open hearth.

"Why don't I go get both of us a cup of coffee? It is rather early to turn in." If he had an opinion on why she was so exhausted, he didn't offer it.

Rachel nodded. A piece by Chopin whispered in her memory. The cool keys drew her fingertips and without a conscious thought, she traced out the opening notes of a piece of music with one hand. She lifted the lid on the piano bench, hoping that Sam hadn't made good on his promise to burn all the sheet music when he told her that he never wanted to hear her play the piano again. To her relief, every leaf was still safe within the depths of the seat.

She settled the score teasing her memory onto the music rack. In the dim light, she strained to see the notes. A lamp from the desk and the lantern on the piano were lit and the black jotting became clear. The word "*largo*" leaped out at her when she set her finger tips onto the keys. "Softly, slowly," she heard her instructor whispering in his thick German accent the first time she ever played the piece, his gnarled fingers on one edge of the sheet to flip the page for her as she sight-read the notes. From that first time she heard the notes form a wordless cry to the heavens, this piece became her favorite.

Her head bent to the keyboard, and her eyes closed. She had committed this prelude to memory within days of first playing it. After one look at the written notes, the remembrance of fingering, hesitations, the delicate touch of the keys as if caressing the face of a loved one all returned. One hand sang the melody, her fingers sliding closer to the body of the piano to change the volume. The middle of the piece was frenzied and almost angry and defiant, before the sound returned to the subtle coaxing of the notes. As the last chord sounded, Rachel lifted her hands and let the last of the resonance seep into the room. The solitude she found at the keyboard wisped away as the notes faded. The solace from the music remained.

The last of the storm whispered into the room as faint, far-distant thunder and the final strong gust of wind lifted the curtains.

"That was beautiful," Harrison said, his voice coming from the doorway.

"One of Chopin's preludes." She didn't turn to him, didn't lift her head, nor open her eyes. "When Daddy told me he never wanted to hear me play again, this was the piece I most missed being able to create." The aroma of coffee mingled with the rain-quenched earth in the room and she opened her eyes. Harrison stood next to her, a steaming cup of the brew in each hand.

The cup he offered her was caramel colored and the sweet scent of sugar mixed with the dark fragrance of the coffee. Warmth oozed through the porcelain into her fingers. "All that money he spent to hire a concert pianist to teach me to play when I was at finishing school, to bring Herr Bauer here during the summer so I could continue my lessons, even to have this piano moved here and he didn't hear me play a single note in more than six years because he was angry with me."

She set the cup on the floor next to her and again settled her fingers onto the keys. After a few notes, Harrison sat next to her on the bench, leaned closer to her, and said, "I will never tell you to stop playing. Even if the music you play sounds like two coyotes fighting, I'd never tell you to stop."

A chuckle broke from her. "Herr Bauer told me I was passable. He would stand over me with a willow switch and if I made a mistake, he'd smack the back of my head with it. I think I have a permanent ridge there." Her hands hesitated for a stop in the notes. "I made him cry though, the last time I played this for him. He said I finally understood that music lets us touch the face of God."

The melody of "Ave Maria" whispered into the room. The hesitation in the music that marred the piece this time came from Harrison settling his arm around her waist and his whispered, "Would it be considered sacrilege if I said it's not the face of God I want to touch right now?"

Her face heated. The weight of his arm on her, his hand spanning along her thigh, burned through the fabric of her dress. "It probably is."

Rachel heard the voice of temptation in his low laughter. He leaned a little closer and his breath feathered across her cheek. "Darlin', I'm absolutely certain what I'm thinking right now places my immortal soul in dire jeopardy, according to the priest I had when I was growing up."

The heat scalding her face increased. His hand

shifted against her leg, lightly squeezing her. His chest pressed against her shoulder and he said, "Aren't you in the least bit curious?"

Her fingers stilled on the keyboard. She couldn't force a single word free. Curious, yes. There were three children who had been born less than nine months after their parents married and that was just in the last year in the little town of Federal. Common sense told her that relations between a husband and wife weren't always something to be feared and avoided. Again, common sense dictated that her experience was not theirs.

"Rachel?"

There was so much he asked in that query composed of only her name.

She forced herself to draw a deep breath. "Yes. But, I'm more frightened than curious."

He shifted on the bench, then caught her shoulders and turned her to him. He studied her face for so long she couldn't continue to meet his gaze. Instead she focused on the length of his thigh pressing against hers. He slipped one finger under her chin and tilted her face up to him, again. "We rather put the cart before the horse, but what's done is done. You deserve to be courted and wooed and seduced. A woman like you has to be won."

Her cheeks had to be the color of ripe beets as hot as they felt. "Isn't it a little late for a courtship?"

His smile heated and sparks smoldered in the depths of his eyes. "It's never too late for a courtship, darlin'. I want to steal kisses from you in the moonlight, hold you against me at a dance, walk hand in hand with you in the rain, and whisper sweet nothings in your ear."

Remembering how to breathe became a priority. "Are you courting me or trying to seduce me?"

It should not have been possible for his smile to grow any hotter. "Let me fill you in on a little secret. Done right, courtship is always a seduction. And, seduction is about anticipation—anticipating the next touch, the next kiss." He moved closer to her, so close she could feel his breath against her skin, so close that if he moved any nearer his lips would be against hers. "Anticipation can be seductive in its own right."

The warmth scalding her face spread into her belly and even lower. She licked suddenly dry lips. "Can...can I kiss you?"

"You can do anything you like."

She leaned into him and pressed her lips to his. They were warm against her, firm without being possessive. A withdrawal broke the kiss and she struggled to draw another breath.

"For a first kiss, that wasn't so bad." One brow quirked up and he asked, "Are you curious enough to try for a second one?"

A shiver skittered across her but she whispered, "Yes. Please, kiss me."

Something shifted in his expression and for a moment, she wasn't sure what it was.

"Put your hands on my chest so you can push me away if you feel you need to."

Her breath caught in her throat. Hesitantly and mindful of the scratches she'd left on him, she pressed her palms to his upper chest. He wrapped an arm around her lower back and she let him pull her fully against him. The pad of his thumb traced her lower lip while his fingers splayed along the line of her jaw.

Her stomach filled in an instant with fluttering. Seemingly of their own accord, her hands slipped to his shoulders as he tilted her head up. She couldn't hold her eyes open.

Anything she thought she knew about a kiss dissolved under his lips. Firm but ever so gentle. An invitation to respond, a coaxing to meet him. There was no crude invasion of her mouth. There was no conquest. It was a negotiation for her to join in a mutual capitulation. She couldn't contain a whimpering cry with the first taste of his tongue.

Not sure when she had wrapped her arms around his neck, she clung to him when he broke the kiss and buried her face in the juncture of his neck and shoulder. She wasn't even sure which of them was shuddering or if it was both of them and gave in to the sudden desire to draw her hands across the width of his back.

He nuzzled into the side of her throat, trailing the length of her neck from her ear to the collar of her mourning dress with short kisses, tiny nips of his teeth, and the hot flick of his tongue against her skin. Her head lolled to the side, granting him more access. The back of his shirt wadded in her fingers with the sensations ricocheting through her.

She should push him away. She knew where this would lead. She couldn't. She didn't want to push him away. She was on fire. Every inch of her felt as if she was burning and deep in her core, that fire raged, leaving her shaking.

One hand blazed a path up her spine, scalding even through the material. His other was at the back of her head, tugging on her hair, pulling her mouth back to his. This time, she opened her mouth willingly to him.

When this kiss ended, he levered back from her. His harsh breaths matched hers. "You're trembling." He untangled his hand from her hair and ran his palm down her arm pausing only when he wove his fingers with hers.

Her heart should have pounded its way free of her chest as rapidly as it raced. She gulped in a breath, then before she lost her nerve, asked, "Will it hurt every time?"

Harrison's mouth dropped open before comprehension eased the furrow in his brow. His breath left him on a sharp exhalation. "No." His fingers tightened on hers. "I don't know how to delicately put this, but what he did was meant to hurt you physically. It was meant to belittle and degrade you."

Rachel lowered her head, staring at a spot in the patterning of the Oriental rug under the piano. No matter how much she scrubbed it there was still one small blood stain that refused to vanish. She didn't know if it was hers or Jason's. The marring of the crème colored wool had faded over the intervening years, but she could still find it. It drew her eye every time she glanced at the rug.

"I know you're frightened. Otherwise you wouldn't be asking that. That's why this is as far as we'll take this tonight. You've had a traumatizing day—"

She reared back, her whole body rigid, her reaction to his words cutting him off. Before she could form a protest, a crooked, half-grin danced across his features. "Quit bristling. I'm not accusing you of hysterics. I am saying I would be an utter cad and blackguard if I took advantage of your curiosity at this moment."

"If I told you I wanted to continue, would the other

terms of our agreement still be in effect?" She didn't even know where that question had come from, but she couldn't stop the words.

Without the slightest hesitation, Harrison said, "Yes." He stood and held his hand down to her. "I think we might be more comfortable on the chesterfield if you really want to continue this."

Rachel let him lead her to the overstuffed couch. He pulled her down next to him and tucked her into his side. Without any coaxing from him, she slid an arm over his stomach, curled her legs up onto the seat, and lowered her head onto his chest. This felt right. It felt like safety. She asked, "Which side of the bed do you sleep on?"

"The middle...you're going to have to snuggle up tight to me to keep from falling out of bed." His arms tightened around her. "Rather like you are now. Though I need to ask if you snore, because if you do, I might have to reconsider."

The teasing quality in his voice brought a fleeting smile to her face. "I do not snore." She hesitated, then added in less than a whisper, "I do have nightmares."

"I know." The depth of his voice, the protective timbre wrapped around her in a wave of warmth. His fingers tightened in her hair and he levered her off his chest just enough to place a soft, lingering kiss on her mouth. "I've heard you the last two nights and I have wanted so much to hold you until you felt safe again. I can't promise the nightmares will go away, but I will promise that you'll never have to face those memories alone anymore."

She buried her face in his chest, pushing away the recollection of the countless times in the past six years she had woken from those nightmares, and spent the rest of the night huddled on her bed, her back pressed to the wall, knees pulled up to her chest, praying for the dawn—if only so the sunlight would banish the worst of the memories.

His low voice, not much above a murmur, intruded on her thoughts. "Tomorrow I want you to ride with me and show me the ranch from your perspective."

"From my perspective?" She pushed herself off his chest and looked down at him. "Why?"

"I can follow fence lines, see where the watering holes are, and even figure out which pastures are in use and which ones aren't. I want you to show me what it is you love so much about this place."

If he was jesting with her, he didn't reveal such in either his tone or his level expression. "You want me to show you why I love the Lazy L," she said, not understanding exactly why he wanted to see such things.

"Yes. If I asked you to tell me why it is this place is home, why it's the only home you've ever wanted, and why it is you love it so, could you tell me?" His brow lifted with his question.

She considered her answer and finally shook her head. "No, I don't think I can explain it. I've tried before, with my father, with girls at the boarding and finishing schools I was sent to. I think it can't be explained."

"But, if I asked you to show me the things you love, the places that you brought to mind when you were at those schools, could you do that?"

Sagebrush Creek as it gurgled and chuckled down the mountainside; the white quartzite on Tableau Mesa glittering in the early morning sun; the strange rock formations the Indians called Vedauwoo in the Medicine Bow range; the manner the aspens turned absolute, shimmering gold in the fall; the ability of a horned toad to completely blend into the gritty soil; the pristine white face of a prickly poppy lifting to the sunlight… She nodded. "I can show you some of those places. Others take more than a day's ride. Some are right in plain sight, but most people never see them."

Harrison pulled her down against him. "Those are the things I want to see. I want to see our home through your perspective."

As she drifted to sleep in his embrace, Rachel added two more items to things that meant home to her—the sound of his steady and firm heart-beat under her ear and the feeling of security and comfort being held in his arms gave her.

## Chapter Eleven

When Harrison woke, the muted gray of the moments just before dawn filled the parlor. He lifted his head from the back of the couch, wincing as stiff muscles protested. A glance down at his right leg explained the weight resting on it. Rachel's head was pillowed on his thigh, her chin tucked into the V formed where she'd crossed her wrists over her chest. His hand was still draped on her shoulder.

Sometime during the night, she had slipped further down the length of the couch and she was so deep in sleep a soft, small snore—sounding more like the purring of a contented cat than anything else—issued from her. He couldn't contain his grin. So much for her claim she didn't snore.

He carefully brushed a tendril of hair from her cheek. She didn't even stir and the thought occurred to him that this was the first time in a long time for her that she had felt safe enough to fall into a deep sleep. Tracing her profile, he noted how relaxed she finally looked.

The blanket he vaguely remembered draping over her during the night had slipped down to her waist and he tugged it up to her shoulders. The pillow was behind her knees, against the back of the chesterfield. He picked it up and positioned it under her head as he stood. Other than a slight twitch of one hand, she didn't move.

The chill in the room was nothing the rapidly rising sun wouldn't banish so he negated the thought of lighting a fire. However, a cup of coffee was a necessity. He gathered up the cups forgotten the night before, pausing to glance at her over his shoulder.

What in the name of heaven could have possessed Sam to castigate her as he had? She was everything Sam had said she was during that damned poker game—beautiful, intelligent, poised and polished—and yet when his plans for her were ruined, the man had deliberately attempted to destroy his only child.

He made his way to the kitchen and rinsed out the cups, then started a fresh pot of coffee. While that brewed, he went upstairs and changed out of the nearly formal mourning suit. A simple white linen shirt and a pair of denims would more than suffice for the day. Before returning to the kitchen and a cup of hot coffee, he looked in on his sleeping wife, again.

A shaft of golden light rested across her legs and must have warmed her as she had kicked the blanket off. He didn't bother to replace the brightly colored fabric as the black wool of her mourning dress would gather the warmth as well.

He took his cup of coffee onto the back porch and sank into the rocking chair. He set the cup onto the rail and rolled a cigarette. The flat roof of the nearest mountain drew his gaze. Shadows and light played across its face and the angle of the rising sun left its base shrouded in darkness. He watched the light slide down the slope, bathing the whole edifice in a rose-tinted glow. Splashes of gold in the tree line marked the first turning aspens.

He had no idea how long he watched the mountains and the landscape shift and alter in the ever-changing light, but when he reached for his coffee, it was cold. He stood and tossed the less than appealing liquid over the rail. The early morning quiet was broken with the sound of horses approaching.

The red dun was easily recognized and Harrison decided he didn't need to reach into the house for the shotgun Rachel kept above the kitchen door. Rather than resume his seat in the rocking chair, he opted to move to the top of the porch steps and leaned a shoulder into the roof support.

As the two riders drew closer, he recognized Royce Majors with Drake Adams. The men drew rein a few feet from the house.

"Gentlemen," Harrison said, adding a slight dip of his head.

"Marshal." Majors returned the greeting. The younger man was silent but he never took his gaze from Harrison. The unsettling sensation he was looking at a ghost rippled through Harrison again.

"What can I do for you two?"

"There's a meeting of the cattlemen this morning and we just thought we'd stop and check on Rachel on our way to town." Majors didn't dismount and Harrison had the distinct feeling neither of them was too sanguine about her well-being.

"She's still sleeping."

Adams snapped his head back. "It's after nine in the morning." The red dun shifted with the immediate tension visible in the younger man's frame.

"I'm aware of the time." Harrison regretted not reaching in the door for Rachel's shotgun.

"It's not like Rachel to still be sleeping at this hour," Adams said, the rigidness in his shoulders increasing.

"She had a very long and emotionally draining day yesterday. She doesn't sleep well, so when she does sleep, I can't bring myself to wake her."

The strained tableau broke with the slamming of the screened door behind him and Rachel's appearance. Without greeting either of the mounted men, she stood at his side and lifted herself onto tiptoe to press a quick kiss to his cheek. "And I appreciate that you didn't wake me when you got up this morning."

That she had slept in her mourning dress was apparent as she was still clothed in the black weeds. Her hair was tousled, and a faint hint of a blush colored her cheeks. Even as disheveled as she appeared from just waking, there was a grace and quiet dignity to her. When she slipped her hand into his, Harrison smiled down at her. "Good morning."

"Good morning." She finally directed her attention to their visitors. "Do you have time for coffee?"

Majors swung from the saddle. "I never refuse a cup of hot coffee."

"Coffee's on the stove," Rachel said as Majors passed them on the porch. "Cups are in the cupboard over the sink."

Adams was slower to dismount. His head dipped to a side and his jaw clenched while his penetrating gaze skipped from Harrison to Rachel. Harrison was sure the younger man was debating whether Rachel's peck to his cheek was a performance.

Rachel squeezed Harrison's hand, then said to the still mounted man, "I'm not bringing your coffee out to you, Drake."

The grin crossing Adams's face was disturbingly familiar as he took Rachel's pointed hint to dismount. He slid from the saddle and followed Majors into the kitchen. Harrison didn't release Rachel's hand and he halted her from entering the house.

"Thank you. Your timing is impeccable. Your arrival prevented what could have been a nasty confrontation."

She looked up into his face, her eyes still dewy with sleep. "I have no idea what you're talking about." A grin found its way to her mouth. "You could have held your own."

Harrison squeezed her hand. "I like what I'm holding right now." He leaned closer and added in an undertone, "I'm looking forward to holding more of you, too."

A blush crept along her cheeks. She continued to meet his gaze as she asked, "Are you courting me now, or trying to seduce me?"

"Pick one." Taking advantage of the moment, he brushed a kiss against her forehead. "Are we still riding out today or do we need to be at the meeting of the cattlemen?"

Exasperation sounded clearly in her deep sigh. "I'm not allowed, even though I own the largest spread in two counties. Those meetings are for 'gentlemen' only. Ben will be there, to represent my—our—interests. However, I'm sure you'd find it fascinating." He couldn't miss the sarcasm layering her last comment.

"What about Joshua?" That she had corrected herself about whose interests Ben represented was heartening.

"Ben won't take him into the drinking parlor." Rachel rolled her eyes. "There's something wrong with the fact I can vote in this territory, but I can't attend meetings my five-year-old son can attend—meetings which have a direct impact on the Lazy L."

"Speaking of direct impacts, why don't I keep our guests entertained while you change your clothes?" Harrison finally and reluctantly released her hand. "I'm not passing up a chance to spend the day alone with my wife."

"Should I pack a picnic, too, if we're going to be out all day?" Her hand was on the pull, but she hadn't opened the screened door.

He decided to push her a little if only to gauge her reaction. "Be sure there's a blanket for that picnic."

She bowed her head, bright color staining her cheeks. Her shoulders lifted with her deep breath but when she twisted her head to him, her smile lanced into his chest. God help him if she ever discovered just how potent that mixture of unrehearsed coquettishness and innocence was to his heart rate.

Her voice drifted out to him. He couldn't make out exactly what she said to the men in the kitchen, though her corresponding laughter raised the startling reaction of jealousy. He tamped that emotion down, reassuring himself that with enough time, she would openly laugh with him, too. He let himself into the kitchen. Majors was seated at the table, while Adams stood near the sink.

Over the gurgling of coffee flowing into a cup, Harrison heard Adams demand, "What is your problem with me?"

Harrison set the pot on the stove before answering. "I don't have a problem with you, Drake. Your resemblance to someone I once knew is unsettling." From the corner of his eye he saw the younger man jerk his head up. How many times had he seen that very reaction from a long dead man he once considered himself closer to than a brother? "You're twenty, twenty-two at the most?"

"I...I don't know."

Harrison glanced from the younger man to Majors. Royce shook his head. "The year after the war, I moved my family from Texas to here. Somewhere in Indian Territory, we found Drake. He was with a tinker named Darby. Drake came with us. We guessed he was about ten, maybe eleven years old."

Majors stood and set his cup in the sink. "I'll be outside. When you're ready, Drake, we need to get going." The man hesitated. "Marshal, we've never been able to discover anything about Drake's life before we got him away from that man. If we hadn't taken him with us, his chances of ending his life at the end of a rope were darn good. My wife once said that we have two sons: the son she gave birth to and the son we chose."

Harrison met Majors's demanding gaze and briefly nodded. The last time he had seen the Drake Adams he knew, the boy was perhaps five or six. That was late in the first summer of the War Between the States. This Drake Adams was the right age to be that boy and his uncanny resemblance to another man was too close for comfort. He also understood the subtle warning in Majors's comment—what would be the point in voicing his strong suspicions of who he believed Drake to be?

Adams hadn't moved away from the sink. "I truly don't remember anything of my life before Darby. When Royce took me away from that man, it was after he caught me stealing from their wagon in the middle of the night."

Movement in the hallway on the other side of the kitchen caught Harrison's eye. Rachel stood a few feet away from the kitchen and she slowly shook her head. He wasn't sure what she was negating but he chose to not alert the other man to her presence.

"You act as if you've seen me before or know me from somewhere, but I don't remember you." Adams set his cup on the counter. "I'm not even one hundred percent certain that Drake Adams is my name. It's the name Darby said was mine."

Harrison walked to the sink and let the flat roof of the mountain he'd watched grow lighter with the advancing day draw his gaze again. He chose his words with deliberation and care. "I'm sure Majors has said something similar to what I'm going to tell you. A man's name—good or bad—is what he makes of it." He angled his head to the younger man. "Whether or not it's your birth name, you've made it yours and you've made it a good name, if I can judge from the little Rachel has told me about you."

Adams pushed off the counter and hesitated. "That man you say I resemble, what kind of a name did he make for himself?"

His gaze returned to the mountain. The image of A.J. Adams flooded Harrison's memory. The recollection of A.J.'s face etched with pain as he struggled to pull himself erect in the office of the commander of a Union run prisoner of war camp was more searing because of Harrison's betrayal. He shut his eyes, trying to force the unrelenting guilt back into whatever dark corner it resided. "He was the most honorable man I have ever known."

The screened door squeaked and then softly slammed. Harrison bowed his head, questioning his decision to not tell Drake of his suspicions. He startled when Rachel placed her hand between his shoulder blades and softly said, "I've known him for almost ten years and for as long as I've known him, he's felt he had to prove to everyone—but mostly to himself—he isn't the horrible things that tinker told him he was: a thief, someone's cast-off and unwanted by even his own blood."

He twisted his head to her. "If he's who I think he is, he might have been forced to be a thief, but he certainly isn't the other things. Telling him who I think he is would serve no purpose. His family is here. The life he's making for himself is here."

Harrison let his gaze drift down her form. She was dressed once more in her denim trousers, scuffed old boots, but this time she wore a more fitted flannel shirt. "How did I ever mistake you for a boy?"

Her smile could have vanquished the deep Wyoming night. "If you saddle the horses, I'll pack that picnic and we can get on our way."

"Yes, ma'am." He paused in the opened doorway, grateful she hadn't remarked on his less than artful attempt to steer the topic of conversation away from Drake Adams. "Don't forget the blanket."

\*\*\*\*

Rachel handed a burlap sack and the brightly colored trade blanket off the chesterfield to Harrison.

He hefted the sack, his brow rising. "Unless the Seventh Cavalry is joining us, I think you packed too much."

"I couldn't decide what to bring and we had so much food left over from everything brought out to the house the past two days, I put a little bit of all of it in the sack." Neighbors who hadn't spoken to her or had avoided her in town had quietly arrived during Sam's visitation. They brought fried chicken, stews, cakes and cookies, loaves of bread, homemade jams and jellies— all with murmured expressions of sympathy and more than a little curiosity about the new lawman in town, the man she happened to be married to.

He secured the blanket at the back of his saddle and then tied the sack to the pommel. Rachel tossed Twinkle's reins up and grabbed the horn. Harrison walked around his mount, a hand trailing on the horse's haunches to avoid a kick. "Let me give you a leg up."

"I don't need…" Rachel trailed off when he caught her arm, halting her swing into the saddle.

"Allow me the honor." He laced his fingers together and bent.

There was no way she could refuse. She slid her knee into his cupped hands, and gripped his shoulder with one hand and the saddle horn with the other. It had been ages since she'd been assisted to mount, and that had been when she had been taught how to ride side-saddle at finishing school. No matter how much she protested she would never again allow herself to be so uncomfortably and insecurely seated on a horse outside the confines of Miss Julianna's School, learning to ride side-saddle had been mandatory. No lady would ever consider riding astride.

Harrison boosted her and she settled into the saddle. She froze when he took hold of her ankle and fit her foot into the stirrup. As he walked around Twinkle, she pushed her other foot deep into the leather covered wood, collected up the reins, and then adjusted her hat. He paused to toss a glance at her foot in the stirrup.

"Are you sure those leathers are adjusted to the right length for you?" He tipped his head back to her. "Perhaps you should stand in the stirrups so I can be sure."

"I assure you, my stirrups are the most comfortable length for me." She looked down at her right leg and then the left. Her knees were slightly bent, her heels behind the cinch. Curiosity won out, though. "Just how would standing in the stirrups accomplish determining if the leathers are the correct length?"

His gaze traveled in degrees up her leg, crawled the length of her torso, to finally settle on her face. "If they're the correct length," he said, his palm sliding up her lower leg to her knee, "there should be exactly a hand's breadth between your rather becoming bottom and the seat of the saddle."

Scalding heat splashed over her face. "My leathers are fine," she said, at the same time pulling Twinkle's head to a side and giving her a slight kick to move her into a slow jog. His laughter sounded behind her.

She checked the mare to a walk when he rode to her side. A sidelong glance at him tightened her throat. The man sat a horse as easily as if he and his huge black were one. His hands were light on the reins, applying minimal contact to the bit. Even though his feet were deep in the iron stirrups, she could tell he didn't rely on them for his balance. He held that with his legs. "That's a McClelland saddle."

"Yes, and no...the McClelland is very generous to the mount but brutal on the rider. I had one modified to a full leather seat with a bit more padding both on the tree and in the seat." He cocked his head to her and grinned. "Are you sure you want to discuss saddles? I still think I should check your—"

"They're fine," she said. "Why did you name him Demon? He seems to be very even tempered."

Harrison ran a hand down the horse's neck. "He's been as black as the depths of Hades since he was born and I didn't want to name him Blackie or anything along those lines. With his pedigree, he deserved an imposing name." He turned to her. "Where's Royce Majors's place?"

"Do you see where the tree line follows the ridge lines to form a W?" she asked, pointing out the natural landmark. "The Rocking Bar M is over that ridge. And, over there"—she gestured in the opposite direction—"is the Crazy TG. Royce, Drake, and Ben make sure that no one tries to stake a claim on Tommy's land. Since Jake's been gone, it's just three hundred and twenty acres of empty land."

"Why haven't you or Majors tried to buy it?"

"Because it's Tommy's home." A ride along the bed of a seasonal though currently shallow creek brought her to an easy exit from the sandy bottom. "He'd have nowhere to go if one of us bought his home."

Harrison nodded and she noted the landscape held his attention. She looked at the place she knew and loved, trying to see it through another's perspective. Gently sloping hills gave way to pine and aspen covered mountains, their roofs of quartzite and mica glittering in the sunlight. Usually dry arroyos scored the land between the hills. More than once, she had witnessed the power of water flowing down from the mountains through those gulches, cutting deeper into the hills and exposing layers in multiple shades of red, yellow, white, and green. After the rain the other night, the wildflowers were blooming in wild abandon before the fall cut them down: black eyed susan, prickly poppy raising its ghost white face to the sun, prairie sunflowers bobbing in the breeze, bright yellow broom waving. Even the sage brush was blossoming with its small, butter-colored flowers. Gravel crunched under the horses' hooves, and a small dust trail rose.

As they rode into the higher elevation, the thick prairie grasses and sage brush gave way to the pines, firs, and aspens and the heat of the valley surrendered to the cooler air. Leading the way through the trees and around boulders tumbled from mountain peaks eons ago, the gurgling of a mountain stream became more pronounced.

Rachel drew Twinkle to a stop in a small clearing on the creek bank. She swung down, dropping a rein, and walked across a small area composed of pulverized granite to the water's edge.

Harrison was still silent and hadn't dismounted. Rachel picked up Twinkle's reins and led her to the stream. The mare bent her head and began to drink.

Sunlight splashed off the creek's rippling surface, throwing brilliant flashes of light. The aspens bending over the water dappled the bottom with ever shifting shadows. Small trout darted through the water, staying close to fallen trees and water weeds while the darker forms of larger fish skimmed over the creek bed. Somewhere in the trees a jay chattered angrily at their intrusion and she saw a momentary flick of a squirrel's tail before the animal vanished into the canopy. The bay lifted her head and the sound of the water dripping from her muzzle added to the chuckling of the stream as it flowed over rocks and tumbled down a tiny waterfall a few feet away. Looking around the sheltered bend, Rachel wondered if this had been the wrong place to bring Harrison.

Harrison's continued silence was unnerving, to say the least. Maybe she should have just followed a fence line and pointed out where the property boundaries were contrary to what he had said he wanted to see. She startled when Demon splashed into the creek a few feet from her and bent his head into the water.

"This is on ranch property?" Harrison asked.

He seemed surprised to find such an oasis in the semi-arid land. She tilted her head up to him. His gaze was on something across the creek. "Yes," she said, peering through the trees to try and see what held his intense concentration. A flash of a white tail, a rustling of the underbrush, and Rachel saw the mule deer he must have seen before she did. "It's Sagebrush Creek and it flows through the Lazy L, a corner of the Rocking Bar M, and another corner of the Crazy TG. The water rights are mi—ours because the creek originates on ranch property. But, I have a written contract with Royce and Tommy, guaranteeing the Lazy L will never dam the creek or cut off their access."

"That's a good wading hole." He jerked his head in the direction of a small area on the river where she had built a wide pool the year before for Joshua. The mountain rocks she used to create the pool were still steady against the current. It had taken her almost a week to stack the small boulders and rock, leaving two sections of the retaining wall open to allow water to flow in and out of the pool. She had also scooped the pool a little deeper than the stream bed.

"I feel comfortable allowing Joshua to play in the creek here." She watched fingerlings dart in and out of the pool, safe from larger predators in its rocky confines. The week she had spent with her son building his wading pool had been a few days of peace and calm. They had fished every day and dined on trout every night, slept on the small beach, and woke each morning to a squirrel scolding them for being in his home. When they weren't wrestling rocks into place, they wandered along the creek bed.

"A pity it's not deeper," Harrison said, his tone snapping her gaze from the tiny, darting trout to him. There wasn't condemnation in his voice but a suggestion of something else, something that heated her cheeks with the warm timbre of the words. He leaned his elbow onto the pommel of the saddle. "Have you ever gone swimming in the nude?"

Even her ears felt warm but she met his gaze. "Not here. But there is a place a little further upstream that I want to show you."

The grin crossing his face was a mixture of feigned shock and genuine amusement. "Why, Mrs. Taylor, you've been keeping secrets from me. You've been swimming in a mountain stream as natural as Eve on the day of creation and haven't told me this?"

"You never asked me." She stepped into the stirrup

and pointed Twinkle upstream. "It's not keeping a secret if you don't ask."

"Oh, darlin', the list of questions I want to ask just got a whole lot longer."

## Chapter Twelve

A few hundred feet from the wading hole, the channel the stream followed narrowed, and the water flowing through it increased in speed. Whitewater marked where it broke over submerged boulders. The banks contracted and the path she followed upward forced them to ride single file. The creek leveled again, though this time it was a good one hundred feet below them and the sound of water breaking over the falls became a distinct reverberation.

She reined Twinkle to a halt when the path seemingly ended. "We have to walk from here. It's passable on foot, but there's too much dead-fall from the winter snows for the horses to make it."

"Should I bring the sack and the blanket?"

She doubted the rain the past few days had swollen the creek so much that the small granite shelf she intended to take him to would be submerged. The water downstream wasn't frothy and colored the same shade as her doctored coffee, both usually indicative of a creek running fast and hard with either snow melt or a heavy rain. "There's an area to picnic where we're going."

She led him along a narrow, winding footpath that followed a secondary ridgeline at a gentle slope down to the stream. When Harrison emerged from the trees behind her onto the massive pink and black granite slab that jutted out over a giant, deep pool at the base of the crashing waterfalls, she heard his audible gasp.

The same granite that created the shelf formed the towering walls, rising into soaring pinnacles of pink rock veined with black. Firs, pines, and aspens clung to the steep walls, partially shading the pool. Whitewater churned under the falls and calmed by the time it reached the other side of the natural depression.

"That's Rachel Falls. My father named it for my mother, right after they were first married." She gestured to the falls. "It's fed by the Upper Sagebrush Creek, Sam Creek, and Rachel Creek. Sam and Rachel Creeks end at the falls and they all form Sagebrush Creek below."

Harrison looked over the edge of the shelf into the depths of the pool. "It looks cold."

Rachel shook her head, smiling. "It's fed not only by the falls but by a hot spring at the bottom. I've been here in the dead of winter and there is always a small area of open water."

He knelt and dipped his hand into the pool. "It's as warm as bath water."

"Yes. When the rains don't come in the summer and the falls almost dry up, it's too hot to swim in it." She backed a step, quelling the sudden urge to push him in.

As if he read her thoughts, he stood. "Don't even think about it, Rachel."

She plastered what she hoped to be an innocent smile to her face. "I wouldn't ever do that."

"I'll just bet." He plopped onto the shelf and pulled off his boots and socks.

Rachel backed another step, until the sheer granite

wall pressed into her spine. Suddenly, bringing him here didn't seem like such a good idea. Her hand crept to her throat. Indecision thrummed through her. She should tell him she wanted to leave and she immediately reminded herself they were married and so far he had done nothing but treat her with deference and respect.

He stood and opened several buttons on his shirt, then tugged the garment over his head and dropped it next to his socks. He hooked his thumb in the still closed waistband of his denims, and asked, "Is something wrong?"

"No." Her mouth was dry. The sight of his bare chest and shoulders dappled with sunlight and shadows did things to her she'd never felt before. Or at least hadn't ever felt until he arrived. She screwed up her courage and said, "I'm just…just thinking the view is good from here." Heat scalded her cheeks as she said the words.

His gaze drifted down her form before he just as deliberately brought it back to her face. There was no way she could define his expression as anything other than a smirk. His lingering perusal increased the warmth in her cheeks. The ground at her feet drew her sight, the gravel a much less confusing alternative than the view of his smirk and bared torso.

A crow scolded from somewhere overhead. The wind whispered through the pine boughs. The thundering of the falls grew louder in the silence. Long toes attached to bare feet came into view. He slid the back of his hand under her chin and tilted her head up. "We don't have to do this."

"I'm not sure what I want to do." A deep breath

filled her lungs with mingling scents: pine and sage brush, the earth still damp from the rains, a lingering trace of the soap he'd washed with, leather, and even his masculine scent. "I'm being ridiculous, aren't I?"

"No." He angled his head, his smile encouraging. "You're being cautious. All things considered, that is definitely not ridiculous."

"It's just that I've never undressed in front of anyone before." She didn't know where to fix her sight, and settled for the hollow at the base of his throat. That seemed safer than the wide expanse of his chest—who would have thought brown hair could have such a gilded appearance? Safer also than the unsettling warmth of his eyes, a shade that was neither green nor blue nor even brown, but seemed to be shifting in color and depth. Much safer than the curve of his mouth, which she wanted pressed against her lips and throat as he'd done the night before.

He flattened his palms against the granite wall on either side of her shoulders and leaned in ever so closer. "I could help."

Her heart sped up. A strange fluttering invaded her stomach and sent molten tendrils coiling lazily through her. She forced herself to meet his gaze. Yes, she could lose herself there.

One hand trailed down her arm, his wrist brushing feather-light over the swell of her breast. She swallowed when he inexorably pulled her shirt in minute degrees from the waistband of her denims. The rough granite bit into her palms but she couldn't force herself to pry her hands from the wall.

The button at her throat parted and then the next button. She was trapped by the weight of his gaze, unable to move, and offered no resistance. A third button separated.

His other hand cradled her cheek. The pad of his thumb traced her chin and then trailed as light as a butterfly's wing along her lower lip. The color in his eyes shifted, deepened, and heated. His fingers curled around her neck, threaded into the hair at her nape. She thought another button had surrendered. He bent his head closer to her, his lips nearly against hers.

Anticipation. Wanting. Wanting him to kiss her, to make the world dissolve. Wanting the fire he stoked in her veins to consume her.

A shift of his head and he blazed a trail of light kisses along her jaw and then down her neck. Her breath shuddered out when his tongue flicked against the skin in the hollow of her throat. His lips followed the curve of her collarbone, teeth grazing with playful nips and she realized she'd pried her hands off the granite face and her fingers were entangled in his hair and her body was arching into his.

His hands were under her shirt, inside her chemise, skimming along her rib cage. She pulled her hands down to his shoulders and pushed him. Harrison rocked back, but didn't withdraw his hands.

Before she lost her nerve, Rachel said, "I want to renegotiate our agreement."

"Name your terms." His breathing was as ragged as hers.

"I...I..." The words wouldn't come. She couldn't meet his heated gaze, and the cliff wall behind her wouldn't allow for a retreat. His chin dropped onto the top of her head and she felt the deep breath he pulled in and slowly released.

"Just tell me what you want, Rachel." His hands curled around her back, gathering her more fully into his embrace.

"I don't want to be afraid." She swallowed, then added, "Promise me I won't be afraid."

The steady beat of his heart under her ear, the warmth of his skin against her, the rise and fall of his chest all calmed her. A short, deep chuckle rumbled in his chest. "Darlin', I'm not doing something right if you're afraid. I'm not sure I can promise that, but I will promise our original terms still apply. Anything we do is entirely up to you."

She pushed him back. "Please don't laugh at me."

A smile crossed his face and he slowly shook his head. "I'm not laughing at you. If anything, I'm laughing because otherwise I'd be furious for what he did. And, don't mistake me, I *am* furious." He lifted his hand and brushed a wisp of hair from her cheek. "I'm furious that you were hurt, furious that anyone would think so little of you. Deeply furious that something which is beautiful and the most wonderful manner of sharing between a couple has been tainted into something to be feared."

Rachel burrowed her head into his chest, struggling to keep her tears in check.

"Anything else you want to renegotiate?"

She lifted her head. This time, she managed to find the words. "I want to be your wife."

"According to the papers we signed at Pruitt's office, you are." His brow lowered with confusion. That wasn't the response she expected. He continued, "Unless you want a church wedding and that might be problematic because we'd have to post banns, and get approval." A grin teased the corner of his mouth. "We're looking at about two months before we could marry in the church."

Rachel pushed his shoulders, staggering him a step back. "Now, you are laughing at me. That is not what I meant, and you know it."

As if verifying her accusation, a full laugh broke from him. She shoved him again, pushing him closer to the edge of the pool. He glanced over his shoulder and threw his hands up in a gesture of surrender.

"I don't want to ride home in wet trousers."

"Too bad," she said, and pushed him again. His eyes widened with surprise and he plunged from sight. Rachel heard a satisfying splash and when she looked over the edge he bobbed in the water, hair plastered to his head, droplets rolling down his face. His voice drifted up to her.

"This means war, Rachel. You'd better at least have your boots off when I get up there because you're going in this pool."

She scampered away from the edge and promptly sat to pull her boots off. She had no doubts he meant it, but she was going to get into that warm water on her own terms. The sounds of splashing in the pool continued as she shrugged out of the flannel shirt. Her denims joined her shirt, boots, and socks and she stood.

The pool was silent and Harrison still wasn't back on the ledge. A glance at the narrow pathway leading down to the pool revealed he wasn't standing there. A thread of unease rippled through her.

She crept to the edge and peered over. He wasn't there. Nor was he downstream. "Harrison?"

His hands closed around her waist and she couldn't

stop her startled yelp. She hadn't even heard him creep up behind her. He lifted her and dangled her over the pool. "If I'm going home in wet trousers, you're going home in wet undergarments. Turnabout is fair play."

She twisted her head over her shoulder. "My chemise is silk. It'll be ruined."

"Too bad," he said, repeating her taunt. "I'll just have to buy you another one."

"But that's so frivolous," she said, hoping for another way to dissuade him from dropping her into the water.

She dangled over the pool for what felt like an eternity before he pulled her back to the ledge. Her relief died in the next instant when he scooped her into his arms and jumped into the pool.

The warm water closed over her head and he shifted his hold on her so her back was to his chest and he pushed her upward. She broke the surface and felt his hands still around her waist, keeping her head above the water. A splash behind her told her he had broken the water.

"Lean back against me," he said even as his arm tightened around her waist. Rachel let herself relax, then dropped her head to his shoulder. He pulled her to the edge. She grabbed the slick rock and hoisted herself onto a ledge in the water's depths and stood. Harrison treaded water in the middle of the pool. "I think I like this view the most."

A glance down revealed how sheer and see-through both her chemise and short knickers were in the water.

He ducked under the water and surfaced mere inches from her. He stepped up onto the submerged outcrop, holding her captive with a hand placed on the rock to either side of her head.

Water beaded on his chest and ran off his shoulders. A slight tug at the end of her braid and he held up the ribbon holding her braid intact. A teasing grin accompanied the toss of the scrap of wet fabric onto a sun-filled, dry ledge. He bent his head to hers, and skimmed his lips over hers. Without any urging, she opened her mouth to him, encouraging him to deepen the kiss.

Confusion filled her when he didn't. Tentatively, she wrapped her arms around his shoulders to lift herself more fully to him. She curled her fingers around the back of his neck and cautiously slid her tongue into him. His quick inhalation halted her and she jerked her head back.

"Don't stop what you're doin'," he said in no more than a whisper, his breath brushing against her skin.

She pulled his head to her, her eyes closing as her opened lips met his. With more confidence, she began a still timid exploration. When he met her tongue with his, a shiver cascaded over her, and her hands tightened in his scalp. His arm wrapped around her, just under her bottom. He nudged her legs apart, braced his knee against the stone and lifted her onto his thigh, driving a deeper shiver to ripple through her.

He held her pinned to the wall. The wet material amplified the sensation of her breasts against his chest. His mouth was hot against her throat, his tongue flicking and teasing her skin, and his roving kisses trailed outward, halting at the wide ribbon of the chemise's shoulder. His hands partially lifted the hem and he hesitated, pulling his head back.

Not a word passed between them, yet she

understood his hesitation. She managed a curt nod. He pulled the now sheer silk up and over her head, tossing the chemise somewhere out of the natural pool, then lowered his gaze. She followed his line of sight to his hands cupping her breasts. The pad of his thumbs rolled over her tightening nipples. Her breath caught at the back of her throat.

He lifted both breasts from the water and brought his mouth to one, while continuing to tease the other. Rachel arched her spine, thrusting herself into his hot mouth, and caught his shoulders. Fire lanced into her, searing her to her core. She couldn't stop the whimper when he momentarily lifted his head to give his attention to her other breast.

His teeth grazed the hardened nipple, his tongue twisted around and around, even as he sucked her deeper into his mouth. Another protest sounded when he lifted his head. "Put your arms around my neck," he said, the words sounding as ragged as her breathing.

Rachel complied. As soon as her arms were locked around him, he lowered his leg. Instead of sinking, she was held up by her hold on him and the buoyancy of the water. He brought a hand to the back of her head, his fingers pegging her scalp, holding her captive. His mouth came down on hers. His tongue thrust into her.

She stiffened to keep from giggling when his hand drifted down her stomach. The pressure on the back of her head eased and the heated assault on her mouth softened. He'd misunderstood her tension. Gripping him around his neck more firmly with one arm, she reached below the water to take his wrist and guided him lower. "I'm ticklish."

Something that sounded like a growl rumbled from

his throat. His possession of her mouth became demanding, a duel for complete surrender. Rachel capitulated, her limbs trembling with her concession.

She barely registered her knickers slipping from her. Her whole body lurched when his fingers slid between her legs. She was crushed between his solid body and the water polished granite. Sensations overwhelmed her—the hair covering his chest rubbing against her stimulated nipples, his skin under her palms, the taste of his tongue in her mouth, his hard rasping breath, his long fingers stroking her but not entering, deliciously tormenting the small bud at her opening. She twisted against his hand, needing more.

Harrison retreated, ending the kiss. Her scalp twinged when he pulled her head back. She stared into his face. The heat in his hooded eyes should have set the water to boiling in an instant. Her mouth fell open as he continued to arouse her, making every inch of her quiver. Her spine arched, her shoulders pressed into the smooth rock, and she splayed her hands on his back, trying to pull him even closer. She rounded his hips, snagging on the waistband of his denims.

In some dim corner of her mind, a voice whispered to stop. She shook her head, trying to silence the words, and realized it wasn't a voice in the back of her mind, but Harrison. His voice rasped, sounding pained. "God help me…if you say 'stop', I will." Every syllable sounded as if it was torn from him.

She shook her head again and tugged ineffectively at the buttons on his trousers, but the water had swelled the fabric. Another growl sounded from him, this one of impatience, and he pushed her hands away so he could force off the obstructing garment. She barely registered the wet slap of the sodden denim landing on the ledge just above their heads.

He lifted her higher, jockeying her so he stood between her legs, with both hands on her buttocks. The heated proof of his arousal pressed against her belly and she stilled, even as she dropped her head. A different shiver, not quite fear, skipped over her. One hand skimmed up her spine until his fingers wove into her hair, but he neither forced her to meet his gaze nor pulled her more tightly against him. He seemed to be waiting for her.

Rachel dragged her gaze upward, pausing at the pulse pounding in a maddened pace in the hollow of his throat, lingering on the almost pained lines around his mouth before she caught his face between her hands, and pressed herself closer to him. "I don't know what to do," she managed in a broken whisper.

His teeth bared in a smile that further melted her. "Wrap your legs around my waist."

She hooked her ankles behind his back and tensed when she felt him at her opening. The gentle pressure he placed on the back of her head to pull her closer to his lips couldn't be denied. He left a slow, lingering kiss against her mouth and rained kisses over her closed eyes, along the slope of her cheek, and nuzzled into the side of her neck. "It's jus' you an' me, darlin'," he whispered, the words breathed against her skin, his drawl thicker than she'd ever heard it.

She sucked in a sharp breath and froze when he entered her. One hand skimmed down her spine, the other still cradled the back of her head. Her breath eased from her and she wrapped her arms around his shoulders, lowering her head into the juncture of his neck. He withdrew and filled her again with a slow, easy motion, continuing in a gentle rhythm.

The warmth pooling in her belly heated, became molten. Her breath caught and she clutched his shoulders. A slight tug at the back of her head and his mouth was on hers, again, his tongue hot and slick in her. She met him with hers, twisting around him. His hands pegged into her bottom, pulling her more fully onto him with each successively quicker thrust. When had he moved his hands there?

She couldn't breathe, couldn't think, couldn't do anything but feel as he delved deeper and deeper into her. The roaring in her ears drowned out the rumble of the falls. She was melting with the sensations.

"Jus' le'go, Rachel," he rasped.

She did, barely able to hear or comprehend his deep growl with his own release.

## Chapter Thirteen

She couldn't or wouldn't meet his eye. Harrison wasn't sure which it was, but either way, it worried him. She wasn't talking, either, other than to answer his attempts at conversation with mumbled, one word responses. The walk from the natural spring pool felt a lot longer than the hike in. Every step they took, she hunched more into herself, as if she could shrink as small as possible.

Demon and Twinkle were right where they'd left them. By the long shadows blackening the ground, there was maybe an hour, ninety minutes at the most, before night fell. He retightened Demon's girth then turned to do the same for Twinkle. Rachel was already in the saddle, the mare's nose pointed in the direction of the Lazy L. Yeah, it might be a really long ride home.

He still wasn't sure where her chemise had gone, but the safe assumption would be somewhere downstream. He made a mental note to get her another one the next time he had to ride into town. The problem was he wasn't exactly sure where a lady would go to purchase those particular garments. He couldn't recall seeing anything like that at Burlington's. Probably the shop-owner could give him some guidance, though.

When they crossed the shallow stream bed, Harrison nudged Demon closer to Twinkle and grabbed the mare's closest rein, forcing her to stop. Rachel twisted her head away from him and toward the ground. He released the rein, settling back into the saddle. The unsettling sensation of defeat crept through him with her pointed refusal to meet his gaze.

"Damn it, Rachel, say something." He wanted to take the words back as soon as he said them. Her shoulders rounded even more and she exhaled sharply. He was well out of his depth here. He tried for a different approach. "Please, say something. I don't know if I should be apologizing—"

Her shoulders hitched with what sounded suspiciously like a choked cry. Wrong thing, again, Taylor. Just dig that hole deeper.

"—or asking if you're all right?"

She tilted her head to him and his heart sank into his boots. Tears drowned the blue of her eyes until all that was visible was pewter gray. "I'm not all right."

"I'm s—"

"Don't you dare apologize to me." The gray depths grew stormy, filled with something he couldn't put his finger on. Her voice dropped to a quivering whisper. "Don't you dare, Harrison Taylor."

Demon shifted under him and without looking away from her, Harrison checked the stallion's sideways motion. "Then, tell me what's wrong."

Her lower lip trembled and she dashed the back of her hand across her eyes. When she spoke, it was still in that shuddering whisper. "I felt beautiful." A deep sob choked her. "For the first time in a very long time, I felt I was worthy of being loved."

His mouth dropped open but before he could think of a single thing to say, the mare exploded into a gallop. Harrison stared at Rachel's retreating figure, her damp hair flowing behind her. With a clenching of his jaw, he put his heels into Demon's sides.

It didn't take the black long to close the distance between them. He momentarily contemplated pushing Demon in front of her to stop the little mare, but that carried too much risk. If Rachel didn't veer off or stop the bay to prevent a collision with Demon, all four of them could be seriously hurt.

Instead, he kept pace with her. He was certain Demon could last longer and that she knew better than he did her horse's limits. She straightened in the saddle, her shifting weight alone slowing Twinkle into a lope and then into a walk. Deciding in this case that silence might be the best route, he bit his tongue.

Rachel reined the mare to a stop and dropped the reins across the bay's black mane. She sat hunched in the saddle, breathing unevenly, her head tilted away from him and to the ground. Twinkle began to graze.

Waiting for her to break her renewed silence, Harrison swung down. He dropped one rein and made his way to the ground that seemed to hold Rachel's undivided attention. Her eyes were screwed shut but tears dripped into the dusty earth. Still feeling he was in way over his head, he took her clenched fist into his hand. A choked sob broke from her.

"Darlin', I'm at a total loss." Her fingers unfurled and entwined with his, though she still didn't open her eyes.

"I was supposed to be the prize for whoever had the biggest ranch so he could build a bigger cattle empire." She openly sobbed. "When he couldn't sell me off like some pedigreed heifer, I wasn't worth anything."

God help him, he was actually glad the man was dead because there wouldn't have been any honor in calling the bastard out for his treatment of his daughter in the condition he had been in.

"I told him I didn't want to marry someone to make the Lazy L bigger. I wouldn't marry for his or anyone's financial benefit." A bitter laugh ripped its way free and she finally opened her eyes. She jerked her hand from his. "But, that's exactly what I did. Eight thousand dollars makes me little more than a high priced..." Her voice faded for a heartbeat. "And then you had to tell me it was supposed to be beautiful and it was and I felt I was, too."

He grabbed Twinkle's rein again, sensing Rachel gathering herself for another headlong dash. He noted she shrank from describing herself as a soiled dove—or whatever word she had thought to use. And, he would be damned before he ever put that label on her. "Stop it, Rachel. I told you before and I'll repeat it every day for the rest of our lives if I have to—you are *not* what anyone has accused you of being."

The steely resolve he had come to know hardened the gray in her eyes.

"If you think I see you as anything other than a beautiful woman I have the honor to be married to, you are sorely mistaken." The anger he fought all his life to keep tightly reined growled in his chest and knotted his stomach. "Your father was a close-minded fool and blinded by his own ambitions. He refused to see what a priceless treasure you are—beautiful, strong, incredibly smart, gracious. All those women in town who've talked about you behind your back and even to your face don't amount to a hill of beans in my estimate. If I ever hear any man defame you or sully your good name I'll call the blackguard out into the street."

The tiniest hint of a smile lifted one corner of her mouth and softened the steel in her gaze. She angled her head away and her fingertip traced the silver concho on the saddle horn. "Why am I seeing drawn pistols at dawn in some foggy swamp?"

His anger subsided and retreated to the dark corner where he tried to keep it subdued. "If I ever call a man out to defend your honor, I'd prefer swords."

Her gaze came back to him. "Why swords?"

"Because a sword is a much more personal weapon." Without releasing Twinkle's rein, he settled his hand on Rachel's knee. "Anyone who attempts to blacken my wife's name makes it very personal to me."

She trailed her gaze to her knee and then to his face. "I'm sorry."

"Whatever for?"

Her shoulders lifted in a helpless little shrug. "I thought...I was afraid you..." She struggled to articulate what she was apologizing for.

Harrison had a good idea what she felt she needed to offer an apology for but he had to be absolutely certain. He released Twinkle's rein and stepped back. "Get down off that horse."

Her hands trembled when she dropped the reins and slid from the mare on the off side. Her chin dipped toward the ground. He caught her face between his palms and forced her to look up at him. "You thought there were eight thousand reasons why what just happened at that waterfall had to happen, didn't you?"

"I'm sorry," she repeated, her voice breaking.

A deep sigh broke from him and he shoved his

hands through his hair, not wanting to give in to the frustration. "Rachel, it wouldn't have mattered if I had eight million to put into the ranch. Not one penny of that money will ever give me the right to force my attentions on you. Ever." He tried for a softer tone and coupled it with a grin. "Are we clear on that now?"

Her short nod didn't expel his misgivings. "There's something else, isn't there?"

A deep blush colored her face. "I...You...I couldn't think of anything else when we...I couldn't even think." She trailed off.

"That's a good thing, isn't it?" If he'd been at a loss a few minutes ago, he was in totally uncharted territory now. "It's been my experience if both partners are unable to think it's more pleasurable for both of us."

He didn't think it was possible for her color to heighten. Like a bolt from the blue he knew why she was blushing so deeply. As if the gnarled old man was standing in front of him, Harrison heard the warnings of his family's priest about the "sins of the flesh" and "taking pleasure in the carnal knowledge of one's spouse." He struggled to keep his laughter contained. "Because you enjoyed having physical intimacy with your spouse and you reciprocated my advances—that makes you some kind of wanton and I'm going to think you're less than a lady?"

She was clearly miserable as she nodded affirmation. He knew if he laughed it would destroy her. He twisted on his heel, struggling to keep his amusement hidden. Twilight caressed the land, painting the sky with shades of red, yellow, orange, blue, and purple and he let the darkening landscape hold his attention until he could respond without a hint of laughter. "In public, I appreciate your sense of propriety and comportment." He craned his head over his shoulder. "Your mannerisms would put the vast majority of ladies I have ever known to shame and I grew up in a society that valued public persona over just about everything." One of the many things wrong with the Old South, he thought but didn't add. "For the rest of the world, be exactly who you are—every inch the proper lady. Behind closed doors, I want that woman at the waterfall. I want the woman willing to give herself unabashedly."

She slowly raised her head to meet his gaze. Her mouth dropped open in disbelief.

He fully faced her and allowed what he hoped to be a suggestive grin cross his face. "In our bedroom, Rachel, the last thing I want is a prim and proper lady."

"I was told a wife's duty was to keep her husband's home—"

"You keep the home already," he said, adding a shake of his head. "It's fairly apparent you were doing that long before you became a wife. Unless you'd rather we hire a maid."

Rachel glared daggers at him. Her response surprised him. There was no doubting she didn't want another woman in her house, caring for her home.

"I was also told a wife's duty is to bear her husband's children."

"It's physically impossible for me to bear a child."

Her glare hardened into steel. He wrapped a hand around the back of his neck, and glanced at the last of the sunset. "I'm not sure I'm ready for more children than Joshua right now but I'm not averse to the idea. Especially the part that involves creating a child."

Even in the rapidly fading light, the color staining her cheeks was visible. "Harrison, I'm trying to tell you what I was repeatedly told."

"Forgive me. Please continue." He bit his tongue to keep both his laughter and a smile subdued.

"Lastly, I was told time and again a well-brought up woman never experiences pleasure while satisfying her husband's physical demands and proclivities."

"*Physical demands and proclivities?*" He managed to quell his laughter but he couldn't keep the amusement from his voice. "Good Lord, that makes it sound like something you have to endure because I'm a total beast. I can't even begin to account how flawed the rest of that statement is."

"I suppose," she said and picked up Twinkle's dropped rein, "as your wife I must endure such things. Though it will be difficult, I will struggle through." The soft chortle of her barely contained laughter took any sting from the words.

"You little minx." Harrison grabbed her around the waist and pulled her against him so her back was to his chest. He nuzzled into the side of her throat and she tilted her head to grant him greater access. "After Joshua is asleep for the night, we'll have to test your endurance, Mrs. Taylor."

**\*\*\*\***

The air had grown markedly cooler by the time they rode up to the house. The home itself was dark and silent. Rachel reined Twinkle to a stop but didn't dismount. "Where are Ben and Joshua?"

Harrison swung off and tugged on Demon's girth. "He probably got here this afternoon, noticed we weren't here and took the boy to his house for the night."

"That's probably it." She slid off the mare but Harrison noted her hesitation in approaching the house.

"If you wait, I'll be done with the horses in a few minutes and we can walk in together."

"It's all right. I'm just being silly. I've never come to this house and seen it dark like that." She drew in a deep breath. "I'll start a pot of coffee if the coals haven't gone out and then I'll get a fire going in the parlor."

"Hot coffee sounds good." Harrison pulled Demon's saddle from the horse and watched her walk to the house. A lamp flared in the kitchen, the warm yellow light spilling out onto the porch.

He caught Twinkle and Demon's reins and led both animals into the small corral, then pulled Demon's bridle off. The black snorted, twisted around and cantered to the middle of the enclosure where he immediately dropped to the ground and began to roll.

Harrison tugged on Twinkle's girth strap. He was lifting the saddle when Rachel's scream tore through the night air. The saddle fell to the ground. Harrison ran across the yard, shouting her name.

His only answer was another scream. He vaulted the three steps onto the porch and raced through the house. Rachel stood in the middle of the parlor, her fingers digging into her scalp. He grabbed her arm at the elbow, spinning her around, and into his chest. She buried her face against him and he wrapped her in the security of his fierce embrace.

In the single light of the lamp she had lit on the desk, the room had the appearance of an abattoir. Someone had filled a bucket with blood and then spun it, painting the walls, ceiling, and furnishings with garish, dripping stripes. The bucket was lodged against a leg of the piano. On the closed lid of the instrument was the chemise that had gone missing at Sagebrush Creek and the head of a young calf, both pooled in a puddle of congealing blood. The chemise dangled from the handle of a fireplace poker. The other end of the poker was buried several inches deep through the calf's eye.

Still holding her face pressed against his chest, Harrison took a step back, needing to get Rachel out of the room, out of the house. He stopped when he saw the writing on the Oriental rug. Whoever wrote this missive had used blood as the ink and had made certain to only write in the crème areas of the rug.

*How dare you allow anyone to touch what's mine?*

Rachel's cries formed a name. "Joshua."

Harrison dragged her backward. "We're going to Ben's. He's there. He's safe."

On the way out, Harrison grabbed his gun belt and his vest. Before he resaddled Demon, he strapped on the belt and pinned the badge to his vest. He followed Rachel on a headlong flight across through the dark night.

Ben's small one-room cabin was as dark and silent as the ranch had been. Rachel slumped in the saddle, an incoherent keening cry tearing from her depths. Harrison leaned out of the saddle and grabbed her arm, startling her enough that she fell silent.

"He probably stayed in town. Where does Ben stay when he overnights in town?"

"If anything's happened to Joshua, I'll never forgive myself."

Harrison lightly shook her. "Nothing's happened to Josh. Ben won't let anything happen to him. Where does Ben stay when he's in town?"

She managed a deep, even if shaking breath. Her gaze settled on the badge pinned on his vest and she gulped in another deep breath. "Morris's. He stays there."

Harrison pulled Demon's head around. "Will Twinkle be able to make the trip to town at a gallop?"

"She's mustang bred. She could run all day if she had to."

Most of Federal was dark when they thundered into town. Only the saloons on the other end of town still had any activity. The raucous laughter of wranglers drifted up the dark streets, and the continual lowing and mooing from the holding pens at the railroad station alerted Harrison that a drive had just completed.

Rachel led the way to Morris's. Harrison was off Demon before she had vaulted from Twinkle. He pounded on the locked door of the hotel. When he didn't receive any response, he pounded on the jamb with the butt of his revolver. This time, a woman's voice answered his summons. "We're full. Check with the Americana down the street."

"Federal Marshal. Open the damn door." He had never thought to use the authority behind the badge he wore in this manner.

Tumblers twisted and fell in the lock and the door was cracked open. Harrison shoved his weight against it, forcing the portly woman behind the door to stagger back. Before she could protest, Rachel darted into the hotel lobby, asking, "Is Ben here?"

The woman gaped at the two of them. Rachel said,

the fear and uncertainty edging her voice, "Helen, I need to know if Ben is here."

"He said to bill the room to the Lazy L. He's in room twenty-two."

Harrison took off after Rachel. Helen called after them, "But he's not here."

He heard Rachel's pained gasp and he rounded on the woman. "Where is he?"

"He's down at the Thirsty Dog. He left the boy here. When I locked up for the night, I checked on him and made sure the door was locked." Helen's mouth pursed with her disapproval. "I am not a nanny and I told your foreman that. He said to put a few extra dollars on the bill."

Before Rachel could continue down the hallway to the room, Harrison caught her arm. "You go pounding on that door and you'll scare the daylights out of the boy." He twisted his head to Helen. "Is there another key to the room?"

"Of course."

When it appeared that Helen had no intention of getting the other key, Harrison said, the growl in his voice evident even to himself, "Go get it."

Helen huffed and flounced across the small lobby to the group of cubbies for the rooms. She picked up a key and carried it to Harrison. He snatched it from her hand. "Will Ben's room key unlock the front door?"

The hotel owner shook her head. "If guests are going to be out after I lock the front doors, I tell them that the door at the top of the outside staircase is always unlocked."

Harrison handed the key to Rachel and together they jogged to Ben's room. Rachel's hands shook so intensely she couldn't fit the key into the lock immediately. It finally slid into the opening and Rachel pushed the door open. The gaslight on the wall near the door was dimmed as far as possible. Harrison spun the valve, raising the illumination.

Joshua sat up, rubbing his eyes. Rachel flew across the room and sank to her knees on the bed. She gathered Joshua into her arms, and smothered him with kisses, all the while murmuring, "You're all right. Thank God, you're all right."

The boy pushed his mother off him. "Momma, stop it. I'm getting too big."

Harrison pulled the key from the lock. He crossed the room and once again handed the key to Rachel. "Josh, your mother got a scare. She and I both just wanted to come into town to check on you and Ben." He paused in the doorway. "Lock the door behind me and don't let anyone other than me in. I'm going to go find our foreman and have a talk with him."

Helen Morris waited at the front doors, arms folded over her chest, and face set in a disapproving glower, complete with fully pursed lips. "I will be locking the door behind you, Marshal."

He paused. "When Jason worked for the Lazy L, did he ever stay here?" He wasn't even sure why he was asking about his half-brother but his suspicions were beginning to point to a man no one had seen in years.

Her disapproval deepened. "Yes, he did. Such a hard-working and polite man and to be accused—"

"Did he know you don't lock the door on the staircase?" Harrison cut her off. His stomach knotted as the pieces of Rachel's so far faceless and nameless note-writer began to fall into place. Too well he knew the deceptive charm Jason wielded like a well-honed blade. On the surface, his half-brother was very charming, the epitome of a gentleman. Scratch that surface, and the only thing that emerged was a violent, cruel, and calculating fiend.

The woman nodded. "He stayed here often."

"Go lock that door." He dropped his hand onto the butt of his revolver when it appeared she was going to refuse. "Now, ma'am."

He waited until the hotel owner returned before he left. "Lock the door behind me and don't let anyone else into this hotel until I get back."

"I don't know where you're going to stay. I told you before we're full."

Harrison hesitated, shook his head, and reasoned it wasn't worth arguing with the woman. Demon and Twinkle stood at the hitching rail with their heads lowered. At least both animals were breathing levelly after the hard gallop into town. As he passed both horses, he patted each on the neck. He had never had any doubts of Demon's stamina and his opinion of the little bay mare increased.

On the boardwalk outside The Thirsty Dog, Harrison paused and looked over the swinging batwing doors. After allowing his sight to adjust to the comparatively bright lights of the saloon, he pushed the doors open. Heads swiveled to him and the bawdy laughter and conversations stuttered to a halt.

The barkeep lifted a hand and Harrison noted two doves trying to blend into the shadows at the back of the saloon. "What can I do for you tonight, Marshal?"

"I'm looking for Ben Hauser."

"You missed him by about thirty minutes. He went down to The Golden Eagle." The man returned to cleaning steins. "I don't offer what he was looking for tonight."

Harrison shifted his gaze to the two women who had moved even further into the shadows behind the piano player. If Ben had left The Thirsty Dog half an hour ago looking for feminine companionship, the foreman probably wouldn't be heading back to the hotel any time soon. Harrison decided he could take a few minutes before he ruined the rest of Hauser's evening. "Neither of those two what he was looking for?"

The barkeep jerked his head up and toward the back of his saloon. "Marshal, I know you're new here, but you ask anyone in this town about my establishment and they'll tell you I run a saloon, not a brothel. I have beer, hard spirits, and poker. That's enough to have the church ladies breathing down my neck. I won't have any doves in here."

"It's Silas, right?" Harrison hadn't taken his gaze from the two doves the saloon owner said he wouldn't have in his establishment.

"Silas Kirk, yeah." A full stein dropped onto the teak bar at Harrison's elbow. "And, those two aren't what you think."

"Even if they are what I'm thinking, you're not breaking any laws that I'm aware of." He glanced at the beer. "If that's a bribe, I'd rather have a bourbon."

Silas laughed and reached behind him for a bottle. The owner's laughter broke the tension in the saloon, and the conversations around the green-felt covered tables resumed. He set a shot glass on the teak counter and poured a generous portion into the small container.

"I guess this is a bribe to look the other way and forget you ever saw those two runaways from The Golden Eagle. Probably have a third one when Ben gets back in a little while. Tomorrow morning, Luke there—" He gestured at a young wrangler sitting guard over the two women with a rifle across his lap. The wrangler touched two fingers to the bill of his hat. "—is going to take them down to Sage Springs, make sure they get on the stage to Denver, and they're going back East." He directed his attention to a table in the front. "Still want another beer, Gabe?"

It seemed Gabe did because Silas drew a beer, and settled it onto the counter. One of the two doves left the shadows. "I'll take it over to him, Mr. Kirk." The smile crossing her face was as shy as a child's. "Marshal."

If this woman was more than sixteen or seventeen, he'd sit right at that saloon bar top and eat his own hat. He shot his gaze to Silas. "Dear God above, she's a child."

"Now you know why we help them run away and try to get them back to their families. It was your wife's idea, about five or six years ago." The saloon owner nudged his head to the back of the room. "Her sister there is even younger."

"They're leaving in those get-ups?" Harrison downed the bourbon and carefully set the shot glass down. That Rachel was involved with saving these little doves was a startling revelation, but wasn't that surprising when he thought about it. Luke wasn't sitting guard on the two, he was protecting them. Harrison doubted the owner of The Golden Eagle took kindly to his "girls" leaving.

"Good Lord, no." The saloon owner refilled the

shot glass. "Miss Callahan owns the dress shop here in town. She makes sure they're outfitted as right proper spinsters or widows. And if she doesn't have time, Burlington sends a few ready-made dresses for them."

The dress maker...Rachel's missing and unfortunately returned chemise...if Silas Kirk was like any other saloon owner, the man knew just about everything about everyone in town. "Any long-lost citizens returned lately?"

"Like who?" Silas hesitated, putting the bourbon bottle away and instead set it on the bar at Harrison's elbow.

"Jason Taylor."

As with so many people in town, the response from Silas was immediate. The heavy moustache covering his upper lip quivered and he stiffened. He then reached under the bar and brought out a sawed-off shot gun. The weapon was slammed onto the bar top so fiercely the bourbon bottle jumped. "You see this, Marshal?"

Harrison let his line of sight drop to the shot-gun.

"I've never fired Big Bertha in all the years I've owned this saloon. I just keep her around to make sure things don't get too rowdy in here. There's a shell in there. It's heavy buck shot. And it has your brother's name on it."

If Jason had returned, it was doubtful he had reacquainted himself with former haunts.

"For what he did to that sweet young lady you're married to, if I ever see him, I'll kill him. Killing an animal like him would be worth the risk of hanging."

To give himself a chance to hide his agreement with Silas and to cover his surprise the man would be so open about his desire to see Jason dead, Harrison slid his gaze to the shot glass at his elbow.

"I've always viewed Rachel like my daughter." Silas's voice lowered. "Her father and Tom Giles and I all came out here together. Three young fools thinking we were going to make it rich. Sam was already married to Rachel Anne but she despised Sam. Hated him with every fiber of her body."

The image of the grave marker Sam had installed over Rachel Anne rose in Harrison's memory. "What?"

"You got a few minutes, Marshal? This may take a while to tell."

Rachel and Joshua were safe at Morris's hotel and from what the saloon owner told him about Ben's whereabouts, the foreman would be back at The Thirsty Dog in a little while. He picked up the second round of bourbon Silas had poured and nodded.

"Rachel Anne hated Sam. Her family forced her to marry him. She'd already married once and her first husband died in one of the last battles of the War of Northern Aggression. Her family considered it a blessing because they thought she'd married below her status."

Harrison quirked up a brow. There was little doubt Silas hailed from south of the Mason-Dixon.

"She had a baby in arms, a boy, when Sam married her. Her family paid Sam handsomely to take her off their hands and to go far away with her. They wanted her to disappear and take the deep shame she brought to them with her." A stein was set onto the counter but the bar-keep didn't fill it with beer. Instead, a pitcher of milk was pulled from a tub of ice water. "I can say by the time Rachel Anne died Sam wasn't too fond of her, either. When they married, Sam was an illiterate wrangler with little more to his name than big dreams. He hoped she would at least tolerate him. Instead she never let him forget it was her family's money that bought him respectability but that money would never buy her affections. And, she never let him forget he was illiterate when they first married. She was fluent in three languages, four if you count the language of ripping a man's heart to ribbons with words."

And this was the woman Sam Leonard held up as the ideal for Rachel? "Everything Rachel believes about her mother is a lie."

"More than you know. On the journey from Texas to here, Tom and I taught Sam to read and write. He kept learning but the one thing he could never grasp was ciphering. That's why he made Rachel start to keep the books for the ranch and insisted every penny be documented. He might not have been able to cipher it, but with enough description, he could figure out what that money was being spent on. All those books at the house, I can tell you for certain Sam read every one of them." Silas drank more than half of the milk in his glass before he continued. "Anyway, after her mother died, Sam moved himself and Rachel into town for a few years. They stayed with me and that's why I've never had any doves, soiled or otherwise, in my saloon. Just didn't seem fitting for a young, impressionable girl to be around that kind of an influence."

"What happened to Rachel Anne's other child?"

"Don't rightly know. About the time the boy was five or six, just before Rachel was born, Rachel Anne insisted the boy be sent to his father's family in New Orleans. She'd been writing back and forth with them for a while and they wanted the boy. They sent a black mammy out here to get the boy and take him back." A half smile pulled at his mouth. "Shoulda heard the tongues wagging in this town when that one stepped off the train. She was a right handsome woman and dressed as fine as any white woman I'd ever known. According to Sam, she'd been Rachel Anne's mammy. Just stayed with the family even after the war was over."

Movement at the back of the room caught his attention. The Lazy L foreman had returned to the saloon. A scantily clad young woman stood at his side, Hauser's jacket draped over her shoulders.

Harrison let his gaze skim over the woman and then Hauser. He acknowledged the rescued dove with a slight dip of his head. The relief that softened her features and rounded her too-thin shoulders tempered some of his anger with Ben for leaving Joshua alone.

Chapter Fourteen

Rachel startled with the soft knock. She glanced in a panic around the room, looking for anything she could use to "even the odds" as Ben had put it when he taught her to fight. The pitcher in the wash stand would have to suffice. She tiptoed to the door and stood brandishing the heavy ceramic. She forced her heart from her throat when Harrison's voice came through the door. "Rachel, it's me."

She lowered the pitcher to the floor, then twisted the lock and pulled the door open. Harrison walked in, followed by Ben. Without any warning, Rachel pulled her fist back and drove a hard right cross into the foreman's jaw.

Ben staggered a step. "What was that for?"

"Keep your voice down so you don't disturb my son," she hissed. She shook her stinging hand and then flexed her fingers. "You know, Joshua. My son. The child you left alone in a hotel room. Alone while Jason is out there, looking for a chance to hurt him."

"No one's seen him since Sam blasted that mine shut," Ben said.

"What makes you certain it's Jason?" Harrison asked.

Rachel held a hand up. "One at a time. Daddy said he had nothing to do with Jason's disappearance and swore he saw both Jason and Jake riding hard to the south the day Jason went missing."

"Yeah, well, Sam swore to a lot of things that weren't true," Ben muttered. "I'd be checking that mine for bodies."

"What are you saying, Ben?" A chill chased the length of her spine.

"I'm saying before his apoplexy, he sent me out to the Domega to be sure it was fully blasted shut so nothing could get out." Ben looked away from her. "Nothing bigger than a mouse could have gotten out of there."

She spun round to Harrison. What was the line about blood being thicker than water? Ben had as much as accused her father of murdering Harrison's brother. "I didn't know."

"I meant what I said the first day I was here, Rachel. I hope he's dead. That hope is considerably more fervent now." Harrison walked to the windows in the room and moved the curtains aside. He nodded his head down to the street. "If we assume Sam blasted a mine closed with Jason in it, what makes you think it's him doing all of this?"

"Only two people on earth know when Jason came out to the house that day, I tried to hide from him in the barn. I never told anyone." A shudder passed over her with the recollection of being dragged by her hair, of his repeated blows to subdue her. "That's how I knew it had to be him who wrote the note at Burlington's."

"What note?" Ben asked.

"Someone's been leaving threatening missives for Rachel," Harrison said. He let the curtain fall into place and turned his back to the window. "At first light, Ben, you and I will ride out to the mine."

"You're going to need more than the two of us to move enough rock out of the way to get in there. I'll head to the Rocking Bar M and ask if they'll help."

Rachel folded her arms across her chest. "And if you think I'm just going to sit alone at the Lazy L, you have another think coming, Harrison Taylor. I'm not staying there by myself."

"No, you're not," he conceded. "I'm taking you and Joshua to the jail."

"Jail?" Surely he had to be attempting levity. "You're arresting me and Joshua?"

A slight smile twisted up his mouth. "It would be an interesting manner to resolve any disputes we might have down the road." A shout from the other end of town penetrated the room and Harrison moved the curtain away again, the disturbance down the street drawing his attention. "I'm not arresting either of you. But, think about it…most people try to break out of a jail, not into it. It's the safest place I can think of for you and Joshua if I'm not around."

He did make several valid points, Rachel conceded, especially about resolving marital disputes.

\*\*\*\*

If she had to spend the day at the jail while Harrison, Ben, Royce, and Drake were attempting to reopen the Domega, Rachel decided she might as well make herself useful.

Cobwebs filled the corners at the ceiling, a thick layer of dust coated the battered desk and chair—the only furnishings in the squat, block building—and that same dust dulled the light of early morning attempting to penetrate the windows.

In the back room, one of two that she guessed were

meant to be living quarters, she found a broom, dust pan, a mop, a bucket, and several rags. She picked up one of the rags and promptly dropped it. Mildew stained the fabric and the musty smell tickled her nose.

"Momma, what's this?"

Rachel twisted around the door to see what Joshua asked about. He was pointing to a locked, barred, and all-together empty gun rack. The key was in the lock. "That's where the marshal keeps rifles."

"Is he the marshal?" Joshua studied the rack. "It's got spots for six. That's a lot."

"Yes, it is. And, yes, Harrison is the marshal." The condition of the mop gave her pause. Like the rags, it was useless because of mildew.

"Do I have a pa?"

His question pulled her up. This was not a conversation she wanted to have with Joshua, though she knew it was something that would have to be answered at some time. Part of her wanted to tell him she didn't want to talk about his father at this exact moment and another part of her argued she had never been anything other than honest with him. She might have sweetened the information but she had never refused to answer his questions. She made her way out of the back rooms. "Yes, Joshua, you have a father."

He looked up at her. "Is he dead, like Donnie's pa?"

To give herself time to carefully construct her answer, she let her gaze sweep over his features. As with every time she looked at him, she never saw anything of Jason Taylor in his features. She saw her father in his jaw and herself in his nose, eyes, and cheekbones. "I don't know. I haven't seen him since before you were born." She wasn't willing to swear it had been Jason by the barn the night it burned.

His little brow furrowed as he puzzled that out but she was saved from answering any more questions by a rap on the locked door, accompanied with the announcement, "It's Kathy and Jessie, Rachel."

Grateful for the interruption, she unlocked and opened the door. "What are you doing here?" Realizing how rude that sounded, she quickly added, "I'm glad you've come, though."

Kathy swept in, a covered basket in her arms. Jessica carried another. Both women set their burdens on the desk and Kathy said, "When Ben woke everyone up at the house this morning and told us what your husband was doing, I decided Jessie and I would come and spend the day with you. We brought breakfast and lunch, and I stopped at Helen's to get coffee."

By mid-afternoon, the jail was scrubbed from floor to ceiling. More than just two meals had been in the baskets Kathy and Jessie brought with them. Lemon oil scented the air and the battered old desk had taken on a new life. Rachel looked around the nondescript interior. The windows in the office area and living quarters still needed curtains. She wanted to make a seat and back cushion for the chair behind the desk, and both cells needed ticking for a mattress and a pillow.

Kathy emerged from the back rooms. "Is there a key for that locked door?"

Rachel lifted her shoulders in a shrug. "I suppose so. I saw a ring of keys in the desk drawer."

One by one, she fitted keys into the lock. At last, a key fit that turned the tumblers. She opened the door and she and Kathy stared at a room filled with furniture, rolled mattresses for the metal bed frames bolted to the walls in the cells, pillows, and even a massive pot-bellied stove.

"Well," Kathy said, sending a conspiratorial grin at Rachel, "at least if you banish him from the house, he'll have someplace to put his head."

Rachel couldn't contain her small laugh. "I just thought the same thing." She clamped her hand over her mouth, abashed she had admitted such a thing. "I shouldn't have said that."

"Yes, you should have." A light, airy chuckle broke from the older woman. She sobered and added in all seriousness, "Sending you away to those schools was a horrible mistake. You never had a chance to foster friendships with women either there or here. I told Sam that."

"You told my father that was a mistake?" Her mouth dropped open with Kathy's revelation.

"Repeatedly. You must have felt like a caged meadowlark in an aviary full of clucking peahens." Kathy dropped her cleaning rag onto a chair. "Your father made it very clear he didn't want me befriending you. He was afraid I'd encourage your 'hare-brained idea'—his words, not mine—that a grown woman has the right to choose her own husband. His argument was an arranged marriage had worked well enough for him and marrying for love was just a ridiculous, romantic notion."

Rachel shook her head with disbelief. "He loved my mother."

"And your mother was the ideal you could never live up to. You need to talk to Silas sometime if you want the truth." She looked at the furniture. "We may as well get this organized and cleaned."

In as many words, Rachel understood Kathy wasn't going to say any more. She shook her head and backed out of the small room. She had struggled so valiantly to just once hear the words "I'm proud of you" and when those words were never uttered, she had believed it was her fault for failing him. Her whole life, the man she had looked up to, and his ideals had been as false as the facades on the buildings across the street. Everything she thought she knew about her father was a sham.

**** 

The four men looked at one another. The last large rock blocking their way into the mine rolled down the slope and came to a halt at the bottom of the steep grade. The clattering and rattling of the smaller stones in the talus pile chattered like some kind of demented laughter in the sudden silence. Without a word, Harrison lit one of the lamps they had brought with them. He lifted it closer to the black hole gaping in the side of the mountain.

He straightened. "I can't see anything. I'll go in. The rest of you stay here in case the damn thing collapses again."

"I'll go with you," Ben said. The foreman struck a match and lit a second lantern. "It'll be hard to crawl through that hole and hold onto a lamp. I'll hand it in to you once you're inside."

"I'd rather you go in first in that case, if it's all the same to you." Harrison sent a hard glare at Ben.

"Give me a lamp," Drake snapped at the same time pulling the lit lantern from Ben's hand. He handed it to Harrison. "Hand this to me when I tell you to."

The younger man climbed onto the tumbled,

jagged shards of the mountain and shimmied through the hole on his belly. The sound of rocks falling against other pieces of stone echoed from the opening. Drake's hand thrust through the black portal. "Hand me both lamps."

Harrison handed them to Drake and he then crawled through the aperture.

"Watch yourself. There's a rock with a nasty edge on it. Darn near sliced my arm open," Drake said.

Harrison dropped to his feet and took a lamp from Drake. The stench of death still lingered in the mine, a sickly-sweet scent of long decayed flesh. A few feet into the darkness, the shadowy form of a dead buckskin entered into the pitifully small circles of light the two lanterns cast. The desiccated hulk of the horse was slumped against a wall. The back half of the animal was trapped under a massive pile of stone, giving the dead horse the appearance of attempting to crawl its way from the rocks. The creature's right hoof was bent up, a shoe with a heart-bar visible. The leather of his bridle was crumbling with dry-rot, though the bit was still within the horse's clamped jaws.

"Terrible way for a horse to die," Drake said. "You recognize him?"

Harrison nodded. "It's Duke. I trained him for Jason. He was born the same week as Demon." Jason would have spent the money to have a special shoe made for Duke. The horse was probably the only living creature Jason truly cared for and a heart-bar shoe to alleviate the pain of a reoccurring founder wouldn't have been out of the question for him. "You found Rachel the morning after she bluffed Jason to fold in front of all those wranglers."

"Yeah." The younger man's voice was tight with something Harrison could only define as anger. "Don't ask me to tell you what that was like."

"Wouldn't even consider it. Why wasn't Jason arrested?" This was the one piece of the whole tale that had never fallen into place. "Until Sam took matters into his own hands, no one thought to charge him with a crime."

Drake stepped closer to the dead horse. "Jake gave him an alibi. Said Rachel spent the night before flirting with Jason and even invited him to come back the next day. He said he went with Jason but left when Rachel said she wanted to be alone with Jason. It was her word against theirs." He twisted around to Harrison. "That son of a bitch was brazen enough to ride it out, until nearly everyone in this town believed his version."

Rachel had told him by the time Sam got home the bruises had faded and she had concocted a story to explain her broken bones. Couple her attempt to hide what had happened to her with Jason's bravado, Jake's alibi and Sam's obsession with public appearance, and Harrison could see how Sam would believe Rachel to be light-skirted. He couldn't understand it, but he could explain it. He said, his gaze resting on Drake, "Not everyone believed him."

"No, not everyone—but enough of them."

Harrison lifted the lantern higher over his head and looked up. Heavy timbers supported the roof, though several of the beams were broken and strained. "Let's find Jason and get out of here."

"If his horse is here, Jason should be here."

"I want to be sure." Harrison started down the carved-out passageway. Within yards, the remains of

Duke were no longer visible. Another dead horse came into view. A massive slab of mica-rich rock glittering in the lamp light hid the animal's head and half its neck. A brand marked its visible hip.

"That's Jake's horse." Drake looked back toward the entrance. "Sam said he saw both Jason and Jake together. Guess he wasn't lying about that."

Just outside the flickering circle of Drake's lamp, Harrison said, "I think I found Jake because this isn't Jason." He looked away from the rictus of the body. Just as the semi-arid environs had desiccated the remains of the two horses, the same conditions preserved the dead man.

"Sam shot him in the back," Drake's voice was filled with disgust.

"Let's play this out. Sam lures Jason and Jake here. How?" Harrison peered into the darkness. "What would convince Jason to go anywhere with Sam? Even if he thought Sam believed him and not Rachel about what he did to her, I don't see Jason being that trusting."

"He was your brother." The disgust in the younger man's voice deepened. "How greedy was he?"

Harrison almost pointed out, for what felt like the millionth time, that Jason was only his half-brother because they had the same father and other than that, he and Jason had nothing else in common. Instead, he said, "If he thought Sam had hit a big silver vein, Jason would probably be greedy enough to take the chance Sam didn't have an ulterior motive. Just how profitable was this mine before it played out?"

"The rumors I heard was it built that house the year Rachel was born and paid Doc Hagar's salary for five years so he'd move out here. It also paid for Rachel to go to boarding schools. Sam never seemed to care if the cattle paid."

"So, we can assume Jason heard the same rumors." After Silas's comments the night before about Rachel Anne's family paying Sam to take their daughter and her son far away, Harrison had his doubts the mine ever even yielded a single flake of silver. "Sam tells those two he found another large vein. They meet him here— because no one saw them riding with Sam the day he blasted the mine." Harrison looked down at the body again. By the lack of a blood trail down his back, Jake had fallen where he'd been shot. "Sam shoots Jake in the back and kills him instantly. Jason can't get out the way they came in. Sam's there with a loaded and ready gun."

"He takes off running—or at least to get behind cover so he can try to shoot his way out." Drake fell silent when one of the old timbers creaked softly. He craned his head at an angle to the beam.

"If you want to leave, go. I'll look for him a little longer," Harrison said.

"And if this mine collapses fully I'd have to explain to your wife why I left you. Thanks, no."

"Then we keep looking." Harrison walked down the main tunnel, ignoring the way his skin crawled with each creak and moan of the timber supporting the walls and ceiling. The more fresh air rushed into the mine through the newly opened entrance, the more those beams protested.

Drake finally halted Harrison. "Look, we could spend years searching every single tunnel and played out shaft in here and still never find his body. The lamps are running low on kerosene. Those braces are deteriorating with all the outside air coming in. We've got to assume his body is in here, somewhere."

Harrison nodded and watched the flame in his lamp flicker. He measured the fuel still in the reservoir. Using his shirt sleeve to protect his hand from the hot glass, he carefully slid the chimney up a few inches. The flame flickered more and bent, as if being pulled. "There's another way out of here."

Without waiting for Drake, Harrison took off in the direction of the flame.

"Damn it, if we get caught in here without any light, I'm going to put a bullet in you."

"You're afraid of the dark?" Harrison came to a halt where a smaller tunnel branched off the main shaft. When he started down the narrowed passage, Drake's obscenity echoed in the corridor.

Both men halted when the passageway opened into a massive, subterranean cave. The air brushing against them came from the other side of the cavern. "That's too much air moving to be a narrow or small opening," Harrison said.

"Yeah. And with our kind of luck, we're going to meet a grumpy bear."

Harrison took off toward the source of the air moving into the depths of the earth. The passage he followed hadn't been dug out by hand, but by running water at one time. The walls were smoothed and the floor stair-stepped upward. At the end of the natural staircase a shaft of light illuminated an area several feet into the earth.

The aperture was just wide enough for him to get out if he moved through the last yard or so of rock sideways. When Drake emerged, Harrison asked,

"Where are we?"

The younger man looked around. "I'm not sure. I need to climb higher to get an idea of where we came out of that."

When he scrambled down from his higher vantage point, he gestured to the southeast. "Royce and Ben are about three hundred feet lower than us and about a quarter of a mile that way."

"If Sam didn't kill Jason, it's conceivable he got out of there." The chill creeping over Harrison had nothing to do with the temperature dropping as the sun sank behind the mountain range.

"Just as conceivable he got lost in the maze of tunnels and shafts in there and never got out."

"I'm not willing to take the chance with Rachel and Joshua's safety by believing that." Harrison looked off in the general direction Drake had said the others were. A narrow, distant pillar of jet black rose on the purpling horizon. He gestured to the column. "That's smoke."

Almost as one, Harrison and Drake broke into a run, scrambling down the steep face of the escarpment toward Royce and Ben. By the time they reached the other two, night had taken hold but the smoke was still visible, highlighted in orange and red from the flames that were at its base.

Darkness hampered their ability to ride as quickly as possible. The risk of a horse breaking a leg was too real, as was serious injury to a rider in that event. The closer they approached the hellish column, the more apparent it was that the fire originated at the Lazy L.

Harrison put his heels into Demon's sides when they started on the road leading up to the house. He reined the stallion in the yard and slumped in the saddle. Drake, Ben, and Royce reined to a stop near him.

There would be no saving the structure. Flames leaped from the windows and through the roof and a deep, almost pained groan sounded seconds before what he assumed to be the second floor crashed down.

"How the hell am I going to tell Rachel?" Harrison asked no one in particular.

"Maybe," Ben said, a growl heard in his voice, "if we weren't chasing ghosts and instead were looking for a living, breathing culprit, none of this would have happened. But you had to be sure your brother was still in that mine."

"Just what is it you're accusing me of, Ben?" Harrison twisted in the saddle to confront the foreman. "The house was empty today because regardless of what you told me and Rachel about Sam and the mine, no one was going to be at the ranch house until that mess was cleaned up."

"All this started just a couple of weeks before you showed up. Maybe you didn't burn the barn or the house, or write those notes to Rachel—"

"What notes?" both Royce and Drake asked at the same time.

"—but it doesn't mean you ain't doing it with a partner."

"Why in the hell would I do any of that?" Demon jumped sideways as an ember drifted close to his nose and forced Harrison to settle back into the saddle. "I've got every reason to make sure the Lazy L stays solvent. Rebuilding the barn and the house doesn't help with solvency."

"And even more reason to try to drive her out so

she signs everything over to you." Ben slapped a spark that landed on his arm. "That would make you a very rich man."

"I'm not trying to drive her out. She and I are married." Harrison lifted Demon's reins. "I've given you a considerable amount of latitude in light of your loyalty to Sam and because Rachel trusts you, but if you're going to lock horns with me, I'll have to let you go."

"Rachel's the ramrod for this ranch, not you, and she's the only one who can tell me to move on."

Harrison lowered his voice, struggling to keep his anger in check. "Take a look around you, Ben. What started out as vandalism and maybe some destruction of rangeland has escalated into arson. At this rate, there isn't going to be a ranch for her to ramrod. I'm not the enemy here."

"What notes?" Royce asked again.

"For the past two weeks or so, someone's been leaving threatening notes for Rachel." Harrison looked at the inferno and slumped a little more in the saddle. "This is going to crush her."

Chapter Fifteen

It was gone. For what felt like a lifetime, all Rachel could do was sit on Twinkle and stare at what had once been her home. She couldn't force herself to dismount, could barely make herself draw a level breath. Her throat tightened and burned with the tears she tried to blink away.

A plaintive meow pulled her gaze to the ground. Joshua's cat sat in front of Twinkle. The old tom broke her inability to move. She swung off the mare and scooped the ragged feline into her arms. In the last two months, he had used up several of his rumored nine lives. A warning rumble from the cat convinced her to set him down. Joshua was the only person he allowed to hold him for any length of time.

Rachel walked around the ruins. There had been the back porch and the kitchen. What appeared to be her massive Hoosier stove leaned awkwardly to one side, the porcelain on it cracked and shattered. Somewhere in the pile was the long hallway from the kitchen to the large foyer and the two parlors. On the other end of the remains of the house, the fireplace and chimney made of granite and quartz defiantly jutted upward. Glass in a multitude of colors littered the ground where the double doors of the formal entrance to the house had been. One piece of the glass survived, the lead beading that held it in place with the other intricately placed pieces melted away in the heat of the inferno. If she closed her eyes, she could still see the roses in the center of both doors, trace the ivy that twisted along the edges of the glass.

She picked up the still warm, ruby-colored glass and tried to convince herself her tears were from the stinging smoke rising from the smoldering remains. It was just a collection of lumber, and fabrics, and glass, and native stone. There had been nothing in the house that couldn't be replaced. The glass tumbled from her fingers, shattering on one of the pink quartz boulders her father had imported from the Dakota Territory. The heat had been so intense even several of those seemingly impervious rocks had cracked.

She finally halted and turned to Harrison.

The wind, howling out of the north, carried the bite of snow and the threat of winter. Low, dark clouds rippled across the sky, spilling an icy mist. Harrison stood with his shoulders hunched against the wind's teeth, holding the reins of both Demon and Twinkle.

"It's too late in the season to start to rebuild, isn't it?"

Harrison nodded. "Probably. And, I'm leery to start any building with our arsonist still on the loose."

A glance over her shoulder one last time at the charred and blackened pile of rubble revealed a bright splash of color. She retraced her steps to where the back porch and the rose trellis had been. A single rose survived the inferno and bravely stood against the wind. She squatted next to the plant and cupped the small bud in her hands. "I planted this from a cutting I kept alive all the way from Boston. I was told it wouldn't survive the trip here, and then it wouldn't survive in Wyoming.

I kept it watered and put a heavy layer of straw on it every fall to keep it alive." All she could detect was the scent of smoke when she bent her head to sniff the petals. A sigh broke from her. "Maybe with enough straw on it, it will survive this winter, too."

She dragged her hands down the front of her denims and wiped most of the soot from her palms before she pushed herself to her feet. "We'll have to sell the dairy cows. Without shelter for the winter, they'll never survive. We're already spending a fortune boarding Demon and Twinkle at the livery. We can't afford to keep the dairy cows anywhere."

"It wouldn't take but a day or two to build a lean-to shelter at the back of the jail. We don't have to get rid of them and we could move Demon and Twinkle to the jail." Harrison tilted his head from the house and her, looking off into the distance. "What about the rest of the cattle?"

Demon tossed his head, his bridle jangling.

"They'll be fine. They hide down in the arroyos and in the stands of trees when the weather gets really bad." She took Twinkle's reins from him and put a foot into the stirrup. "There is a silver lining to all this, I suppose. It's easier for Joshua to get to school now."

"I never planned on anyone living at the jail." Leather creaked as he swung into the saddle. "It's just until spring when I can get a house built for us. Or, we could hire a builder. James Murphey out of Laramie City has an advertisement in *The Federal Eagle* today. I can do the finishing work on the interior, but I don't know the first thing about home construction."

The defensiveness in his tone caused her to hesitate moving Twinkle forward. "I'm not blaming you. It's just material things lost." She attempted a smile. "I don't think like Ben does, that you're involved with any of this." Rachel pressed her heels into Twinkle and rode to Harrison's side. "As long as Jason's out there somewhere, I feel safer at the jail. Like you said, people don't usually break into jails." She drew a breath and added, "We do need to stop at Burlington's and purchase a few items."

"Such as?" He tossed a glance in her direction.

"Other than the clothes on our backs, none of us have any other clothing. I also need cooking utensils and we have no bedding." She attempted another smile. "Whoever furnished the jail didn't plan too well."

"We're not busted, so get whatever we need." He didn't look at her as he added, "It's not an ideal situation but you're right. It could be worse. We could be without a roof over our heads."

****

"What happened to fall?" Harrison asked as he closed the door between the jail and the living quarters. "It's only the first of October."

Though the living arrangements were cramped, and she missed some of the luxuries the ranch house had provided, Rachel admitted to herself that this was pleasant. The two rooms attached to the jail had begun to feel like home, especially when both Joshua and Harrison were present. She laughed with his observation. "We don't have the long seasons here that you had in Kentucky. I heard a wrangler once say that Wyoming's seasons are 'winter,' 'still winter', 'not quite summer', and 'winter, again'." She dipped her head to the small table and set the iron on the pot-bellied stove to reheat it. "Dale left a telegram for you."

The crackle of paper unfolding reached her, followed immediately with Harrison's deep sigh. "I have to go to Laramie City to transport a prisoner to the federal court in Denver for trial. Knowing how long these things take, I'll probably be gone for about two weeks."

"Why for so long? It only takes a day to get to Laramie by train and two at the most to Denver." She looked over her shoulder at Joshua. The child was engrossed with several tiny toy soldiers, marching them up a hill made of a pillow and across a battle field composed of a blanket. "Two weeks is a long time."

"Unfortunately, it'll take that long. I have to be there the whole time to make sure the jurors all show up, as do the witnesses. The minute I sign Wallace out of the penitentiary in Laramie City, he's my responsibility. It's part of the job. At least I don't have to rent someplace to serve as a courtroom." He pulled her against him and kissed the top of her head. "I don't like that I have to be gone for two weeks any more than you do."

"Is this Wallace dangerous?"

"I don't know. I'm not even sure who he is." Harrison released her. "Did *The Sentinel* get delivered?"

"Yes. You walked by it. It's on the desk in the other room." Rachel picked the iron up and sprinkled water on the collar of his shirt. The soft hiss of the heated iron on the damp fabric filled the silence.

Harrison returned, the weekly newspaper under his arm. "Whatever you're cooking smells good."

"It's starch for your shirts. Supper is in the warmer. I went to The Americana and got two of their meat pies." She hung up the ironed garment, then blurted out, "Take Ben with you."

He shook his head and sat at the small table. "No. I want him here while I'm gone." The paper snapped open and the news of the land drew his attention.

"Nothing has happened in the six weeks we've been here. Maybe, he got what he wanted by burning everything to the ground." Rachel shook another shirt onto the ironing board. An unnamed fear nibbled at her and no matter how she reasoned with herself that she was being foolish, she couldn't quell that unease. "Please, take Ben with you—at least to Laramie City. You can decide when you get that man from the prison if you need Ben's assistance."

Harrison met her gaze over the top of the newspaper. "Wallace will be removed from the prison and transported to Denver in wrist and ankle shackles. I want Ben here, with you and Joshua. I'm not willing to take the chance that Jason's gotten what he wanted with those arsons."

Realizing she had found the proverbial immovable object in Harrison's insistence that Ben remain to keep guard over her and Joshua, Rachel allowed herself a small sigh. "What time do you have to leave? Do you want me to pack your frock coat?"

His attention returned to the page. "Train leaves about seven in the morning. Be sure to put my tie in there, too, please." A chuckle broke from him. "How is this reporting on anything?" He read from the paper, "'The *Cheyenne Ledger News* assures us the wind blew so hard it blew the horns off a goat. We don't doubt it.' It wasn't that windy three days ago when this was reported."

"It's Cheyenne. Look at all those politicians there. It has to be windier there."

Another chuckle broke from him. "You have a point."

After Joshua had fallen asleep, Rachel set Harrison's saddle bags on their bed. She took his frock coat off the hanger in the small armoire and laid it out next to the saddle bags. She brushed her hand over the wool, smoothing the lapel down. Her heart sped up when Harrison slipped his arms around her waist and pulled her against his chest. She tilted her head to a side when he nuzzled under her hair and left a trail of small kisses on her skin. "Can't you hire a deputy or two to take care of this?"

"I intend to do that, but I don't have time to do it before morning. I don't want to leave, darlin'."

His teeth grazed the sensitive spot behind her ear and Rachel sharply sucked her breath in. Warmth pooled deep in her and spread throughout her limbs.

"It's my job, though. I'll be back as soon as I can," he said. "Are you going to miss me?"

She twisted around in his arms and tilted her face up to him. "Of course. What kind of a question is that?"

He bent his head to hers, his lips coaxing hers to open. The warmth he so easily started in her flared into fire. He broke the kiss, a crooked, heated grin crossing his face. "Why don't I go close the door to Joshua's room and you can show me how much you'll miss me?"

"It's already closed." A small squeak of surprise sounded from her when he scooped her into his arms, then carried her to their bed. He lowered her to the thick ticking and Rachel flung her arms around his neck and pulled him down.

****

Laramie City was a thriving metropolis compared to the sleepy town of Federal. Harrison stepped off the train, threw his saddle bag over his shoulder, and looked down the street. The porter was assisting a woman and two small children from the train and as soon as the man was finished with that task, Harrison asked, "Where's the livery?"

The porter pointed and said, "About two blocks that way on Garfield. Can't miss it. It's right on the corner of Third and Garfield."

"And, which way to the penitentiary?" He noted the railroad employee studying the badge he'd pinned to his great coat when the train pulled into the self-proclaimed gem city of the plains.

"Once you leave the livery," the porter said, pointing in the opposite direction from the livery, "it's south-west of town, that way, across the Big Laramie River. Bridge is fixed, so you don't have to ford the river."

"Thank you." Harrison tugged the collar of his coat up. He should have loaded Demon into one of the livestock cars, but he doubted he could be reimbursed for the horse's transport. Renting a horse at the livery wouldn't raise a question of repayment.

As he rode to the penitentiary, Harrison studied the massive walls of the prison. Located about a mile outside the city limits, the edifice rose on the plain of the Laramie Valley. Vertical bars, spaced less than six inches apart, halted any attempt to leave through the few windows penetrating the thick walls. Before he reached the heavy wooden doors a guard halted him with an order to state his business.

"Harrison Taylor, Federal Marshal. I'm here to transport a prisoner to Denver to stand trial." The rented horse tried to lower her head to graze and Harrison pulled her up.

"We don't have anyone scheduled for transportation. Are you sure?"

Unease wrapped around Harrison's spine. "I wouldn't be here if I wasn't." The mare tried again to drop her head. "Is the warden in? Maybe he can straighten this out."

After the unmistakable sound of a large brace being lifted on the inside of the doors, one door swung open. Another guard, carbine in hand, gestured to Harrison. "Dismount. Leave the horse tied out there. I'll show you to the warden's office."

Harrison swung down and looped the reins over the hitching rail. The guard who let him through the massive brick walls stayed behind Harrison as he directed him to the warden's office. The cold in the corridor was bone-chilling, the kind that seeped deep into a body and wouldn't let go. The echo of his boot heels on the bricked floor raised gooseflesh on Harrison and he suppressed a shudder. The uncanny silence was utterly unnerving, broken only by the footfalls of the two men and the jangling of the keys on the guard's belt. If the intent was to make men unwilling to ever return to custody, this building was perfectly designed. Even though he wasn't going to be a resident, the oppression weighed down on him.

The guard stopped Harrison outside an office with a closed door. The brass nameplate under the frosted half-glass of the door read "H. K. Bostick" while the gold lettering on the glass stated "Warden."

Bostick rose to his feet when Harrison entered. He removed his hat, stripped off his leather gloves and tossed them into the hat, then extended a hand to the warden. At least, it was warm in this room. A pot-bellied stove in a corner radiated heat and a tea-kettle wisped steam.

The warden's piercing gaze swept over Harrison, lingering for a moment on the badge. At long last, he shook Harrison's hand. "What can I do for you?"

Something wasn't right. He wasn't sure what it was, but something was very wrong. Harrison pulled the telegram from his pocket. "I'm supposed to be transporting an Edwin Wallace to Denver to stand trial." He handed the small paper to Boswell.

The warden took the paper, then walked to the door. "Fuller!"

The guard who'd walked Harrison in appeared from a small room directly across from the warden's office. "Sir?"

"Where is Edwin Wallace?" Bostick shoved the telegram into his own pocket.

"He's in the broom factory right now." Fuller glanced from Boswell to Harrison. "You want me to go get him?"

"No. Check his paperwork. Before you do that, though, send Powell in here." Bostick returned his scrutiny to Harrison. "Until I get this straightened out, why don't you have a seat, *Marshal*?"

The hair on the back of Harrison's neck lifted with Bostick's emphasis on his title. He knew of Bostick's reputation. The warden wasn't a man to be trifled with and was rumored to be as cold-blooded as a snake.

Harrison sat in the only chair other than the warden's—a rather uncomfortable ladder-back chair in the corner of the room, situated furthest from the door and which forced the occupant to cross by the warden's desk to reach the exit. Bostick resumed his seat at the desk and pulled a side drawer open. The heavy weight of a revolver settled onto the desk.

"We have a problem. I never sent that telegram." The icy and decidedly unamused smile tipping one corner of the man's mouth increased Harrison's earlier unease and again lifted the hairs at his nape. "As attempted escapes go, this is a first for me. Why don't you tell me who you really are and why Wallace, of all people? He's in for a short term."

"I'm not attempting to help a prisoner escape." Harrison was very aware of Bostick's hand resting next to the gun. He kept his own hands on his knees, far away from his Colt. "Send a telegram to Dale White down in Federal. He'll verify that one in your pocket came in last night."

The guard Harrison assumed to be Powell entered the warden's office. Bostick finally picked up his weapon and pointed it directly at Harrison. "Mr. Powell is going to take your weapon, *Marshal*, and then he's going to escort you to a cell. You can wait there while I get to the bottom of this."

Harrison had no choice but to allow Powell to remove his Colt from the holster. Powell then said, "Stand up," and handed Harrison's gun to the warden.

There wouldn't be any point in refusing. Once he was on his feet, Harrison said, "You're making a mistake, Warden."

Bostick's icy smile deepened. "I've heard that

before."

"Should I take him across the hall and process him?"

The warden seemed to consider that, then shook his head. "No. Just take him down to solitary." Bostick held his hand out. "I'll take that badge. If you're who you say you are, I'll return it to you."

Though he grit his teeth and clenched his jaw, Harrison did as the warden demanded. The man flipped the badge over and Harrison waited, refusing to move even when Powell shoved him toward the door. He knew what Bostick was looking at on the reverse of the badge.

"What did you say your name was?" Bostick hadn't looked away from the badge.

"Harrison Mark Taylor." He ground his full name out, knowing the engraving on the back of the badge was the initials to his first and middle names as well as his full last name.

His badge was tossed onto the desk. "As soon as I hear from Mr. White in Federal, I'll know what to do with you," the warden said. "In the meantime, you're going to go quietly with Powell."

"And if I refuse?" Harrison clenched his hands, wondering if it was breaking out of prison if he'd not been arrested and charged with any crime and he fought his way out.

"I don't think you want to do that." Bostick jacked the hammer back on his revolver. "Fuller, we need assistance over here. I have a prisoner refusing orders."

Fuller entered the office, a heavy cudgel looped around his wrist. Harrison raised his hands to shoulder height. He knew a losing battle when he faced one.

"Just send that telegram to Dale White, Warden."

"I will. I'm glad you came to your senses, Mr. Taylor." Bostick gestured with the muzzle of his revolver. "Turn around and take two steps into the hallway."

Harrison took one step out the door. Stars exploded in his vision and he dropped to his knees. A second blow fell against the back of his head and everything turned black.

****

A knock startled Rachel. She bolted to her feet and ran to the door. A surreptitious peek between the closed green blind and the window revealed Dale White outside the jail door. She unlocked and opened the door.

Dale stood with hat in hand. "I really hate to bring this to you, but I relayed a message from the warden at the penitentiary to the U.S. Marshal in Denver a few hours ago. He says he's holding a man there for impersonating a marshal and attempting to break a prisoner out."

"What?" The unease she felt the night before increased. "Harrison's not impersonating a marshal."

"That's not the problem. It'll be straightened out as soon as I can contact the marshal in Denver. Problem is that message didn't go through. I think the telegraph lines south of town are down. With the wind we had a few days ago, it's possible the poles blew over. The Sioux are always chopping the poles down and cutting the wire. Heck, we've had cattle rubbing against them and pushing them over and snapping the wires." Dale gestured down the street. "I'm going to ride down to Eagle Springs and send the message from there. As soon as I hear anything, I'll be back. Usually, them folks in Denver are real quick about answering."

Rachel closed the door behind the telegraph operator and leaned her back onto the glass. She stared across the room. Everything Dale said made sense about why or how the message didn't go through. The unrest with the Sioux had been increasing, though usually not around Laramie or Cheyenne. Just the month before, up in the Sweetwater Valley, Tom Sun had said his Sun Ranch had been over-run, though no violence had erupted. More than once, cattle had rubbed so much against the poles they pushed the telegraph poles over. Before the cattle, bison had done the same. She couldn't count the times it had been reported high winds had taken out the telegraph wires. Yet, there was something wrong. She felt it, as surely as if a severe thunderstorm was brewing.

The clock ticking over the desk drew her attention. Joshua would be home from school soon. Though she couldn't quiet her own growing concern, she had to keep that hidden from him. She had to start supper preparations. Joshua came home from school ravenous. There were two or three oatmeal cookies left he could have with a glass of milk. Surely that would keep him until supper.

She went into the living quarters of the jail and got the pitcher of milk from the ice bucket. The lack of space negated an ice box. She was pouring a glass for Joshua when the bells over the door jingled. The unease she'd felt earlier waned with his return from school. "Joshua, leave your coat on the tree out there and lock the door, please."

Even in the living area, Rachel heard the tumblers

clattering on each other. "I've got cookies and milk for you. How was school?"

A loud, telltale double click of metal on metal shattered any sense of relief.

Rachel spun to the doorway separating the jail from the rest of the building. Joshua stood a single step away from the living quarters and as still as a statue. His left shoulder was held under a white-knuckled grip and the muzzle of a heavy revolver pressed into his temple.

She faced her worst nightmare.

## Chapter Sixteen

Jason Taylor held her son. She should have locked the door. She should have agreed when Harrison wanted to buy her a revolver. She never should have argued that all the eyes in town were enough to keep watch on her and her son. The sense of security living in the jail provided was false and the temporary domicile hadn't kept them safe from Jason. Worse yet, there was nothing within reach to use as a weapon to defend and protect her son.

"Please, let him go."

The curl of his lip turned her as cold as a mountain lake in January.

Her fingers tightened on the back of the chair. "Please, don't hurt him. I'll give you anything you want." She gulped and added in a whisper. "I'll do anything you want. Just don't hurt him."

Joshua cringed with Jason's fingers biting into his shoulder. A small cry broke from him.

"I would never want to be accused of not acceding to a lady's request." That curl of his lip grew. "But then you're not a lady, are you?"

Rachel couldn't keep her helpless sob contained. Jason jabbed the muzzle harder against Joshua, tilting the boy's head to the right. Joshua's pained cry cut across her heart with the intensity of a mortal wound.

"You're not a lady, *are you?*"

Harrison's voice rang in her head, insisting she was every inch the lady, even as she managed a broken, "No."

Jason shoved Joshua toward her. As quickly as she could, Rachel gathered him into her arms and shoved him behind her at the same time, using her body as a shield. Joshua clung to her and she whispered, "You're all right."

The clicking of the hammer easing down gave her some strength. She straightened, keeping Joshua behind her, and forced herself to meet Jason's gaze. "If you leave now, no one will know you've been here. I promise, we won't say anything."

"Why would I want to leave such a scene of domestic bliss and tranquility?" His laugh was the ugliest sound she had ever heard. "We're going to wait here until after dark."

Rachel looked down into Joshua's terrified face. "Go to your room."

"No." Jason gestured with the muzzle of the revolver. "I want my son to sit right at that table."

Rachel's heart sank. Joshua didn't move. "You ain't my pa."

Jason's features tightened and mottled shades of red and purple colored his face. She moved even further in front of her son, and braced herself for Jason's explosion. His gaze darted from her face to the child cowering behind her and he rubbed his thumb over his lower lip.

"Now, darlin', just what lies have you been telling my boy?"

Her stomach knotted and the bile rose in the back of her throat. To hear Jason use that endearment in the same drawl and with the same inflection as Harrison made her physically ill.

"You *ain't* my pa," Joshua repeated. "Tell him, Momma."

"Hush." Rachel wrapped an arm behind her, enveloping him and pressing him closer to her even as she withdrew a step.

"You need to start being honest with my son, darlin'."

Rachel clenched her jaw with the endearment. Jason must have noticed her reaction because a renewed smile crossed his face. He closed the distance between them, faster than Rachel could back away. His hand shot out, catching her jaw in a painful vise. Even though she trembled from head to toe, she still forced herself to meet his gaze.

"You don't like it when I call you that? Because he calls you that?"

Jason leaned so close to her she could see the black flecking in the dark, dark brown of his eyes. His breath was rancid, coated with the stench of beer. No longer built like a bull bison, now so lean he was nearly skeletal, there still was terrifying strength in his hand.

"When Harrison says that, I know he means it."

"Yeah, ever the honorable one, that brother of mine, except when he turned his back on his country and enlisted with the Union forces." Jason's grip tightened on her jaw and he twisted her head up. "I was raised with the same devotion to keeping my word. I promised you a long time ago that I'd be back to finish what I started." A leer crossed his face. "'Course, I'm not real strong on being sweet when I want something. But, you already know that, don't you, *darlin'*?"

He released her with a snarl. Rachel gulped in a breath and sagged forward.

"Tell that boy to sit down at the table or I'm going to get angry. You know what happens when I get angry." He gestured to the table with his gun. "I told him to do something and if he won't do it, I'm going to have to teach my son the manners you haven't taught him."

Rachel took a step away from Joshua. "Do as he says, Josh. Go sit down."

Joshua had just settled into the chair when a loud knock on the door startled all three of them. Jason immediately brought the revolver up and pointed at her son's head. Ben shouted through the door, "Rachel, it's me."

"One word, and I blow a hole clean through his head," Jason promised.

"If I don't answer the door, Ben will know something is wrong." Rachel looked over her shoulder into the jail. "I'll tell him everything is fine and send him on his way."

Jason shook his head. "I have a better idea." He pulled Joshua from the chair and pressed the muzzle to the boy's temple again. "Bring him in here. One wrong word, and the boy dies."

Rachel nodded her understanding. She tried to compose herself on the short walk from the living area to the door. Her hand shook as she twisted the lock and then pulled the door open. She plastered a smile on her face when the door opened enough for her to see Ben's face.

"Supper's almost ready. Are you joining us?"

Her tone of voice was too bright, the words sharp.

Ben's brow shot up and his line of sight darted past her toward the living area. "No, I don't think I will tonight."

Her hand shot out and grabbed his wrist. "Please. Stay. You've been a stranger for the last couple of days." She pulled his arm, as much as to stop him from leaving as to tug him into the jail.

Ben relented and walked into the office area. Rachel quickly shut the door and twisted the lock. Before she moved away from the door, Ben's curse sounded. "What the hell is this?"

"Ben, I'm sorry."

The foreman twisted his head over his shoulder. "Don't think you're the one who's got anything to be apologizing for."

The arm draped over her son's shoulder and down his chest would appear almost paternal, were it not for the heavy revolver pressing into Joshua's skull. "Get a set of those wrist shackles and shackle him to the bed in one of the cells." Jason tipped his head into a cell. "Get in there, Hauser."

Without any argument, Ben strode into an open cell and sat on the bed.

Rachel clamped one side of the shackles to one of Ben's wrists and started to clamp the other end to the metal frame bolted to the wall.

"No," Jason said. "Through the frame and around both wrists."

Again, Rachel said, "I'm sorry," to the foreman. Her hands shook as she closed the second cuff around Ben's wrist. She pressed the key into his palm and didn't dare make eye contact. As she straightened she hoped the flare of her dress would hide Ben's attempt to further secret the key away.

"Sit down against that back wall," Jason said. Wordless, Rachel slid down the wall. What little hope she had that so far Jason hadn't noticed the missing key was crushed with her rising panic and terror. Jason shoved Joshua into the cell. "Go sit next to your mother."

Rachel pulled her son into her embrace, holding him tightly, trying to calm him. Jason leaned against the bars, his gun pointing at her. "You sure that boy's mine? He doesn't look anything like me."

Rachel dipped her head, thanking God that her son looked nothing like Jason.

"What's your brother's role in all of this?" Ben pulled against the shackles as he asked the question, as if testing the strength of the metal.

"He gets to die for her." Jason gestured with the revolver at Rachel. "What do you think, Hauser? Should I let her watch him die before I kill her, or just kill the bitch and then kill him when he comes for her?"

Rachel hugged Joshua more tightly to her, the side of her face pressed to the top of his head. She screwed her eyes shut. She was not going to cry. She was not going to give Jason the satisfaction.

"I'm sorry, Rachel. I was wrong about him."

Ben's apology almost shattered her tenuous self-control. She forced herself to draw a gulping breath and clenched her jaw to keep a frightened cry contained. She had no idea how long Jason held her and Joshua at gun point. The light through the windows grew fainter and before the jail was plunged into darkness, Jason lit a single lantern. Some time later, Joshua squirmed against her and whispered, "I have to go to the outhouse."

Jason must have heard him because he shook his head. "You're not going outside."

"He's a child, Jason." Rachel nudged her head toward the living area. "There's a chamber pot in his room."

"Hurry up, then," Jason said, gesturing with the gun to the other room. "Don't think about sneaking out a window and going for help. If you're not back here in five minutes, I'll kill your mother."

When Joshua returned, Jason caught him and draped an arm over his shoulders and pressed the muzzle once again to the boy's head. "Go get a chair, Rachel, and find some rope."

"There isn't any rope in here." She forced stiff muscles to move and stood.

"You've got bed sheets. Tear one of those up." Jason finally moved the gun away from her son's head, using it to gesture to the living area of the jail. "Hurry up."

Rachel brought a chair into the cell. The low shriek of the fabric rending as she tore the bed sheet into long strips skittered across her as painfully as the feel of stinging nettle on bare skin. With his arm still around Joshua, Jason frog-stepped the boy to the chair and pushed him onto the seat. "Tie him up. Hands behind the chair, each ankle to a leg, and his arms to the back. Make sure he's tied up tight because I'm watching. If you don't, I put a bullet into his head, right here. Right in front of you."

To emphasize his point, Jason pushed the muzzle against the back of Joshua's head. Rachel was unable to stop the few tears that trickled down her cheeks.

"It's okay, Momma," Joshua said. His attempted bravery hurt her as deeply as any physical pain ever had.

She tied Joshua as ordered and then faced their captor. "Now, what?"

He bent and tossed a strip to her. "Gag both of them."

She shook her head. "Please, don't make—"

Jason grabbed the thin pillow off the bunk near Ben and wrapped it around the revolver. He fired, the pillow muffling the bark of the gun, and a chunk of the wall over Ben's shoulder fell onto the thin mattress. "The next shot will be a gut shot. Gag them both or watch Hauser and your son die very slowly."

Rachel bent to pick up the cloth, the slow spiral of a feather from the pillow to the floor holding her attention for a few seconds. She didn't apologize to Ben this time as she gagged him. When she tied the gag on Joshua she felt as if she was choking on her own tears. She caught his head between her hands and kissed his crown. "I love you," she managed to whisper.

Ben's unintelligible, garbled words alerted her that Jason was right behind her. When he grabbed her arm at the elbow, she didn't resist. Her son's life and Ben's life were still in her hands. The cold metal closing on her wrists behind her back ratcheted up her fear with each click of the shackles contracting. An uncontrollable shudder of terror convulsed her.

Jason dragged her to the door of the cell. "Anything else you want to tell them before we leave?"

Leave? Where on earth did he think he could go that he wouldn't be recognized in this town? Even with his hair nearly all gray, thin to the point of being skeletal, he was still easy to recognize.

Realizing she had spent precious moments trying to understand where Jason was taking her, Rachel blurted out, "Tell Harrison I love him." A new sob broke from her. She'd never told him that herself. She never would be able to, either, now.

"Touching," Jason muttered. "I have a message for him, too. Tell him I've always had a hankering to see Rachel Falls."

****

Harrison slowly became aware of his surroundings. He was freezing. His greatcoat was gone, as was his frock coat, his holster—not that it did him a lot of good without his Peacemaker—and his boots. He stood and smacked his head on the low ceiling. A curse broke from him. The tiniest amount of light seeped into the confining area. By stretching his arms out, he was able to determine where he was being held wasn't as wide as his arm span.

He stumbled to the black wall where the light seeped in. This wasn't brick. It was metal. Harrison pounded on the door, shouting for anyone to hear. He yelled until he was hoarse and beat on the metal until his fists were aching and he assumed bruised.

Dejected, he made his way to a back corner and slid down the wall. At least the physical activity had warmed him up, but now the cold from the stone floor was seeping into him again. He watched the miniscule thread of light fade into blackness.

He brought Rachel to his memory. Even if he was stuck here, Ben was looking out for her. She wasn't totally without protection. And, she was right about most everyone in town helping to keep a lookout for

Jason.

With no manner to keep track of the time, he wasn't sure how long he had been sitting in the corner, arms wrapped around his knees in an effort to keep warm, when a key grated into the lock. He was so cold he couldn't make himself stand when the door slid to a side.

Bostick stood in the corridor with Powell and Fuller. Both guards held a lantern. Harrison ducked his head away from the harsh light flooding the near complete darkness of the cell.

"Marshal, I have to offer you an apology."

With deliberation, unwilling to let this man see his struggle, Harrison used the walls to help him gain his feet. As his eyes became accustomed to the light, he noted Fuller held all his personal belongings. "I will assume by that I'm free to go."

Bostick nodded. "It appears, for whatever reason, you and I have been the victims of an elaborate hoax."

Harrison grabbed his frock coat from Fuller and pulled it on. Before he stomped into his boots, he pulled his greatcoat on. His badge was neatly pinned to the coat, right where he had worn it earlier that day. At least, he assumed it had been that day. "Would you care to elaborate on that, Warden? And, where in the hell is my gun?"

The warden reared back with Harrison's curse but with a deep breath, the man smoothed his features into a calm mask. "In my office. If you'll follow me there, I'll elaborate."

Though he had had enough of Bostick and the man's arrogance, Harrison knew if he wanted out of the prison he was going to have to dance to the warden's tune for a bit longer. "After you."

Fuller and Powell took the lead. The silence within the depths of the brick walls was beyond unnerving. He knew most penitentiaries had rules forbidding prisoners to speak to one another, but this silence went well beyond that. The miasma of fear and desperation clung to the stone as thick as moss.

"Three days ago, I was sent a telegram by someone I assumed to be you. I was informed that someone had stolen your badge and would arrive here, posing as you in an attempt to free Wallace." Bostick spoke as if it was Harrison's fault he had been duped. "When you arrived, I immediately assumed you were an imposter."

They navigated a corner and the light of the warden's office spilled onto the brick floor of the hall. Harrison bit his tongue to keep any comment about making assumptions corralled.

"What I couldn't understand was why Wallace. He has less than a month on his sentence. Why risk escape and being caught and having more time added to his penalty?" Bostick halted outside his office and gestured for Harrison to enter. "Mr. Fuller, please get the marshal's horse from the stables."

Harrison walked into the office. His hat, gun, and holster were on the seat of the chair he'd been in earlier. Without a word to the warden, he picked up the holster and strapped it on, then bent to tie it down around his thigh. That task completed he asked, "What changed your mind?"

"Several things." Bostick closed the door and crossed the floor to the stove. "Tea, Marshal?"

"No, thank you." He shoved his gloves into the depths of a pocket of his greatcoat. "I just want that rented nag brought up so I can get back to Laramie City, get on the next train out of here, and go home to my wife."

"Understandable." The warden poured a cup of steaming water into a cup, then carefully measured a spoon of tea into a steeper and dropped it into the cup. "The next train west doesn't leave until tomorrow afternoon."

"I'm not going west. Federal is east of here." As soon as the words came out of his mouth, Harrison realized his direction of travel had been a final test from Bostick to prove his identity. The warden picked up his cup and with a barely perceptible nod agreed as to the direction in which Federal lay.

"So, what else changed your mind?"

"I deeply questioned why anyone would bother with Wallace. He's a failure at everything he has attempted, including train robbery. When I questioned him, he swore he knew nothing about a planned attempt to release him early." The warden lifted the steeping ball from the cup and delicately spooned sugar into the brew. "I also telegraphed Mr. White and the U.S. Marshal in Denver. Mr. White verified you had received that telegram you gave me the night before. The marshal in Denver vouched for you, and verified your middle name and even a physical description. The Kentucky drawl was the final proof. The east bound train leaves at nine in the morning."

Harrison sent a silent prayer of thanks heavenward that he'd known Federal Marshal Warren Hagstrom for better than a decade and the man took great delight in mimicking his Kentucky drawl. "Thank you."

"I can recommend either the hotel at the depot or

the Rawlins' House for overnight lodging." Bostick took a long sip from his tea.

"The hotel at the depot is fine with me. It's closer to the train out of here," Harrison said as Fuller entered the office. Not giving the guard a chance to say anything, Harrison added, "Warden, I hope I never have to come back here, for any reason."

He clamped his hat on his head and walked from the prison.

Chapter Seventeen

Defeat hammered down on Rachel so fiercely even her bones felt pummeled. Not a soul had been on the streets when Jason pulled her gagged and shackled from the jail. Families were sitting down to supper and it was too early for the men who might frequent the saloons to arrive. A blanket tossed over her head and shoulders, a solicitous arm around her shoulder as if she wasn't feeling well, and she became a stranger passing through town with a drifter. The blanket also hid from sight the revolver digging into her ribs.

Forced to ride in front of Jason with that blanket over her head and subsequently also blindfolded, she spent the time planning just how she was going to kill him. Kill him for the terror he had inflicted on Joshua. Kill him for the helplessness on Ben's face. Kill him for the pain she was certain her capture was going to inflict on Harrison. Kill him for making her father into a murderer and an attempted murderer. As the list of reasons to kill him grew, her method of ending his life became more prolonged. She promised herself that every hurt he had ever inflicted on her, on her loved ones, would be repaid tenfold. If she could have laughed at the ludicrousness of her bravado, she would have.

The horse stopped. Jason's weight shifted behind her and he pulled her from the horse. Off-balance without her sight or the ability to use her hands she fell heavily to the ground. Gravel bit into her hip and shoulder. The gag hadn't prevented her biting her tongue with the jarring halt. She refused to give him the satisfaction of hearing her cry.

He grabbed her upper arm and dragged her to her feet. Rachel stumbled at his side, struggling to keep upright. She was almost certain they weren't anywhere near either Sagebrush Creek or the falls. There wasn't the sound of water tumbling over rocks or gurgling through the streambed. The earth near the creek had its own scent: moist earth and mosses, the air heavily laced with pine and the musky, tannic scent of the aspens.

The sound of his footstep on a wooden structure drove a new blade of terror into her. She twisted around, trying to pull free. Where she could run blindfolded with her hands shackled behind her she didn't know, but she wasn't letting him drag her into a building. He would have to kill her before she'd ever submit to him again. She couldn't hit him, she couldn't bite him, but she could kick and she aimed a kick where she thought he was.

All Rachel did was succeed in throwing herself off balance again and only his punishing grip on her elbow kept her from falling on her face.

"Stop being coy, darlin'." The taunt in his voice twisted the blade. "We'll get to that soon enough."

She screamed against the gag. Jason's hand fisted in the hair at the back of her head and his voice hissed against her ear. "Stop fighting with me. You're going to upset Tommy."

*Tommy?*

"Why did you bring Rachel here?" The voice of

her neighbor, eerie and sounding more slurred and confused than usual, reached her. Jason had brought her to the Crazy TG, the home she, and Royce, and Ben, and Drake had all protected from dishonest homesteaders attempting to file a claim on the ranch. How many times had she ridden to this small home to visit with Tommy after Jake vanished, to make sure he was eating properly, and taking care of himself? Rachel screamed Tommy's name but all she emitted was a garbled cry of betrayal and anger.

Jason's fist twisted more firmly in her hair, pinching and ripping against her scalp.

"Because the man who killed your brother will come to get her." Jason's voice had a softer cadence to it, as if he was trying to carefully explain something to a child. In a real sense, Rachel knew, Tommy was still a child, despite being five or six years older than she.

"But, he's the man who made her smile again." A heavy measured tread echoed on the boards. "Why would he kill Jake?"

Another set of hands closed on her and she was lifted into the air by her arm. A cry of pain she couldn't halt broke from her. She was dropped but that second set of hands kept her from falling completely down. Both men forced her into the house—the sound of their combined footsteps changed when they crossed the threshold.

"I told you why he killed Jake. Rachel wouldn't believe me but he wants to kill her, too. He wants her land."

Rachel shook her head in violent protest even as she was forced into a chair. A hand touched the back of her head and she jerked away. The knots in her stomach were painful, and grew to fill her chest.

"Don't be scared," Tommy said. He drew a hand down the back of her head. "Jason only wants to help."

Sweet, gullible, and simple-minded Tommy, incapable of book learning… The hand he ran down the back of her head felt as if he was trying to calm her. How often had she seen him calm a terrified animal in the same manner? The vivid recollection of Tommy kneeling next to a colicky horse, stroking the animal's sweated neck to quiet it before he managed to get the animal onto its feet and walk the belly-ache out flooded her mind.

"Did you do what I told you?" Jason sounded as if he was on the other side of the room.

"Yes." There was a long pause. "I don't like to lie. Telling lies is wrong."

"I told you that sometimes, something bad has to be done to make something good happen." A metal object of some sort dropped onto what sounded like the stove. "Rather like when the people in this little town said what Rachel did was a bad thing. But, now she has Joshua because of that bad thing. He's a good thing, isn't he?"

Rachel choked on the angry sob the gag wouldn't let her release. How dare he?

"Rachel said you did the bad thing." A hint of revolt colored Tommy's voice.

Jason's laugh sounded so much like his brother's that her heart felt ripped into pieces. "Tommy, when women do the bad thing and find themselves in a delicate condition, they almost always blame the man and say he did the bad thing. Now, did you take your medicine today?"

"Yes." Again that hint of rebellion. "I don't like taking it. It makes me feel funny."

Footsteps sounded. "I know. But, if you don't take it, you know what happens. Things that don't belong to you burn, and when you don't take it you get sick, too."

Tears burned against the blindfold with Tommy's almost inaudible whisper, "I know. I'm sorry, Rachel. Your house was so pretty."

"I'm sure she forgives you. Now, help me a little more and get something for Rachel to drink."

The blindfold was pulled up and off, ripping hair with it. Her scalp twinged. She blinked, the bright lantern light burning her eyes. Jason bent over her, the leer on his face further chilling her. "He's such a good helper. I couldn't have done all of this without Tommy's help. Hiding me here for the last several years, helping me deliver love notes to you, and the whole time keeping it a secret." He cupped her face, his thumb digging painfully into the underside of her jaw. "Tomorrow you and I are going to Rachel Falls. If Tommy and I did this right, that very bad man who killed Jake will be on the morning train from Laramie City."

In what she knew was a total show for Tommy, Jason leaned even closer to her and the pressure of his thumb under her jaw increased. The bile rose into the back of her throat with the feel of his lips against her forehead.

"I'm going to take the gag off if you promise to behave. No screaming and no lies to Tommy. He's so easily confused."

Rachel nodded, wincing as each movement of her head made the pain of his thumb in the underside of her jaw increase. Jason untied the gag and she gulped in a deep breath.

Jason straightened and took the cup of water Tommy held out. "Get your medicine and put some in her water."

Rachel shook her head, afraid to speak for fear Jason would gag her again.

"Why are you giving her my medicine?" There was more than a hint of rebellion in Tommy's voice now.

"Do you remember how sleepy it made you when you first started taking it? Rachel is afraid to sleep and look at how tired she is." The solicitousness in his voice was patently false but it convinced Tommy because he tilted a small, dark amber bottle over the cup.

Jason held the highly-doctored water to Rachel's lips. She twisted her head away. "I won't drink it." She ground the words out through compressed lips.

He leaned into her, his tongue brushing against her ear, the cup still at her mouth. Rachel couldn't suppress a shudder.

"Yes, you will or I'll just turn around and shoot him." His teeth closed painfully on the outside edge of her ear. "Drink it or he dies."

The tears she fought to keep at bay slipped down her face as she gulped down the bitter water.

****

Harrison leaped off the train before it came to a complete stop. He tossed a quick sweeping glance up the street. Not even noon and already several horses were tied outside both The Thirsty Dog and The Golden Eagle. He let a half-smile cross his face as he wondered if Ben and Silas had liberated any doves in the last few days. One day, and probably soon, he was going to

239

have to figure out what to do about that, because he'd already gotten an earful from Dan Sanders at The Golden Eagle. There had to be some legal manner to keep Sanders from getting those girls.

He tugged his gloves on, raised up the collar of the great coat, and shouldered his saddle bag. The blacksmith stopped pounding out a horseshoe long enough to wave when Harrison walked past. On the other end of town, the bell at St. Margaret's rang out the noon hour. He passed Gabe McKinnon's office, but the attorney wasn't in. Harrison made a mental note to talk to McKinnon in the next day or so about the situation at The Golden Eagle.

A short walk up Washington Street brought him to Federal Avenue and the marshal's office. He tried the door, relieved it was locked. With only one key, he left that with Rachel. He added another activity to his growing list of things he had to do. He had to get a locksmith into town to replace the locks on the jail and manufacture more than one key.

"Rachel, I'm back," he said, rapping on the glass at the same time. What felt like several long minutes passed without the door opening, though when he pressed his ear to the glass, he thought he heard someone inside.

He rapped on the glass again.

"Marshal, I'm glad to see you."

Harrison twisted his head to the side. Miss Perry, the young school marm, walked in a brisk manner toward him. She was a handsome woman and both he and Rachel had speculated how long it would be before one of the local bachelors started sparking her and the town would have to hire another teacher. He dipped his head in greeting. "Is there something I can help you with?"

"Joshua didn't come to school today." The teacher tugged her shawl more tightly around her shoulders when the wind gusted. "I sent one of the older children here to see if he was ill, and Clara said no one answered when she knocked on the door."

"Rachel probably didn't hear her knock. If Josh didn't come to school today, it's probably because he's ill and if she's with him in the back room, it would be hard to hear a child's knock on the door." It was a lot of "ifs", and a sense of unease settled into his gut.

"That's probably it," she said. "I must return to my students. Please let me know later how Joshua is feeling."

"Yes, ma'am, I will do that." *If I can get into the damn building*, he thought but didn't add.

A loud "clang" sounded from inside. Harrison rattled the door knob and rapped as hard as he could on the door when the clang repeated. Still no one unlocked the door. He pulled his revolver from the holster.

The cylinder fit into his hand and he used the grip to break the glass. He flipped the heavy Colt around and reached through the broken pane to unlock the door. The revolver led his way into the jail. He came to a halt, his mouth dropping open at the scene in a closed cell.

Joshua was confined in a chair, that chair tipped over on its side. Ben was shackled to the metal bed frame. Both were gagged and at that moment, the foreman was pulling futilely against the metal wrist shackles.

"Rachel!" Harrison shouted her name, hoping

against hope for her answer.

The foreman's struggles to free himself ceased as he shook his head. Harrison's gut twisted, dropped somewhere to the vicinity of his boot soles, and drawing a breath was an impossibility. He crossed the jail at a dead run and took hold of the door. The hard clang when he pulled on it repeated the sound he'd heard outside.

He bolted to the desk and jerked open the center drawer. The keys should have been in there. The instant heavy weight of combined fear, panic and a growing rage pressing down on his chest forced a growl. The drawer was pulled out completely and tipped upside down on the desk. A quick swipe through the sparse contents revealed what he already knew. The keys were gone.

There was only one way to open the cell. Harrison pushed the muzzle of his revolver against the locking mechanism of the door and stepped to the side. "Ben, can you pull Joshua closer to you?"

He didn't want metal shards hitting the child when he shot.

The foreman nodded and stretched his legs as far as he could and hooked a foot around a leg of the chair. Sweat broke out on his forehead as he fought to pull the boy out of the potential line of fire.

"That's good enough. Josh, keep your face turned away from the door.' Harrison lined up where the bullet might go after he fired and angled the muzzle slightly higher to the ceiling. He hesitated a second when Ben lurched as close as he could to Joshua within the limits of the shackles and lifted his legs onto the chair back to protect the boy's head.

Harrison spared a tight nod to the foreman and pulled the trigger. The sound of the shot in the jail rang, vibrating through the bars on the cell. The shattered lock released with Harrison's hard tug on the door. He holstered his revolver and entered the cell.

Joshua was his first priority. He righted the chair and pulled the gag down, deciding in an instant not to mention the odor of urine that clung to the boy. "Are you all right?"

The boy wouldn't meet his eye. "I had to use the outhouse during the night. I couldn't get loose and I—"

"It's okay, Josh. It's understandable." Harrison tugged on the bindings around the boy's wrists. The knots weren't giving. He stripped off his gloves, dropping them to the floor, and tried again to untie the knots. There was still not an iota of give. "I'll be right back. I need to find a knife."

Ben's garbled protest halted him. Harrison paused and shook his head. "I should leave you gagged. At least you're not locking horns with me," he said, even as he pulled the material down around the foreman's neck.

"Jason's got Rachel. He said he's taking her to the falls."

"Until I get the two of you freed, I can't do much about that." He welcomed the rage surging through him. Anything other than the chilling, sickening panic. This time he wasn't going to force that unreasoning, destructive beast into retreat.

Once Joshua was cut loose, Harrison dropped to his knees and pulled him into his arms. For the space of a heartbeat, the boy remained stiff in his embrace. Then as if a dam broke, Joshua crumbled against him, sobbing. "He said he was my pa. It ain't true. He ain't. He ain't. My pa would never hurt Momma."

He pressed Joshua's head to his shoulder, not knowing what to say and met Ben's eyes over the child's shaking shoulder. The foreman lowered his gaze to the floor. At length, Harrison gently pushed Joshua out to arm's length. "I will bring your mother home, but first I have to get Ben out of those shackles."

Joshua sniffled and wiped his nose with his shirt sleeve, then rubbed dry the tears hanging from his lashes. His eyes, so much like his mother's, darkened when his sight latched onto the U.S. Marshal's star on the great coat. "Does that badge mean you can kill him?"

"No." Harrison sucked in a long breath. "All that does is allow me to arrest him. I can't kill him unless he tries to kill me."

The boy's stormy gaze rose. "He hurt Momma."

"And, as much as I want to kill him for that, my badge doesn't give me that right. Why don't you go get washed up and get some clean clothes on?" Harrison stood. He waited until Joshua went into the other area of the jail building, then pulled his gun from the holster and walked to Ben.

"What the hell are you doing?" Ben recoiled as far as he could and brought his foot up as if to kick Harrison away.

"The keys are all gone. I've got to shoot those—"

"*No!*" Ben shook his head. "When Jason made Rachel shackle me to this damn thing, she managed to hide the key in her hand. She got it to me, but I dropped it. It's under the bed."

Harrison reached under the bed and swept his hand

across the floor. He found the key, covered with cobwebs. With more force than necessary, he shoved the key into the shackle attached to Ben's left wrist and twisted it, unlocking the iron restraint. Bruises were already forming around Hauser's wrists from his desperate though wholly futile attempt to break free. A hesitation on Harrison's part caused Ben to grab the key from his hand.

"Are you really just going to arrest that bastard?" Ben asked as he twisted the key in the shackle encircling his other wrist. "Because if you are, you might want to take these with you."

Harrison paused in the doorway, his hand tightening on a bar of the cell. The shattered glass in the entrance door of the jail drew his gaze. "He'll draw first." He lowered his head, reining in the anger searing him. "Stay with Joshua, please. He's probably hungry and thirsty and he's scared."

"I'll bet she is, too."

The tautness in Hauser's voice tilted Harrison's head a degree to the side. He held his silence as he walked from the cell to the desk. The drawer on the lower right side held the ammunition for his Colt. The cylinder flipped open and methodically, he reloaded.

His hand was on the door knob when Ben spoke, stopping him.

"Before Jason took her out of here, Rachel asked me to tell you—"

He craned his head over his shoulder and Ben fell silent. Harrison said, softly, "She can tell me herself. I will bring her back. Alive."

Chapter Eighteen

Sounds began to register…the clomping of a horse's hooves in an unsteady rhythm against the ground, the labored breathing of that horse, the angry chattering and scolding of squirrels, the gurgle of water to her right, the hissing of gravel over gravel when the horse stumbled and slid… Rachel couldn't hold her head up and she felt herself slipping again into the black oblivion Tommy's medicine induced.

She tried to fight the darkness. Tried to focus on what she could sense without alerting Jason she was awake. Blindfolded, but not in total darkness, she could see a thin sliver of the landscape under the bottom edge of the cloth. The squirrels wouldn't be scolding at night. The horse was a mousy buckskin, with white and gray strands in its black mane. Gagged again, but this time with fabric of some kind stuffed into her mouth and held tightly in place with a thin strip of material that bit into the corners of her mouth and her cheeks. The weave of the cloth rubbed harsh against her tongue and tasted metallic. Still shackled. The memory of Jason swallowing the key before he had taken her from Federal made her stomach churn. The scent of rain—or was it snow?—heightened the sharp tang of pine and the earthy odor of the aspens. Cold air touched her face and the opened throat of her dress…her stomach twisted. The bodice gapped to her waist.

A shiver that had nothing to do with the cold rippled across her and she couldn't contain a choked, soft cry.

"You are awake, darlin'."

She wanted to scream at him to stop using that endearment but couldn't. And even if she asked him to stop, it wouldn't change how he taunted her with it. Once he knew that it was almost a physical hurt, he'd used that word as a finely-honed blade to slice across her heart.

His fingers bit into the back of her skull, pulling her hair, forcing her head over her shoulder and his mouth closed over hers in a bruising manner. Her stomach lurched and she shoved her shoulder against him. If she vomited with the gag...

"There's my little hell-cat." He sounded amused. "I missed that last night."

She struggled to remember but after he forced her to drink the bitter brew, nothing was clear. It was difficult to remember anything after that vile drink. She shook her head, not even sure what she was negating.

"No sense denying it." The amusement became a cruel taunt. He pulled her head further back and his teeth bit into the side of her throat. "I much prefer the fight."

Don't respond. Don't move. Don't make a sound. Don't give him the satisfaction.

"Shall I tell you what I have planned for us after I've killed that bastard she tried to pass off as my father's son? Or should I tell you why I'm going to kill him?"

Her skin crawled with the deceptively gentle brush of his fingers against her throat.

"He's dead because he touched what's mine. Twin Creeks is mine, but my father decided that her bastard was better suited to be the owner." Jason's fingers tightened on her throat. "And he dared to lay a hand on you...what a whore you've become." His fingers continued to tighten and black spots peppered the minimal light penetrating the blindfold. Rachel thrashed, trying to break his hold. His other hand closed around her throat, choking her further.

"You know what happens when you humiliate me. Spreading your legs for him, letting him have you. When I'm done with you this time, you'll beg me to kill you."

He released the pressure. She tried to suck in a deep breath into her burning lungs but the gag prevented it. His chest pressed into her back and his harsh whisper sounded in her ear. "How fitting that I chose this place, don't you think? Such an idyllic spot for a seduction. Oh, but I forgot to bring a picnic and a blanket. That's all right, isn't it? We're going to be too busy to eat."

Sick with terror, she slumped forward. Would God forgive her if she threw herself off the side of the shelf extending over the pool and aimed her head into a granite boulder? Everything she had been taught, every Catechism lesson had said God would not forgive the taking of one's own life.

A prayer to the Virgin Mary she had often whispered in the throes of homesickness entered her memory and she latched onto those words promising the intercession of the Mother of God in an attempt to make her terror ebb.

She didn't want to die. Her son needed her. She

was not going to die. Not today. Not tomorrow. Harrison would come for her. If Jason was intent on killing her, she was not going to make it easy for him. Perhaps, God would forgive her if she somehow managed to kill him.

The horse stopped and without warning, Jason pushed her from its back. Rachel landed awkwardly, her upper arm crashing against a large rock half-buried in the gritty soil. The gag muted her deep scream of pain with the bone breaking and she struggled to hold onto consciousness.

Jason grabbed her other arm and pulled her to her feet. Another scream was muffled and her knees buckled. To her horror, she started retching.

The blindfold was pulled off and then the gag, just as her stomach emptied. Jason released her as if scalded. Her knees gave out and she dropped, racked with dry heaves. The pain in her arm left her dizzy and nauseated. Unable to catch her breath, she folded closer to the ground.

The gritty soil crunched as he rounded her and came to a stop in front of her. "Time for your gag, darlin'."

"Please, don't. I can't breathe with it and if I vomit again, I'll choke." Even as she pleaded with him, self-loathing for her weakness ignited in her, more caustic than the bile still burning at the back of her throat. "I don't want to die. Please, I don't want to die."

His hand closed on the top of her head, forcing her to look up at him. "We can't have that. You're not allowed to die until I'm done with you."

"My son—" She tried for another manner to appeal to any empathy Jason might have. "Our son needs me."

Still holding her hair, Jason bent over her. "My son would be better off dead than living with a whore like you as his mother. My son is dead. He and Hauser both. Poor Tommy thinks he set another fire."

Her baby, her sweet and beautiful little boy…A pain so searing, so intense it should have killed her on the spot ripped into her chest, clenching around her heart. Her fear and her pain and her anger broke free on an enraged shriek.

\*\*\*\*

Harrison drove his spurs into Demon's sides and slashed him with the ends of the reins. Sweat rolled off the stallion, despite the cold mist that had settled across the land. He knew he wasn't far behind Jason because the small stream that had to be crossed to reach the path along Sagebrush Creek and up to the falls was still clouded where Jason's horse had crossed. As the horse struggled up the bank Harrison knew he had to let the black slow down or he risked killing him. Not even the incredible stamina on the Arabian side of his pedigree could withstand the grueling pace.

The wind carried a faint, almost inaudible keening cry.

"I'm sorry, Demon." There was nothing to be done for it but risk the stallion. He put his spurs into the horse again.

When he reached the point on the trail where he had to continue on foot, Jason's horse—another raw-boned buckskin as Duke had been—was on its side, heaving its life away. The animal's front knees were skinned where it had apparently slipped in the loose gravel. Its hip bones and ribs were clearly visible and the trek up the mountainside under two riders had been too much for it. Under any other circumstance, Harrison would have put a bullet into its head to put it out of its misery. He couldn't spare the time and was not going to alert Jason to how close he was.

Harrison scrambled over a newly fallen aspen blocking the foot path to the pool A glance back revealed Demon was still standing, though he was breathing hard, a deep rattle at the bottom of each exhaled breath. In the short time from when he swung off Demon to climbing over the new obstacle on the footpath, the mist had thickened to a clinging, frigid fog that was coating everything with a thin veneer of ice.

About to edge around a massive, moss-covered boulder, Harrison ducked back behind it. Jason and Rachel were less than fifteen feet from him and almost to the pool. Their forms were shadowy and indistinct with the swirling, freezing fog and the deepening gloom of approaching night. He only had one chance to get this right. If he shot Jason in the back, there would be questions. Yet, if he confronted him, there was the real possibility Jason would use Rachel as a shield, or worse—shoot her.

Mind made up, Harrison pulled his revolver from the holster, stepped out from behind the boulder, and drew aim. He immediately lowered the gun. The fog at the pool was so heavy he couldn't make out a clear target and he wasn't sure if he could discern which figure was either Rachel or Jason. He crept closer, praying the same thick fog created by the heated waters of the pool would cover his approach as well as it hindered his ability to get a clear shot.

What he could see as he moved nearer was that Jason stood on the overhang over the natural pool, with

Rachel closest to the edge. Jason shook her like a rag-doll and she was fighting a losing battle to keep from being pushed any further backward.

Harrison pulled his gun up again, aiming for Jason's back, between his shoulder blades. The revolver was perfectly steady in his hand as he pulled the trigger. Jason's head snapped back in nearly the same instant the loud percussion of the Colt firing sounded. He still held the bodice of Rachel's dress and his head twisted over his shoulder. Across the short distance, Jason's grimace was visible and he shoved Rachel backward.

She disappeared over the edge and Jason staggered around to face him.

"Rachel!" Harrison broke into a run, skidding to a halt as Jason pulled his gun and brought it up and pointed. A bubble of blood, black in the last watery light of the gloomy day, broke at Jason's mouth and he fell to his knees.

"She was mine," Jason rasped. The gun wavered as he struggled to pull the hammer to cock the gun. "Mine…"

Before Jason could jack the hammer back, Harrison brought his Colt up and fired again, hitting Jason squarely in the chest. "She was never yours," he said.

He halted at the very edge of the overhang and stripped off his greatcoat as he scanned the pool. The surface was obscured with the dense steam and what ripples there were came from the water spilling over the falls. He couldn't see her. She hadn't surfaced. He dove into the warm depths, searching. His hand brushed against long strands of something silky—her hair. He grabbed a fistful, pulling her unmoving form closer to him and into his arms even as he swam as hard as he could to the surface.

His head broke the water. Rachel was limp in his arms. He pushed her to the wall of the pool and onto a smaller ledge just out of the water. She wasn't breathing. A deep cut was almost hidden in her hairline at her temple.

"Rachel, no. You can't leave me." He ripped off the gag. He pushed on her chest to try to force the water from her lungs. "Don't do this, Rachel."

Her eyes flew open and she gulped in a deep breath that immediately became a cough. Harrison pulled her up into him, holding her as if afraid she was going to fade away into the thick fog. For only the second time that he could ever remember, he broke down in tears.

"My arm…stop…please." Her voice was muffled against him.

Harrison eased his hold on her but didn't release her. He lightly brushed his fingertips over the bruises on her jaw, her cheek, and her throat. When he drew his hands down her arms, she cringed and a thin cry of pain broke from her.

"It's broken," she managed. Her voice broke. "He killed Joshua and Ben. He killed my baby."

He caught her face between his hands. "No! Joshua is fine. It was just a lie to hurt you as much as he could. Joshua is fine. So is Ben."

Her face crumbled with the sobs of relief. "I want to go home. I want to see him."

Harrison nodded. "I'm going to get you out of here, I promise. Where's the key to the shackles?"

A visible shudder rippled over her. "Jason swallowed it."

"Oh, God…If I help you, can you walk up to Demon? I'd carry you, but I'm afraid I'll jolt your arm." He couldn't stop touching her. He needed to reassure himself she was alive and other than bruising and a broken bone, relatively unscathed. He traced his hand over her head, moving her hair away from the cut at her temple. The bleeding was slowing down. She was going to need a doctor as soon as he got her back to town.

"I can try." She suddenly looked around. "Where's Jason?"

"He's dead." Harrison lifted her in his arms and settled her on her feet. "Demon's up on the ridge." He hoped the stallion was still capable of carrying Rachel. "We're going to walk right past Jason and keep on walking."

Rachel nodded. She was shaking, her teeth chattering, and without warning, she began to whimper. The sound grew until it was a thin, furious keen.

Once more, Harrison gathered her into his embrace, careful to avoid jarring her broken arm. "It's all right, now." He rained kisses over the top of her head. "You're safe. He'll never hurt you again, darlin'."

A violent shudder shook her and she stiffened in his embrace. "Don't call me that, please. He kept calling me that and now all I can hear is him."

"You won't hear him forever." He gently tilted her head up to him and with a light touch, followed her lower lip with the pad of his thumb. "Sweetheart isn't enough to express how much I love you. There isn't an endearment I can think of, so I will just tell you that I love you more than my own life. I'd walk through the fires of hell for you. I love you, Rachel."

Her smile was tremulous at best. "Did Ben tell you what I asked him to tell you?"

Harrison shook his head. "I told him you could tell me yourself."

Her eyes filled with tears and her lower lip trembled with the struggle to keep the tears from falling. "I was so afraid I wouldn't be able to tell you this and I wanted you to know." She gulped in a shuddering breath. "I love you. I knew you'd come for me. I prayed that it would be in time so I could tell you."

He thought about kissing her but not sure what Jason had done to her, he hesitated. Instead, he pulled her against his chest again and murmured, "Let's go home."

Chapter Nineteen

Even with Harrison's greatcoat wrapped around her, Rachel couldn't stop shaking. Every step Demon took shuddered into her arm. More than once, she had been racked with dry heaves from the pain. It was the rattles deep in the stallion's chest though and Harrison's dogged determination to continue to lead the horse with her weight on him that worried her.

"Harrison, stop. I can walk. You're going to kill him."

"He'll make it." The words sounded in the fog shrouded darkness.

"Harrison, stop, now. My arm is broken, not my leg." When he didn't halt, Rachel tried pleading. "Jason took too much from us. Please, don't add Demon to that. I'm begging you to stop and get me off him. Please."

To her relief, he stopped. Demon dropped his nose even further. Harrison tilted his head over his shoulder and her heart sank with the clench of his jaw and his repeated, "He'll make it."

"If you don't take me off him, I will throw myself off this horse." She wasn't sure she could follow through on the threat but to further emphasize her so far hollow promise, she kicked her feet out of the stirrups. "I won't let you kill him to save me."

"He's just a horse, Rachel." The flare of pain

across his face belied his callous words.

"Damn it, he's more than that. He's what you said you and your father were trying to perfect before the war put your breeding operation under. You can't continue to perfect that if he's dead." She swung her leg over Demon's haunches, relieved when Harrison caught her before she hit the ground.

"You are the most stubborn thing I have ever met." He settled her on her feet.

"Pot meet kettle," she shot right back. "If it takes all night to walk back to town, I don't care. You promised me Josh and Ben are safe, so even though I want to see for myself and see my son, I will not let you kill this horse just to get me there a few minutes sooner."

He shook his head in a mixture of anger and bemusement. "Half an hour and then I'm putting you back up on him."

"Half an hour and we'll discuss it." She started walking, gritting her teeth as each step throbbed up her arm into her head. With her hands shackled behind her back she couldn't even cradle the broken arm to herself.

They hadn't walked more than five minutes before her strength gave out and she collapsed to the ground. Harrison dropped to his knees next to her. "I'm putting you back up on him."

She managed to shake her head. "No. Pull his saddle and get the girth. I want you to use that to secure my arm to me. If it stops moving with every step, I hope it won't hurt so much."

"That's going to hurt like hell."

"No more than it is now." She shivered in the depths of his coat. Behind her, the thud of the saddle dropping to the ground reverberated through her.

Harrison gently lifted his coat from her shoulders. "I'm going to have to double it. There isn't a hole far enough back to hold it tight on you to keep your arm from moving."

The several inches wide leather was wrapped twice around her, just below her shoulder and above her elbow. Rachel fought a moment of panic. Harrison hesitated, his gaze searching her face, and asked, "Are you sure about this?"

She drew a deep breath, forcing the panic to subside. It was Harrison. He wasn't restraining her. He wasn't going to intentionally hurt her. "It should be just like pulling a corset tight, I think."

Her attempt at levity earned her a short chuckle from him. "Actually, da—Rachel, I'd rather be unlacing your corset."

That he caught himself in time from using that endearment banished the last of her panic. She forced a smile to her mouth. "Pull it tight."

When she came to, Harrison was carrying her, cradled to his chest. Despite the cold, his sweat dampened the side of her face. He was breathing heavily, and his rapid heartbeat thundered in her ear. Over that, she heard the steady, slow hoof falls from Demon as the stallion plodded along behind them.

Harrison halted but didn't set her down. "I'm going to put you up on Demon now."

"I can walk. Where are we?"

He set her down. "I think we're about two miles from town. We'll make better time if you're up on Demon. He's not rattling now."

Even though her arm still throbbed, it wasn't the

continual, bright sears of pain with each motion. Stabilizing the break had brought some relief. She glanced back at the horse.

Demon had dropped his head and was nibbling the ice coated scrub grasses. His attempt to eat lifted another burden from her. Dying horses didn't try to graze.

"Getting me up on him without a saddle isn't going to be easy." It had been difficult enough with a saddle and a stirrup to help get her weight onto the horse. "I'd rather walk."

Harrison carefully drew her into his side and tugged his great coat more securely around her. "I still say you're the most stubborn thing I have ever met."

Other than the saloons on the far end of town, Federal was silent and dark when they finally walked into town. As they approached the jail, the windows in the squat sturdy building spilled light into the night. Rachel burst into tears at the sight of the jail still intact. "He's really safe, isn't he?"

"I wouldn't lie to you about something that important, Rachel. He's fine. Both he and Ben are fine."

The door was locked, so Harrison rapped on the frosted glass. The sound of feet scrambling across the floor reached both of them and then the door was flung open. Her last reserve spent, Rachel felt Harrison's arms close around her again and he guided her into the office space and into the chair behind the desk as her legs buckled.

"I'm going for Doc," Ben said and headed out the door.

Harrison snagged the key to the shackles off the

desk and as he bent to open the iron restraints, Rachel said, her voice breaking with the tears she still couldn't contain, "I want to see Joshua."

Harrison dipped his head in a terse nod. Through a haze of tears, Rachel watched him disappear into the living area. Joshua's shout of "Momma!" preceded his rapid exit from the living area. Harrison caught the back of the boy's nightshirt just before Joshua flung himself against Rachel.

"Whoa, Josh. Your momma's got a broken arm. Gently."

Joshua eased up against her, his slender arms wrapping around her neck. "I was scared, Momma, but he said he'd bring you home." He nudged his head in Harrison's direction.

"I know, sweetie. I was scared, too." Rachel rattled the shackles. "Get these off me."

"I'm trying. The keys aren't interchangeable." Frustration lent a sharp edge to Harrison's voice. "As soon as Ben gets back here with Doc, I'll go wake Keith up and we'll get those off."

Joshua disentangled his arms from his mother and stepped back. "I can go wake Mr. McKay up."

"No." She was startled to hear both herself and Harrison snap the word at the same time. Rachel tried to soften her denial of Joshua's offer of assistance. "Sweetie, it's much too late for a young boy to be out in the streets, even if you're going to get Mr. McKay. I want you to stay here."

Joshua spun around to Harrison. "I want to help Momma."

Fresh tears stung her eyes when Harrison tousled her son's hair. "You can help her by doing what she told you to do, son."

Her son's shoulders slumped. "But, I'm not your son. That other man—he's my pa, isn't he?"

Harrison dropped to one knee to be on eye level with the boy. "It takes a lot more to be someone's father than to just point at you and say 'He's my son.' Being a father means teaching a boy the things that make a good man. Being a man isn't just about growing up."

"I wish you was my father." Joshua rubbed his nose, tilting his head to the floor.

Rachel waited with her breath caught in her throat for Harrison's response. He never even looked over at her as he drew Joshua into his arms.

"Josh, a man'd be right proud to have you as his son."

****

Harrison stood in the doorway between the office and the living area of the jail, watching Rachel sleep. Getting the shackles off had involved a walk across town to the blacksmith's shop and a shot of morphine from Doc to help block any further pain when McKay struck the locks. Setting the broken bone had been more complicated and required even more morphine to sedate Rachel because when Doc tried to put her under with chloroform she had fought against the cloth held over her nose and mouth with the ferocity of a wildcat.

"You look like you're ready to fall over," Ben said from the bed he'd made on a bunk in the cell nearest to the living quarters.

"I thought you were asleep." Harrison rubbed the back of his neck, hoping to ease some of the tension pounding in his head. He wanted a cup of coffee, but that would involve being in the living quarters and he didn't want to wake either Rachel or Joshua.

"Can't sleep any more than it seems you can." Ben swung his legs to the floor and stood. "Any little noise and I'm wide awake."

"Yeah, I know. I'm jumping at shadows." Harrison sat on the edge of the desk. "She told me where Jason took her before he dragged her up to the falls. I'm sending you to the Crazy TG to bring Tommy in."

"Tommy? He wouldn't hurt a fly." Ben rolled up the mattress. "What's he got to do with this?"

"According to Rachel, Tommy kept Jason hidden for the last year or more. Tommy's our arsonist." Harrison pulled a side drawer open and tossed a badge to the foreman. "Consider yourself deputized."

"You're not arresting Tommy," Rachel said from the doorway.

Harrison twisted to her. Her head was deeply bruised and swollen where she had hit it when she was pushed into the pool. She cradled her cast arm to her, and the dark smudges under her eyes were more pronounced by the pale cast to her features. She swayed with the after effects of the morphine and chloroform and sheer exhaustion. He stood and went to her, snaking an arm around her waist to keep her from falling.

"Anything Tommy did was because Jason told him to do it." Rachel tilted her face to him. "If Jason hadn't been giving him laudanum, Tommy wouldn't have done any of the things Jason told him to."

"He's still responsible. He didn't have to do what Jason told him to."

Rachel shook her head. "You don't know Tommy. Ben's right. He wouldn't hurt a fly. Ask Doc what laudanum does to a person. Now, with Jason gone, Tommy won't have it. If you send Ben out there, it's to bring him into town so Doc can help him. You're not arresting him."

"Boss, I've seen what having to have that stuff does to a man—it messes his thinking up. Tommy ain't known for being a deep thinker to start with." Ben pinned the badge to his shirt. "I'll go out to the Crazy TG to bring him in, but only so Doc can get him over needing that garbage."

Rachel placed her hand on Harrison's chest. "Please, don't punish him for something he wouldn't have done usually. He's not like other people. He's really a child in a man's body."

Harrison looked down at her hand and nodded. "All right. Ben, go bring him in. And, when you get back, go over to Bob's and send him up to the falls to bring Jason's remains down."

Her face paled even more. Ben muttered, "We can't just leave him there for the buzzards and coyotes?"

Even though he answered Ben, Harrison skimmed his hand over Rachel's cheek. "He was my father's son. As much as I'd like to just drag him higher into the mountains to let the scavengers have him, I won't hurt my father like that. Father always held out hope that Jason could defeat whatever demons drove him. I can at least let him know that his son's war is finally over."

"There's only one Catholic cemetery here." The fear sparkling in her eyes knifed through Harrison. It was as if even from beyond the grave, Jason might be able to still reach out and harm her if he was buried too close.

"He'll go home to Twin Creeks. The family burial plot there is sanctified." He drew a deep breath and slowly released it. "Like it or not, someday Josh might have questions about the man who was his father. I don't want to have to explain to him that we just left his body."

A ragged breath broke from her and then another. Harrison gently pulled her against him, enveloping her in his embrace. She shuddered with violent tremors and Harrison scooped her into his arms. He carried her to their bed, lowering her onto the mattress.

As he straightened, Rachel caught his wrist. "Don't go, please. I don't want to be alone."

The door to the jail opened and closed he assumed with Ben's departure. Harrison sat on the edge of the bed. "I sleep in the middle of the bed, remember?"

Though her lips trembled with a watery smile, she still managed one. She moved further into the bed to make room for him. He pulled the quilt up over her shaking limbs and then lowered himself to her, gathering her once more into the protective circle of his arms. He curled around her, attempting to shield her as much as he could, and remained there until she fell into a restless sleep.

Harrison dozed in the chair at the desk until Ben returned several hours later. The quiet click of the door opening jolted Harrison to his feet. Realizing it was just Ben, he sank once more into the chair. Rachel was still asleep and Joshua played quietly with his toy soldiers in a corner of the office. The seriousness and solemnity of the boy's play gave Harrison pause. Though he didn't say a word, the aggression that one soldier exhibited to bayonet another was telling.

"Tommy's at Doc's and Bob and his son are headed up to the falls." Ben looked over his shoulder at Joshua. "Is there any coffee?"

Harrison hooked his thumb in the direction of the living quarters. "On the stove. There's biscuits and gravy in the warmer, too."

"You made biscuits and gravy?" The skepticism in Ben's voice was palpable.

Harrison stood, stretching the knots out of his back and shoulders. "Helen Morris brought the coffee and breakfast down from the hotel. It's all over town what happened. Seems she wants to make amends for judging Rachel so harshly."

Ben snorted. "She and about half this town need to make amends."

"I won't dispute that." Harrison glanced around Ben's form into the bedroom area of the jail. Rachel's restless sleep had finally deepened. He was exhausted. He could only imagine how bone deep Rachel's exhaustion ran. "While you're eating breakfast, Josh and I are heading over to Burlington's. I hear he still has a runt puppy that needs a good home."

Joshua bolted to his feet. "I can get a puppy?" The solemnity vanished.

"Yes. I think as brave as you've been the last day or so, you've earned a puppy." Harrison gestured to the coat tree. "Get your coat."

"Boss, what do I tell her if she wakes up when you're gone?"

Harrison paused with Ben's reference to him as "Boss." He looked down at Joshua and then back to his deputy. "Tell her the truth. We're getting a puppy."

Hauser heaved a deep breath. "I was wrong and she

was right about you."

"It's not a problem, Ben." Harrison helped Joshua into his coat. "I respect and value the loyalty you had for Sam and appreciate your protectiveness of both Rachel and Josh." He pulled the door open and allowed Joshua to walk out first.

"I wasn't brave," Joshua said as they walked along the street to the mercantile. "I was scared."

Harrison dropped a hand onto the boy's shoulder. "Just because you were scared doesn't mean you weren't brave."

The boy stopped walking, forcing Harrison to pause. He let his gaze skim the child's tormented expression as he waited for Joshua to tell him why he halted. At last, he said, "You're not mad that I didn't try to stop him?"

"I'm very grateful you didn't try to stop him." Harrison's deep exhalation plumed in the cold air. "If you had tried, he would have hurt you very badly. He might have even killed you. That would have broken your mother's heart. Mine, too."

"It's okay to be scared sometimes?" Joshua lifted his gaze to Harrison's face. His eyes were dark with his own self-recrimination.

Harrison bent closer to the child. "When I fought in the War Between the States I had people shooting at me and I was scared. But, not as scared as I was when I found you and Ben shackled and tied up in that cell, and nowhere near as scared as I was when Ben told me who took your mother. There is no shame in being scared."

## Chapter Twenty

"We'll wait outside while you get dressed." Kathy Majors patted Rachel's arm. "You really need to get out, get some fresh air. Jessie and I are going to Madeline's to pick out dresses for the Christmas Ball at the Cattlemen's Association. It will be fun."

Rachel noticed Kathy didn't give her a chance to refuse before she stepped outside onto the boardwalk. She turned to Harrison as soon as the door closed. "Was this your idea?"

He took a long drink from the coffee cup he held before he answered. "No. But I agree with her. You need to get out of this building. You haven't been out those doors in thirty days."

"I can't." Her throat tightened with the thought of walking out the door and her heart hammered so fiercely it hurt.

"Can't or won't?" The sharp edge to his voice was unusual. "You're perfectly capable of walking down the street to the dress-maker."

"I can't." The words were repeated on a wail. "I can't listen to them gossip again and, in here I'm safe."

"In here you're a coward."

Her gasp sounded in the sudden silence between them. The accusation hit her as hard as a punch.

Harrison set his cup down and closed the distance between them. "I'm sorry. That was uncalled for. But it's not the gossips you fear. It's being vulnerable. If you hide in here, he's done exactly what he wanted to do to you. You hide in here and Jason's destroyed you."

Rachel batted his hand away when he reached for her. "Don't." She backed a step. "You have no idea everything he did. I don't even know for sure what he did because I can't remember what happened at the Crazy TG."

"We are *not* having this conversation again, Rachel." He pulled both hands through his hair, clearly frustrated. "I will never accuse you of infidelity because that requires consent and I know beyond the shadow of all doubt, there was none."

Rachel stared out the windows. Fat, thick flakes of snow drifted lazily past the glass. He might not ever say those words, but what other reason could he have for not resuming their intimate relationship? Every time she tried to tell him she wanted that intimacy, her throat seized up and he seemed to pull further away.

"Either you go get dressed or I'll just wrap you in a blanket and carry you over my shoulder down to Madeline's." His voice broke into her pained thoughts. "It's your choice."

She craned her head to him in degrees. "You wouldn't dare."

"Try me." He took a step closer. "I'll give you the same ten seconds to make up your mind that you gave me when I first rode up. Do you go to the dress-maker's in clothing or in your night clothes and wrapped up in a blanket and over my shoulder?" His head jerked to the living area. "Time starts now…nine…eight."

"You're really going to make me do this?"

"Five…" He walked into the living area. "Four…"

He stood in the doorway with the quilt draped over his arm. "Three…"

The gossips would have a field day with the sight of her carried over his shoulder like a sack of potatoes. His intractability on this was puzzling, as well. She recognized a losing battle. "I only have one day dress that fits over this cast and I can't button it without help."

"I can help." Harrison dropped the blanket into his chair behind the desk. "Thank you. I really didn't want to cart you to Madeline's over my shoulder."

Once she was garbed in the simple day dress, Harrison picked up her hair brush and began to draw the boar's bristles through her hair. "I don't think I can put it up in a chignon for you, but I should be able to manage a simple braid."

Her stomach was churning in anticipation of walking out the door. "Just tie it back with a ribbon. That will be fine." She clenched her hands on her lap, concentrating on the repetitive motion of the brush down the length of her hair. She stilled when he caught her hair in both hands and pulled it back, his hands skimming her neck. Disappointment crashed through her when he did no more than wrap a bright yellow ribbon around her hair and tie it. Before he would have kissed her nape, or trailed his fingertips the length of her neck, or even just told her how much better he liked it when she wore her hair down.

He helped her to her feet. Before he moved away, she caught his sleeve. His gaze dropped to her hand and Rachel uncurled her fingers from the fabric.

"I'll get your coat." There was something akin to resignation in his voice and lining his expression.

As she walked down Federal Avenue, flanked by Kathy and Jessie, Rachel didn't hear more than two words the women said. She stopped a few feet from the door to the dress-maker's shop and blurted out, "Kathy, I need to talk to you alone, please."

Kathy grabbed her hand. "Will the back fitting room here be alone enough?"

Rachel nodded, afraid to speak and start the threatening tears to fall. Jessie pulled the door open and Rachel was instantly smothered in Madeline Callahan's more than ample embrace. Kathy immediately took charge. "Maddy, would you bring a pot of coffee for Rachel and me? If you wouldn't mind fitting Jessie first, I'd appreciate it. That should take at least an hour, won't it?"

In the private room, Rachel sank into a small settee. Madeline brought in the coffee, pausing only long enough to say, "It's good to see you out again, Rachel."

On her way out, Madeline pulled the door closed. Kathy poured a cup of coffee for both of them, then sat next to Rachel. "Tell me what's wrong."

The coffee cup Kathy handed her was ignored. Never having had another woman to be able to confide in, Rachel hesitated. Kathy, for her part, seemed content to let her find the words and Rachel wondered if that was because of the relationship the older woman and her daughter shared. She stared down at her fingers emerging from the wrist to shoulder cast she wore. Finally, she said, in little more than a whisper, "I'm pregnant and I think Harrison wants to leave me."

"What makes you think that?"

Her cheeks heated with the inappropriateness of

this conversation but she truly felt she had nowhere else to turn for advice. "My monthly cycle is late. The only other time I was late was with Joshua."

"Not that. Most women know pretty much the moment they start to carry a child, especially a second baby." Kathy responded with as much nonchalance as if they were discussing the weather. "I knew the morning after I was in a delicate condition with Trevor. The other part—what makes you think Harrison wants to leave you?"

"It's not like it was before." Horrified at the tears suddenly streaming down her face, Rachel wiped her eyes. "He doesn't even try...he doesn't...he won't touch me. When he does, I may as well be his sister. He doesn't kiss me. The only time he holds me is in his sleep." The tears wouldn't stop. "He says what happened that night at the Crazy TG doesn't matter, but it has to. This baby might not be his and I can't say for sure it is because I can't remember anything of that night."

Kathy set her cup down and shifted on the settee so she fully faced Rachel. "Have you told him any of this?"

"I told him I can't remember. I truly can't. Jason knocked me out with laudanum." She bent forward, burying her face in her hand.

"He hasn't struck me as the type of man who would leave you." Kathy's arms closed around her. "Tell him you want your marriage to be what it was. He might be refraining from intimacy with you because he's afraid anything he would do could remind you of something that happened that night, whether you consciously remember it or not. More importantly, tell him about the baby."

\*\*\*\*

Harrison stepped out of the jail and looked up the street. Even though he knew Rachel was perfectly safe, that she was with Kathy and Jessie, and he hoped that being out with the two women had her completely occupied with dresses and fabrics and notions, there was still the sense of unease when she wasn't right by him. If he was this rattled by what had happened to her, how much more was she?

Maybe, he shouldn't have insisted she spend the afternoon with the two women. Doc had said to give her time. Six years ago, it had taken her months to regain her sense of independence and to find the courage to leave her room. The difference then was Jason wasn't dead. He was now. The telegram two weeks ago from his father had been succinct, just five words.

"Jason laid to rest today."

Jason was buried and Doc had written up an official death certificate, on file in the Territorial capital. The other shoe was going to fall. It wasn't a question of "if" but "when." Doc had to examine the body to write that certificate. There was no way he could miss the back shot. The thought of returning to the prison in Laramie City held no appeal, but when he took that shot at Jason he knew the risk involved. Saving Rachel's life far outweighed any risk of prison or worse.

Once the weather broke in the spring, the barn and the house would be rebuilt and were already paid for. Even with those expenses, there would be operating capital for Rachel to be able to purchase more stock and if the price of beef continued on its current upward rate, she wasn't going to be left without funds or resources.

He reached into his pocket and pulled out tobacco and papers. While he rolled a cigarette, Harrison took the time to scan what was visible of the town from the jail. The heavy wet flakes of earlier were drier, smaller and falling faster as they were pushed by a rising wind. Their accumulation in protected corners was growing. The change in the wind and weather forced most of Federal's citizens to hurry about their business outdoors.

Harrison inhaled deeply of the lit tobacco, welcoming the sharp tannic taste. Through the swirling snow, two figures walked across the open space of the town center, heads bent into the wind. When the snow parted enough that he could make out features, he knew the proverbial other shoe was dropping. Royce Majors—the newly appointed prosecutor for the county of Albany—and Ben continued in an unerring path toward the jail and Ben's badge became visible.

The two men halted at the jail, but didn't step up onto the boardwalk. Harrison took a final drag off the cigarette and flicked the butt away.

"Is Rachel here?" Majors asked.

Harrison noted Ben's hand on the butt of his revolver. "No. She's with your wife and daughter. I'm assuming they're still at Madeline's."

The bell on the Catholic church rang three times. Harrison looked to Ben. "Which of us is going to the school house to walk Josh home?"

Considering he was certain why both men were there Harrison wasn't surprised when Ben struck out in the direction of the small, one-roomed building without a word. After his form vanished in the snow, Majors asked, "Can we go inside?"

Harrison gestured to the door and followed the prosecutor into the jail. Royce made his way to the middle of the office space, his gaze seemingly intent on the far wall. When he closed the door, Majors's attention didn't alter from the far wall, though he asked, "Do you have coffee made?"

Harrison unbuckled his gun belt and placed both the weapon and his badge on the middle of the desk. "Do you want coffee or is this going to require something stronger because honestly, you look like I need a drink."

"Something stronger." The other man craned his head over his shoulder.

Harrison followed Majors's gaze to the desk and his holstered Peacemaker. He walked around the desk and pulled open the lower left side drawer, then withdrew a corked bottle of bourbon and two small glasses. He set the tumblers on the desk and poured a generous portion into both. He said, as he handed a glass to Majors, "Can we get this over with before Josh or Rachel get here?"

"I have no idea what you're talking about." Royce sipped from the tumbler. "This is smooth."

Harrison hadn't lifted his glass. He drew a deep breath. "So you're telling me you're not here to ask for my badge and arrest me for killing Jason?"

"Again, I have no idea what you're talking about." Majors took a seat in a chair in front of the battered desk in the office. "I read Doc's report. Jason died from a single gunshot to the chest. It was through and through." He inclined his head to the chair on the other side of the desk. "You might want to take a seat, Harrison."

Doc had falsified the death certificate. He wasn't going to look the gift horse in the mouth. After he sat, he finally picked up his drink and waited for the prosecutor to tell him why he was there, if it wasn't to arrest him for shooting Jason in the back.

"Doc's report said Jason had a long-healed gunshot wound to the left shoulder."

Jason was left-handed. A gunshot wound to that shoulder would have left him unable to use his gun hand. As far as he knew, Jason hadn't received that injury in the War of Southern Rebellion.

"Doc wrote in that report at one time, several of the bones in Jason's right hand had been broken. They were never properly set and didn't heal right." Majors took what Harrison could only define as a fortifying drink of the amber colored alcohol. "He mentioned other, old wounds in his report and he seemed to believe the gunshot to his shoulder, the broken bones, and the other wounds all happened at the same time. So, I went and had a talk with Doc."

The door opened and Ben walked in, brushing snow from his shoulders. Joshua wasn't with him. Before Harrison could ask, the foreman said, "He's with his mother and I sent the three ladies and Josh to Morris's for pie and coffee."

"Thank you," Majors said, gesturing to the chair next to him.

Harrison quelled the sense that Rachel being out of the office and Joshua delayed from returning after school had been carefully orchestrated.

Ben plunked down and said, "If you have another

glass, I could use a drink."

Harrison pulled the drawer open and took out the last tumbler. He poured and pushed the glass across to Ben.

"You might want to put your badge back on, Boss." Ben downed the alcohol in one swallow. "I told you that Sam sent me out to the mine, to make sure that nothing was getting out of it. He told me what he did." Ben set the tumbler down as gently as if it was made of finely spun sugar.

Harrison pushed the bottle closer to his deputy.

"It happened pretty much like you and Drake thought it did when we were all at the mine. Sam lured Jason there with the story of a new, big silver vein. Jake just happened to be with him when he went to meet Sam there. Sam shot Jake in the back and had Jason trapped. He shot him in the shoulder so he couldn't use his gun and then when Jason tried to shoot his way out with his off hand, Sam just let him run out of bullets." Ben turned to look out the office windows. "He told me he broke Jason's right hand with the butt of his own gun. After he broke Jason's hand, he castrated him, left him for dead and blew the mine."

Harrison reared back in the chair and forced out a short breath.

Majors picked up the bottle and poured another drink for Ben and then himself. "Tommy's been telling Doc everything that happened since Jake disappeared. More importantly, he told Doc he stood guard over Rachel so Jason couldn't hurt her in any manner the night she was at the Crazy TG."

Harrison pulled both hands back through his hair, then with his fingers interlaced at his nape, dropped his head forward. The horrific images that had tormented him, images of the abuse he imagined Jason had heaped on Rachel, vanished. A shuddering breath escaped him as he lowered his hands and lifted his head. "Is he still at Doc's?"

Both Royce and Ben nodded. Harrison stood and buckled his gun belt on, then pinned his badge to his shirt. "I'm going to Morris's to walk my wife and son home. But first, I need to stop at Doc's and eat a fair portion of crow."

"I can keep Joshua with me at Morris's tonight." Ben rose to his feet. "It would do Tommy good to see Rachel, too. He's been asking about her."

The three of them made their way through the snow down Federal Avenue. Before they reached the hotel, Harrison craned his head to Ben. "If you knew all this when we were at the mine, why didn't you tell me then?"

"I was pretty sure Jason was in there, deader than a doornail." His shoulders hunched against the wind. "I was pretty surprised when you didn't find him in there."

Ben entered the hotel/restaurant's lobby first. Harrison pulled his hat off and swept the snow from his shoulders. He debated pressuring Ben for a straight answer to why he didn't reveal what he knew when they had all been at the mine, but decided with Jason's death, Ben's knowledge was little more than a side note to a sordid, ugly tale.

The muted sounds of indistinct conversations came from the dining area and Harrison made his way there. He saw Rachel before she saw him. A smile lifted her mouth and even across the room, he could see the tension was gone from her expression. She met his gaze as he approached and her smile faltered but didn't fade.

With his hat pressed to his thigh, Harrison offered her what he hoped was a warm smile. "If you'd let me, I'd like to walk you home when you're ready."

A faint splash of color filled her cheeks. From the corner of his eye, he saw Royce assisting both Kathy and Jessica's departure from the table. He nudged his head at an empty chair. "May I?"

Rachel nodded. Harrison sat and moved the empty pie plate away, then set his hat on the table. "I need to talk to you. If you're comfortable with the idea, Ben said he can keep Josh with him here tonight."

Joshua leaned forward in his chair. "Can I, Momma?"

Her smile was gone, as was the blush from her cheeks. If anything, she looked as if she was going to burst into tears at any moment. She nodded, then said, her words sounding pained, "Yes. Ben's over in the doorway. I will see you tomorrow."

Joshua jumped out of his chair and walked as fast as he could without running to the foreman. Harrison watched his progress over his shoulder and once Ben had the boy's hand in his, turned his attention to Rachel. She toyed with her fork, rearranging its position on the table next to a plate of half-eaten apple pie.

"You're leaving us, aren't you?"

Harrison reached across the table and took her hand into his. She met his gaze when he softly said, "No, I'm not."

Her fingers tightened around his. "You've been so distant."

"I have, and I'm sorry if my actions led you to believe that I have even thought for one second about leaving you." He reached across the table and took her other hand into his. "I've been waiting for you to come to me—because honestly, I've been terrified if I kissed you, or held you, or anything else, you'd push me away. Half the time, I was afraid anything I'd say would be the wrong thing. That's the only reason I've kept my distance."

Her head bent and he watched her shoulders rise with the shuddering breath she drew. He leaned closer to her. "Let me walk you home, Mrs. Taylor, and steal kisses from you in the dark."

"Is it stealing a kiss if I want you to kiss me?"

If he leaned any further toward her, he would shock the whole town with a very public display of affection. He lifted her hand and pressed a lingering kiss to the back. "Let me get your coat."

As they walked through the falling snow, Harrison kept one arm around her waist. When she leaned into him, he tightened his arm. Even though she was firmly tucked into him, he still felt her tension. "What's wrong?"

She stopped, her head dipped to the snowy ground. Harrison placed his hands on her shoulders, unwilling to force her to meet his gaze. He waited for the silence to weigh enough on her. In the distance, the bell on St. Margaret's tolled seven times, the usual clear tones muted.

Without lifting her head, she whispered, "I'm pregnant. But, I'm not sure if you're the father—"

"You can be sure," he said, even though his head was reeling. He was going to be a father. You are a father, he reminded himself. There's a little boy who already calls you his father.

"How can you say that when I don't remember anything that happened at the Crazy TG?" She finally looked up at him. "I'm not sure."

His long breath plumed the air. "I am. Jason didn't do anything." He chose not to tell her what her father had done. "Tommy stood guard over you the whole night so he couldn't hurt you."

"Tommy?" Her brow knit even as her mouth dropped open.

Harrison nodded. "Tommy. I want you to understand something. I meant what I said to Josh that a man would be proud to have him as a son. He's more my son than he's ever been Jason's. Even if we couldn't be sure, I'm the only father this child will have." He brushed a stray wisp of hair from her cheek. "Before I take you home, I want to go to Doc's and thank Tommy."

A smile he hadn't seen in better than a month lifted her mouth. "Can't that wait until tomorrow?"

"Are you propositioning me, Mrs. Taylor?" He wanted to kiss her senseless right there in the street, but he wanted to be sure he was reading this right.

Her smile deepened and the gray of her eyes warmed. "Is it against the law to attempt to seduce a federal marshal?"

"Sure is." He couldn't contain his chuckle. "I'd have to arrest you."

"Would you now?" She ran her hand up his chest and wrapped her arm around his neck. "And what's the sentence if I'm found guilty?"

Harrison pulled her fully into his embrace and lifted her off her feet. "Life, darlin'. Life."

## Author's Note:

As with *Seize the Flame*, in *West of Forgotten* I dealt with a topic that is a darker one than usually found in a romance novel. I am a survivor of sexual assault and abuse. You have no idea how difficult those words have always been for me to say because of the shame and the guilt, that somehow it was my fault. It was never my fault. I can say those words now. I can write them for the whole world to see. It has taken me years—decades, actually—to be able to free myself of the guilt and the shame. I have been blessed to be married to a man who has attempted to understand my inability to trust, has been accepting of how often I have distanced myself emotionally, and who still just holds me when almost thirty years later I still wake in the middle of the night with horrific nightmares.

However, there is help and hope for victims of sexual assault and abuse. If you are a survivor of sexual assault and live in the United States, contact RAINN at https://www.rainn.org/ or at 1-800-656-HOPE. The call is completely confidential. Please, take the first step to healing. You are *not to blame*.

~*Lynda J. Cox*

## A word about the author...

Once upon a time there was little girl who fell in love with the wide open spaces of the American West, cowboys, horses, and collies. She blames a steady diet of syndicated Western programs and John Wayne movies as well as Lassie for these loves. That girl grew up but never outgrew her first loves.

Lynda J. Cox writes predominantly western historical romance. When she isn't writing, she can be found on the road, traveling to the next dog show to exhibit her award-winning collies. She loves to talk about books, writing, the lure of the vastness of the American West landscape, the mythos of the cowboy, and the insanity which is the sport of showing dogs. She can be reached at www.facebook.com/LyndaJCox or via e-mail at lynda.cox@aol.com.